VAMPIRE MORNING

VAMPIRE MORNING

THE DAYWALKER CHRONICLES™ BOOK 1

THEOPHILUS MONROE

MICHAEL ANDERLE

LMBPN Publishing
PMB 196, 2540 South Maryland Pkwy
Las Vegas, NV 89109

Version 1.00, March 2023
ebook ISBN: 979-8-88541-795-2
Print ISBN: 979-8-88878-093-0

THE VAMPIRE MORNING TEAM

Thanks to our Beta Team

John Ashmore, David Laughlin, Kelly O'Donnell, Malyssa
Brannon

Thanks to our JIT Readers

Dave Hicks
Diane L. Smith
Veronica Stephan-Miller
Dorothy Lloyd
Wendy L Bonell
Christopher Gilliard

If We've missed anyone, please let us know!

Editor
The SkyFyre Editing Team

CHAPTER ONE

You'd think a road trip with Dracula would be fun. The dude was like a billion years old. Well, maybe not *that* old. Whenever you talk about years BT (before technology) it all kind of blends together. You could also call those years BS (before showers) since, as I understood it, back when Dracula was a mortal, if you bathed more than twice a year you were probably royalty.

I can be a bit of an airhead at times, but I'm a smart airhead. Yeah, that's a thing. *Legally Blonde,* hello! I wasn't blonde. Not a law-student, either. Before I became a daywalker—a vampire whose more monstrous self only shows up under sunlight—I was a redheaded computer geek. I suppose that hadn't changed, but I had fangs now, so I was way cooler than I used to be. Something about this new self was more confident than the old Sienna Cartwright used to be. Having the Grim Reaper's daughter—well, his sister, now that her brother took over the family business—as a best friend, and saving the world together a few times helped.

Of course, if I hadn't met Zoey, I never would have become what I am. Human-ish at night. A bloodsucker during the day. Long story short. Vampires abducted me. They tried to turn me. Zoey caught me. Her brother reaped my soul. The theory was if they kept my body alive until the vampiric venom was gone, they could put my soul back in my body and keep me human. It didn't do exactly what they hoped. It made me what we called a "day-walker." Human and vulnerable in all the usual ways humans are at night. Only a few minor features remained. My fangs, for one. My senses were improved, but not at all comparable to regular vampires who could see in the dark just as well as in the day. My vampirism wasn't totally gone during the day, but it was absent enough that I barely noticed it and no one else did either. Unless I smiled too widely. Then, well, I looked like the failed experiment of an orthodontist.

I was *almost* indestructible during the day. In some ways, I was the opposite of regular vampires. The sun made me stronger (and deadlier), and if I wasn't jonesin' for blood, I *loved* garlic. A stake to the heart could ruin my day. I hadn't tested it, for obvious reasons, but beheading might do the trick, too. I had a brooch, a device enchanted by a goddess and given to the reapers, that allowed me to keep my blood thirst under control during the day most of the time. So long as I didn't encounter any blood or anyone with an open wound, it worked. It also had the ability to allow me to travel the astral plane. Basically, go invisible. I could use that ability day or night.

Why was I riding with Dracula? Well, that's another long story. I'll get to it. I'll just say that *this* Dracula was half the villain he used to be. Probably less than half, but that doesn't have the same ring to it. His quirky weird sisters—you might have read about them in the book about my newest travel companion—worked a little dark magic, Scholomance mumbo jumbo on the old Count, divided him up into something that resembled a Borg collective, and isolated anything about his personality that was non-villainous in only one of his various manifestations.

Yes, Dracula had been a *master* of the Scholomance. A mystical school that had trained sorcerers for centuries. According to legend, the devil himself was the school's headmaster. Well, Zoey and I shook things up in hell a bit. We replaced Hades with Athena. She had a bitchy streak, herself—Zoey could tell that story better than I could—but the other gods on Olympus had her under control. Besides, ruling hell suited her. She did it well, and while she was always a goddess who wanted more power, and in a sense she had it, she was never the destroy-the-world-out-of-spite kind of devil. With her in charge at the Scholomance, Zoey and I learned that the school also offered another path. The path of light. Zoey and I went through it. We were able to isolate the one part of Dracula, after the sisters had divided his essence, where any semblance of goodness remained. We got him back to the Scholomance and, though he had been a master of the darkness before, he engaged the trials to become an initiate in the path of light. He passed. Throw the confetti. Toot a few horns. By combining our powers gleaned from the Scholomance, Dracula, Zoey, and I were able to destroy what remained of his darkness. That is, whatever of it the sisters hadn't held on to themselves.

That was the guy I had riding with me. Dracula sans the evil. Still as eccentric as ever. But, you know, look who's talking, right?

I'd say he was my new sugar daddy, but it wasn't like that. The weird sisters were setting up a club down in New Orleans. Zoey and I took down the club they'd set up in Kansas City already. Zoey was preggers, so she was sitting this adventure out, but I bit Dracula, turned him into a daywalker like me, and we hit the open road. Not any daywalker could turn other vampires into our kind. I was the alpha daywalker. I'd been made by an accident, through a botched attempt by the reapers to shield my soul while the vampiric curse left my body. You had to be made like me to pass on the daywalker "variance" to other bloodsuckers.

Before we left town, Dracula got me a new vehicle. Quite generous from a vampire I'd only known a short while. I think he was grateful that he had a chance to live life as someone other than the most famous monster in the history of horror.

He bought me a Toyota Sienna, a minivan. He thought it was *hilarious*. Sienna driving a Sienna. You know, I used to love my name. I thought it was cool, unique, and kind of badass. That was before people started associating it with the number-one rated vehicle in safety and functionality among soccer moms nationwide.

He insisted we needed the space. Even as daywalkers it was good to have a place to take cover, especially since we were vulnerable at night. Besides, the van was a hybrid. More irony, I know, since I was a hybrid of a sort myself. It got great gas mileage, though.

Since Drac was an old fart, I thought I'd go retro with my music choices. What's better for a road trip than a little Journey? I belted it out as we headed down the open road.

"Don't stop… believing!"

Dracula tilted his head. "Please keep the volume down."

"Party pooper. I thought you'd like old music. You know, since you're so old."

"This is not old."

I turned the radio down. "I know what you'd like. You enjoy the king?"

Dracula raised an eyebrow. "The king of where?"

"The King of Rock 'n Roll, genius. Look, we can even make the song our own. 'I ain't nothin' but a vampire, bitin' all the time. I ain't never killed a rabbit 'cause they taste like… turpentine.'"

Dracula shuddered. "Do they? I never bit one. I stay away from bunny rabbits."

I shuddered. "You're scared of bunnies? Maybe I don't want to know."

"Have you ever fed from a bunny and lived to tell the tale?"

I shook my head. "Only bunnies I ever ate were made of chocolate."

"I imagine your song is accurate. I wouldn't be surprised if they were turpentine-flavored rodents."

"Not that I have a clue what turpentine tastes like. What can I say? I needed something to rhyme."

"You can get an idea of what something might taste like by how it smells. People say things taste like shit all the time, but I doubt most of those people have ever had a sample."

I snorted. "Good point, I guess."

"This music still isn't old."

"Oh, come on. Elvis is way old. What do you like, anyway?"

"Do you have any Brahms?" he requested.

"Brahms? Is that like a death metal band or something?"

"No. Brahms composed his symphonies while he was yet alive."

I huffed. "You can't listen to a symphony on a road trip, dude. The idea is to stay awake. It's gotta be something you can sing along with."

"I know that song by Sir Mix-A-Lot."

I laughed. *"Baby Got Back?"*

"I thought it was written by a knight," Dracula explained. "Why else would he be called 'sir'? So, I purchased the cassette. Then I couldn't stop listening to it."

I chuckled. "Well, I'm sure we can stream it if you're really that into it."

"If Brahms is out, then yes, Sir Mix-A-Lot is my choice."

I didn't know Brahms. I suspected he was one of those many dead classical composers whose stuff all sounded the same to me. I knew the gulf between Brahms and early nineties raps about butts was wider than the Grand Canyon. Okay, a massive crevice in the earth might not be the best metaphor when we're talking about big butts, but you get the idea. If Dracula had a playlist, or even a smartphone, I'd be curious to see what it looked like.

I was driving. Dracula drove a little at the start of the trip, but I took over straight away. He wasn't the fiend he was famous for most of the time, but on the road, he was downright terrifying. He didn't exactly respect the concept of lanes on the highway.

Turn signals weren't his style, either. As a wealthy count in Romania, I suppose he wasn't used to driving. Given his previous aversion to sunlight, he didn't travel much, either.

My phone was mounted to the dash. I glanced at it repeatedly to see if Dylan texted me back. He was a werewolf that Zoey and I had saved when he was being held prisoner by a Greek goddess a while back. The sparks were there, and he and I hit it off quickly. Obviously, we didn't do anything during a full moon. I'm not into hairy dudes, and certainly don't dig quadrupeds, but ever since he'd left and rejoined his pack in Louisiana, I'd been looking for a chance to go see him. I won't say we had a long-distance relationship. What we had wasn't at relationship status. But we stayed in contact, sent flirty texts back and forth, and a few photos of each other that I won't tell you about. When I sent him a message to let him know I was heading his direction and to warn him about the weird sisters, he didn't respond. I thought he'd be excited. It wasn't like I was pressuring him or anything. Our flirtations were mutual, and he instigated it more often than I did. How many more times could I text without receiving a response before it got *Fatal Attraction* freaky, though?

It had only been a day since I told him I was coming. He was a werewolf, and a full moon was coming in a couple days. Maybe he and his pack were off on a retreat somewhere off the grid, where they could shift and run free while minimizing the body count they'd wake up to in the morning. I hoped that's all it was. As often as we texted, it was a little weird he hadn't said something. Like I said, though. We weren't in a relationship. He didn't have to tell me anything. Still, I was checking my phone constantly, hoping for a response. Despite being a daywalking vampire, I'd only been on the earth for nineteen years. This sort of thing, anxiously checking my phone waiting for a boy to text, was pretty normal, all things considered, even if there was nothing normal about either of us, individually speaking.

Dracula didn't get it. He hadn't had much luck with romance

through the years. Most of the people he'd ever found attractive ended up as a meal, and that sort of thing doesn't do much for building a relationship with someone. He was even more confused why I'd be interested in a werewolf. "Vile creatures," he insisted. When *we* fed, we were refined. We left two little bite marks on someone's body. Most of *our* victims survived. Were-wolves, though? Well, dismemberment was common. They feasted on people's hearts. If you had to pick a monster to come after you, you were better off with a vampire than a werewolf. If you survived a werewolf attack, you'd become one. Most likely, though, you wouldn't live through it. If a vampire bit you, unless you were bitten several times and sufficient venom was passed into your body, you wouldn't likely turn. You'd be sick for a while, get better, and move on with your life.

My bite was different. Maybe it was because, as a daywalker, I was more-or-less human half of the time. More than that, really, since if I stayed indoors during the day my vampirism remained dormant. One bite from me and you'd find yourself craving blood the next time you went out in the sun.

At the moment, Dracula was the only one like me. I'd made others, but for various reasons, they were all gone. Some died. Others became human again—long story. I was a black swan. Some regular vampires hunted me, not to hurt me, but to bait me into biting them. They missed the daylight. Others feared me. Especially since my brooch gave me an advantage. I could disap-pear and, in astral form, push my fist through a vampire's torso then touch my brooch to take physical form again and rip their icy hearts from their chests. It was as good as staking, but messier. A lot messier. I was the kind of girl who didn't mind getting a little dirty, or bloody, in a fight, though.

Dracula and I drove all night. When sunlight began to show on the horizon, it made my ancient companion visibly uneasy, shifting in his seat. Since I made him a daywalker, he'd had a couple of days under the sun, but it was still an adjustment.

Mornings are hard. Hell, they're hard for everyone. The most I'd ever had to worry about in the morning was the condition of my hair. Historically, sunrises hadn't done much for Dracula's complexion. Things were different now.

"Can you pull over?" Dracula asked.

"Sure. I need a pee break, myself. Shouldn't have gotten that forty-four-ounce Mountain Dew at the last pit stop."

Dracula chuckled. "I don't have to pee. It's just I haven't enjoyed a sunrise in ages."

I pulled over at the next stop, just the other side of the Louisiana border.

Dracula didn't have a brooch or any other device to suppress his vampiric urges when the sun rose. He did have a lot of practice. When it came to controlling one's cravings and restraining one's urges, he was a master. Without my brooch, well, I was less predictable.

That was the funny thing about my relationship with Dracula. In most ways that mattered, he was the mentor. His life experience—if you can call centuries as one of the undead a life—was impressive. He knew how to handle cravings and how to operate in the shadows. I knew how to handle the daylight, how to navigate the world of the living, and more importantly, how to play well with others. Dracula didn't have a lot of human friends, for several obvious reasons. Probably for the same reason omnivorous humans don't usually befriend a lot of cows. I'd never befriended a vampire. All the ones I ever encountered in the past were my enemies.

In theory—we hadn't put it to the test yet—we were a great team. We complemented each other. My weaknesses were his strengths, and vice versa.

I parked the car at the Louisiana visitor's center. We had the back seats folded down in the van, and I double-checked to make sure the blanket was still covering all our wares. We brought a lot of weapons with us. I borrowed several items from Zoey, things useful for slaying vampires like stakes and crossbows. Dracula had several weapons of his own. Real medieval shit. Swords, spears, chain-mail armor. It was smart. Chain mail could stop a stake.

Anyone who might peek through the windows would have a lot of questions. Best keep it covered.

We were the only ones parked there, but anyone else could show at any moment. I was probably more anxious than was necessary, but I didn't want to attract any unneeded attention. If we were going to find the weird sisters and stop them, it was best they didn't know we were coming. Dracula said they could influence people's minds. One bite and people would do almost anything to please them. We were moving in on their territory, and the closer we got to New Orleans, the more I worried someone under their thrall might spot us and warn them we were on the way.

Dracula wasn't as nervous about that as I was. I suppose this wasn't the first time someone—human or vampire—had him in their crosshairs. His anxiety was all about the sun.

We stepped out of the van, and Dracula had the widest grin on his face. He couldn't hide his fangs like that.

His nervousness about facing the sun was mixed with excitement. Like when a boy asks a girl out for the first time. He can't wait for her to say yes, but he's also terrified of rejection. The sun wouldn't burn Dracula, but it would take a while before he really believed that.

We stepped across the grass and sat on the top of a picnic table to watch the sunrise. Dracula gasped when the light hit his face. Then he laughed. "It's beautiful. And it's warm."

I smiled. "Been a while since I watched a sunrise. You sort of take it for granted, you know?"

Dracula shook his head. "I never will. I've never properly thanked you, Sienna."

"For biting you? No problem."

Dracula chuckled. "It's more than that. You trusted me."

I shrugged. "Well, when the sisters divided your essence, they left you with anything that was good that had lingered in you for thousands of years."

Dracula smirked. "Hundreds. I'm old, but I'm not that old."

"How old are you, exactly?"

Dracula shrugged. "I haven't done the math in a while. I'll just say I'm old enough to be your great, great, great, great, great, add a few more greats, grandfather."

I snorted. "Well, hate to break it to you, buddy, but I'm not into older men."

Dracula laughed. "I'm not coming on to you, Sienna. I'm not into younger women."

I snorted. "Well, in that case, you're going to have a real hard time dating. I mean, I think eHarmony has a section for mature dating, but ancient is a category they've never opened up."

"I haven't thought about love in a long time. Romance isn't even on my radar."

I shrugged. "Give it time. I'm sure there are plenty of elderly spring-chickens out there who'd think you were quite the catch."

"Maybe you're right. Until then, how about we do a little training."

I raised an eyebrow. "Training?"

"Look, you're good. That little disappearing act works against low-level vampires. You already know that back at my club in Kansas City we had black lights, illuminated with power from the underworld. They made your brooch useless."

I shrugged. "We'll find another way."

"We will. And when that time comes, you need to know how to fight. How'd you like to learn how to handle a blade?"

CHAPTER TWO

Dracula and I stood in the grass, each holding a double-edged sword. I swung mine around in my right hand.

"This isn't a katana, Sienna. I know you're strong, invigorated by the sun and whatnot, but you need to grip it with both hands."

I shrugged and took a swing at Dracula. He raised his sword to block my strike, parried to the side and brought his blade down over my shoulder. "Your enemies aren't going to be human. They're strong, too."

"Not in the sun, they aren't."

"You really think the sisters, or any vampires we're going after, are going to face you in the sun? You need to be ready to fight in the dark, when you don't have extra strength and your opponent does."

Dracula pulled his blade back.

"Let's try this again. Two hands. Come at me."

"I don't want to hurt you."

"You won't. Besides, even if you got a lucky hit on me, it's not like I can be killed like that."

"Then what's the point?"

"Just because you can't kill a vampire with a cut to the arm, leg, or torso doesn't mean you can't maim him. Do that, and you'll have an advantage."

"I don't want to maim you either!"

"I heal fast. Not fast enough, though, that if we were enemies, you couldn't gain the upper hand if you took out a leg or an arm."

I gripped my sword with two hands. I took another swing. Dracula ducked and swept his leg, kicking my feet out from beneath me. I fell on my butt.

"Damn it!"

"Widen your stance. Half of what makes a good swordsman is in the legs, not the arms."

I cleared my throat. "Swordswoman, thank you very much."

Dracula smirked. "I'm ancient. I'm a little slow on the uptake when it comes to political correctness."

I grinned. "You'd never make it in my gender studies course."

"I didn't know you were in school."

"I was studying computer science. Then, you know, saving the world, becoming a vampire, shit like that got in the way. Maybe I'll find a school down here where I can pick up a few credits. If the weird sisters don't turn up straight away."

"If you were studying computers, why were you studying gender?"

I chuckled. "Just getting my gen ed requirements out of the way. My plan was originally to transfer to a university. Money was tight, you know? You can save a lot by starting at community college."

"Why do they teach you about gender as a college requirement? Don't they handle that in kindergarten?"

"You have no idea, buddy. You have to be careful. If you say that boys have a penis, girls have a vagina, someone might construe that as hate speech. You can't ever be too careful."

Dracula shook his head. "How do people even talk to each other these days? It's almost impossible to say anything without someone taking offense."

I sighed. "Tell me about it. I hate it when people use the v-word with me."

"You're a virgin?" Dracula raised an eyebrow.

"*Vampire*. And it's none of your business, mister."

"Why would you be offended if someone calls you a vampire?"

"It's not the word itself," I explained. "It's what's behind the word when they say it. Someone says 'vampire' and they immediately think of…"

"Me?"

I laughed. "Well, yes! A count in a castle who wears a long cape, can turn into a bat, and *vants* to *suck* your *blood*. Muahaha!"

Dracula shook his head. "Bloody stereotypes."

"Literally!" I pointed out.

"Doesn't offend me, though. That people think I'm a monster. I mean, I kind of earned it. But besides that, other people's ignorance doesn't make me who I am."

I raised an eyebrow. "So you just *decide* not to be offended at people?"

Dracula shrugged. "It's called *taking* offense. No one offends me. It's always up to me if I take it or leave it."

"You can't just ignore it when people are hateful and ignorant."

"Why not? I mean, it makes even less sense for humans to get worked up over things like that. When you've lived for centuries, human lifespans seem shorter and shorter even though they are actually longer on average than they used to be. Even as vampires, though, a hunter could stake us tomorrow and it would be over. No one is truly immortal. Every minute I obsess over someone else's ignorance or hate, or stupidity, is a minute I'll never get back. Besides, when you allow ignorant people to affect you, you give them power. The best thing to do with ignorant folk is to ignore them."

I pressed my lips together and twirled my sword around in my hands. "Don't let assholes get free rent in your head."

Dracula tilted his head. "Don't tell me they teach weird biology now, too."

"What do you mean?"

"Assholes aren't on the head. They're between the glutes."

I rolled my eyes. "Sometimes I forget you don't get modern idioms."

"Or, perhaps, an asshole is a very cheap stable. If you can't build a place for your ass, you could dig a hole for one. It won't wander off that way."

"Right. When your ass wanders off, it can really ruin your day."

Dracula waved his hand through the air. "You don't need an ass, anyway. You have a new minivan."

"A lot of people might say that if you drive a van, you won't get any ass," I cautioned.

"Asses are overrated. Your van has your name on the back. The only way to put your name on an ass would be to shave and tattoo it."

This could go on forever. I wasn't sure if Dracula was really that naive, or if he was screwing with me as much as I was him. Either way, it was entertaining.

I widened my stance and gripped my sword by the hilt with both hands. "Ready to go again?"

Dracula nodded. "Remember, use your legs as much as your arms."

I grinned. "And my ass."

"A strong strike requires the whole body," he instructed.

"The *whole* body?" I raised an eyebrow.

"Just about. Even your eyes are important. Where you're looking can tell your opponent where you plan to strike. A good fighter will pick up on any tell. If your lip quivers when you go for a jab, if you furrow your brow before a swipe, you need to know it. If you're fighting an opponent stronger than you, adept at discerning your tells, you can broadcast a tell, then use it to throw them off. Let your lip quiver, but instead of swinging your sword, go for a jab the next time."

"So it's like poker."

"The card game?"

"Yes. You learn to bluff, trick your opponent into thinking you're doing one thing when you're doing another."

Dracula grinned. "Precisely. A great swordsman—swordswoman, sorry—doesn't win a battle through brute strength alone, but through skill and deception."

I kept my feet wide but put one directly in front of the other.

"That's not a great stance, Sienna. You'll be off balance."

I grinned and swung my sword down at Dracula. He widened his stance and blocked my strike. Exactly as I planned. Then, I kicked him in the balls.

"Owwww! Sienna, what the hell?"

"Skill and deception," I announced.

Dracula dropped his sword and grabbed his groin. "Very good… You got me."

CHAPTER THREE

We tossed our swords into the back of the van and I pulled the blanket back over them. I got in the driver's seat while Dracula made his way around to the passenger side. I checked my phone, still on the dashboard mount. Three missed calls. All from Dylan.

"Damn it!"

"What is it?" Dracula asked as he climbed into his seat and buckled his seatbelt.

I shook my head. "Dylan tried to call. I missed it. He didn't text, either. He always texts before he calls."

Dracula shrugged. "So call him back?"

I started the van and let my phone connect to Bluetooth. This wasn't the vehicle I'd have chosen, but Dracula wanted to surprise me. It was a gracious gesture. It had all the bells and whistles. Sure, things like Bluetooth were standard in most new cars, but I'd never had a *new* car before. I called Dylan's number.

The phone rang through the van's speakers.

"Well, hello!" It was a woman's voice.

"Who the hell are you?"

"I'm the girl who's fucking your boyfriend."

I almost choked on my own tongue.

Dracula shook his head. "Sorina?"

I huffed. Sorina was one of the weird sisters. She was the sole blonde. The other two had long, dark hair with aquiline noses that resembled Dracula's hooked beak. Sorina was the pretty one, the one who spoke while the others listened and mostly did her bidding. The brunettes were Ana and Elena. I hadn't heard them speak two words when Zoey and I encountered them in Kansas City, but Dracula said they were every bit as formidable as their more vocal sister.

Sorina laughed. "If it isn't our puppy!"

"I'm no puppy," Dracula huffed.

"Our Lord always had a soft spot, a weakness. Lingerings of his humanity that held him back. We've taken your strength. I'd say puppy-dog describes what's left of you well enough."

"Why do you have Dylan's phone?" I asked.

"Sienna, isn't it? Tell me, where's your reaper friend? You're nothing but a warped hybrid, half-turned. It's your friend who is the real threat."

"Maybe she's right behind you, ready to reap your ass to hell," I suggested.

Sorina laughed. "Hardly. No matter, dear. We'll find her soon enough. Before she finds us, I'm sure of it."

"Yeah, good luck with that." If Sorina thought Zoey was hunting her, all the better. I wasn't about to tell her that Zoey was off the grid with her detective fiancé preparing to start a family. If she underestimated me and thought Zoey was after her, we could use that to our advantage.

"To answer your question, dear, as I said. Your boyfriend is in my bed. If you think he's virile as a man, you should try him doggy style."

I rolled my eyes. "If he was in his werewolf form, you wouldn't stand a chance. Besides, there hasn't been a full moon since you left Kansas City."

"The moon doesn't awaken the wolf, dear." Sorina sounded delighted to share this with me. "The wolf is always there, eager to emerge. The moon merely renders the human soul that keeps the wolf in his cage weak enough that the werewolf's true self can emerge. There's more than one way to weaken a human spirit, doll."

I glanced at Dracula. He nodded to confirm that what Sorina was saying was true. "What are you saying?"

"I'm saying your boyfriend won't be coming back. He and his pack serve me, now. And we have marvelous plans for them."

"What are you planning, Sorina?" Dracula demanded. "Are you still harvesting human souls, replicating my dark essence?"

Sorina laughed. "Well, that would make things easy for you, wouldn't it? You've already figured out how to stop that. You have the power of light from the Scholomance. Or, at least you did. Do you really think I'd play into your hand that way?"

"Then what is your plan?" Dracula asked again.

"As if I'd tell you. I'm not stupid, even if you treated me that way for the last three hundred years."

Dracula sighed. "I never thought you were stupid, Sorina."

"You always underestimated us. We were nothing to you but errand girls. Go find me a meal, you'd say. And yes, for years, we did exactly what the mighty Count asked us to do. We were women, and you thought that was our place. To feed you. To take care of your needs. What about our needs? What about our desires, our aspirations? Not once did you ask us what we wanted. It didn't matter, so long as the Count got his meals and luxuries. So long as the Count got his rocks off, who cares what the women wanted, what the sisters *needed*?"

"It wasn't like that! I cared for you. I loved you."

Sorina huffed. "Love. Please. That was your greatest weakness of all. It remains so. Tell me, *Lord,* what would that daywalker think if she knew about your perversions? Oh, who am I kidding? I've seen the girl. She's a redheaded Mina. How could you possibly resist?"

I glanced at Dracula. "What is she talking about?"

Dracula shook his head. "Never mind that. Sorina, all of that was a part of my darkness. You took care of that. I have no such intention for her, or anyone else."

"Sure you don't. Listen to me, doll. Darkness or not, that's still the same Dracula. Don't say I didn't warn you."

I snorted. "I don't care about that. What are you doing with Dylan? Tell me!"

"I already did."

Sorina hung up the phone. I called back, but it went to voice-mail. "What the hell was that all about?"

"Have you read my story? That Stoker novel?" Dracula asked.

"Once or twice," I admitted.

"Then you know about Mina. You and she do share a common resemblance, but I truly hadn't noticed it until Sorina mentioned it."

"In the book they kill you, she recovers from your curse, and lives the rest of her life with her husband, Jonathan."

He looked away from me. "That book never would have sold without a happy ending. That's not how it ended."

"Clearly not. You're not dead, after all. I mean, not in the vampiric sense."

"They didn't kill me. I let them think they did. I was wearing chain mail. They staked a pillow and a bag of pig blood. Since I turned Mina, and she was bound to my sire bond, I charged her to return to Harker. She killed her husband and returned to me. Some time later, Van Helsing killed my love while she slumbered in my bed."

"They fell for that? If Mina was a vampire, wouldn't they figure it out? She couldn't go out in the sun, for one."

Dracula shook his head. "As you know, I was a master of the

Scholomance. I cast a spell that suppressed her vampirism for three months. The ruse worked well. She didn't even know the plan until she awoke again with her true nature restored."

"What perversions was Sorina talking about?"

Dracula took a deep breath. "For decades, I made her play the role of Mina. She played the part. It assuaged my anguish for a time. Still, I knew the truth. I forced Sorina to do many unspeakable things. When even that wasn't enough, I cast her and the sisters out for nearly a century. When they returned, they'd found a way to sever the sire bond. Until then, I presumed that a sire bond could only be severed in death. Still, the sisters found a way. I suspected sorcery was involved. They were no longer in my thrall, but they continued to serve me in my castle."

"Why would they do that?"

"Pity, perhaps?" Dracula mused. "Maybe that was it at first. That's what I believed. I was happy to have them back. I never questioned their loyalty. That was a mistake."

"They were biding their time, looking for a way to take your power."

Dracula nodded. "Darkness has its side effects. Dark magic, the Scholomance, gives you power. But it leaves a hole. It leaves you in a dark place. I couldn't bear it."

"You were depressed?"

"Maybe it was the dark magic. I was still mourning Mina. I think that darkness made it impossible to move through the stages of grief. I was stuck. Sorina and the sisters offered to help, to carry the darkness for me."

"Wait, you're saying that you consented to everything they did in Kansas City?"

Dracula nodded. "I was lost. I was desperate. I taught them the ways of the Scholomance. We came to America. We started a few clubs. It was supposed to end there. With my darkness gone, I had a new mission. I was going to use what power I had to do good, to atone for my past evil deeds by making the world better."

"But they decided to replicate your power, to create new Draculas they could manipulate. Why didn't they just stake you, then, and be done with it?"

"Because if they did, the dark power they took from me would die with me. Light and dark always go hand in hand. It's why I always had a little light, flickering within me, even at my worst. The darkness needed it to thrive."

I bit my lip. "You're not saying—"

"If I could stake myself and be done with it, I'd do it. It's beyond that, now. They aren't merely wielding my darkness. They've used it to acquire a dark power of their own."

"What about Dylan and the other werewolves?"

Dracula sighed. "What Sorina said is true. Werewolf blood is like poison to vampires. A bite from a werewolf won't kill us. It will leave us paralyzed for a hundred years. If we were to bite a werewolf, twice as long."

"Then why would Sorina and the sisters mess with the wolves at all?"

Dracula scratched the back of his head. "A master of the Scholomance can resist the effects. The trick is we have to be prepared for it. If a wolf takes us by surprise, we're still vulnerable. If we cast the spell before biting a wolf, ourselves, we can assume control over the wolf like a vampire's sire might his progeny. I showed the sisters as much years ago when I claimed a pack, bit its alpha, and used them to do my bidding for nearly a decade. Until a few Van Helsings, you know, what I call hunters, took out the pack."

I took a deep breath. "So, now that the sisters are masters of the Scholomance, they've done the same to Dylan and his pack?"

Dracula nodded. "It sounds that way."

"Is there any way to save them?"

"They can only control the pack through the alpha. That's the only way it works. If we can figure out who the alpha is and kill him, the others will be released."

I shook my head. "Dylan never told me who his alpha was."

"He wouldn't. It doesn't matter how close you were to him. It's a sacred oath among wolves, they'll never tell anyone the identity of their alpha. It could be any of them."

"So, we kill one alpha and it's over?"

Dracula shook his head. "Not exactly. Kill a pack's alpha, and they'll hunt down whoever did it. The one who kills their alpha's slayer will become the new alpha. If you kill Dylan's alpha, Sienna, Dylan will try to kill you."

"He wouldn't do that!"

"As a werewolf, he won't have a choice. Whatever he was, whoever Dylan is, isn't in control when the wolf's instincts take over."

I sighed. "There must be another way."

"There is, but it's unpredictable. If the alpha dies some other way, if he happens to fall on a silver stake, or steps into a trap that he triggers himself and dies as a result, the other wolves will fight among themselves to determine which wolf will take the alpha's place."

"So we lure the alpha into a trap, a pit in the ground covered with leaves, silver stakes waiting to impale him below."

"The swords we trained with before are made from an alloy with silver. They'd do the trick before, provided you or I weren't wielding the sword at the time."

"So we mount the sword to something in the pit."

"Maybe. Werewolves have keen senses. They aren't easy to trick or trap. Besides, I'd keep your sword on hand. We don't know who the alpha is. We might need our swords to defend ourselves."

"Okay. Back to the silver stakes in the pit. Maybe a silver

blade that gets triggered by a trip wire, you know, like a booby trap."

"There's something else to consider, Sienna. The bond between wolves is strong. Even if this idea works, and we kill the alpha, Dylan might not forgive you."

I pressed my lips together. "But he'd be free."

"He'd be free, sure," Dracula agreed. "But would you? Werewolves are normal people all but a couple nights out of the month. They have families, human lives. If this pack is responsible, if they take precautions not to kill under a full moon, you'd be murdering an innocent man. The alpha, like all the wolves, is a victim of what Sorina and the sisters have done. Could you live with that guilt?"

I tightened my grip on the steering wheel. "I don't know. But if these wolves remain under Sorina's control, they *will* kill. If I have to bear the burden of guilt as a killer so they don't have to be killers themselves, then I'll find a way to deal."

"There's another matter to consider."

I huffed. "As if this isn't going to be hard enough?"

"Sorina's plans are surely larger than claiming a pack of wolves and using them to wreak havoc on a city. Under her thrall, sure, they can do a lot of damage. The carnage they'll leave behind will be unspeakable. It will undoubtedly attract the attention of hunters from all over the continent. Sorina knows, having learned from my experience when I claimed a pack in the same way, that it's just a matter of time before the pack is eliminated. When that happens, if the hunters are worth their weight in salt, they'll turn on Sorina and the sisters. We barely survived the onslaught before."

"So this isn't her master plan, then?"

"Definitely not. At best, it's a distraction. There's a reason why she went after this pack. She knew you'd try to save them. In the meantime, she and the sisters will have something else in the works, something much worse."

"Any idea what that might be?"

Dracula took a deep breath. "The world knows about vampires now. Sure, the average person might not know what's going on, but after all that happened in Kansas City, the authorities and the powers-that-be know all about our kind."

I bit my lip. "From what I understand, the police department in New Orleans is prepared to deal with vampires."

Dracula nodded. "We've known for some time that it was just a matter of time before our existence was known. In an age with infrared cameras on every corner, with social media and everything else, it was inevitable that—pardon the expression—that the truth about vampires would come to light. The sisters and I had a plan to deal with that. It was, in part, Sorina's idea."

"So what was this plan you and the sisters cooked up in your castle in Transylvania?"

"When the powers-that-be become our biggest threat, we *become* the powers-that-be."

I furrowed my brow. "The vampires fight to take control of the government?"

"Not exactly. We *infiltrate* the government. We turn the most powerful people, bind them as their sires to our will, and use them as our pawns."

I winced. "That's brilliant. Devious and downright evil, but certainly clever."

"We knew that getting to someone like the president wouldn't be easy. The plan was to start with local governments. Mayors are easy to reach and turn. State representatives and senators. From there, we'd work our way up the ranks."

"Trying to do that, without going into the sunlight, wouldn't be easy, either."

"A complication, for sure. But it wouldn't be impossible. With enough patience, I have no doubt that Sorina can pull it off. I believe that's why she suggested we come to America. If we were to take the American government, there isn't a leader in the world who wouldn't give an audience to the president of the United States. Your former president even managed to meet with the supreme leader of North Korea once. Those few nations whose leaders might be reluctant to meet with your president, well, if he secured an audience with just one of them, and they got to the others, eventually vampires would rule the world."

CHAPTER FOUR

Save the boy or save the world? I'd say it's a tough call, and if Dylan and I were more than we were, maybe it would have been more difficult. If Sorina was going to carry out the plan that Dracula suggested, stopping the sisters was the higher priority. If it was so easy as that, well, we'd thwart the bigger plan and worry about the wolves later. The problem was that we didn't know where Sorina and the weird sisters were. We didn't know where they had Dylan and his pack. Were they with the weird sisters, like guard dogs, or were they out and about terrorizing the city in a way that we couldn't ignore?

If the sisters had designs on local authorities or politicians, who would they target first? The mayor of New Orleans? Would they go big and start with the governor? Or would they start even smaller with a city councilman, the police chief, or the school board?

Okay, probably not the school board. Unless reeducating the youth on systemic anti-vampire bias was their *real* diabolical plan. Anyone who thought there was a systemic bias against vampires hadn't read *Twilight*, *The Vampire Diaries*, or anything else listed under vampire romances on Amazon's Kindle store. If anything, we were eroticized. Even if a lot of people still found vampires terrifying, there were a healthy number of people—young people especially—who were fascinated, wanted to date vampires, or hoped to become one. The truth of our existence was only beginning to leak out to the public.

People didn't know about me, though. A lot of vampires knew about me. Zoey and I had been thorns in the side of a number of powerful vampires before. According to Dracula, the murmurs from the vampire community he'd picked up on while he was still on the dark side, was less a desire to eliminate me and more a hope to capture me, to force me to turn others. If enough vampires could walk in the sun, invigorated by the light, while some remained committed to the night, humans wouldn't have any way to hide.

The one saving grace was that so far, none of the daywalkers I turned could turn others. I was like a queen bee, the only one in a hive who could hatch younglings. Since I'd be the sire of any daywalkers I made, I could control them. A sire's bond wasn't absolute, but if a vampire's progeny received a command from his or her sire, they'd have no choice but to comply. Resisting a sire's command was possible, with intense pain and anguish. The weird sisters, though, knew how to break a sire bond. They had done it with Dracula.

Sorina and the sisters were the biggest threat out there to me, personally. Dracula was convinced that I was also the biggest barrier to their ultimate plan.

Maybe it was because I was the only one who could work alongside Dracula, who was the only one who knew what they were up to. Sure, I could be formidable in the daylight, but vampires were susceptible to the sun already. If I was well-fed, I could step out of the sunlight and maintain my vampiric strength for a while. It was hard to know how long it would last. Some-times I'd gone as long as half an hour before my vampirism went dormant. At other times, my strength faded after a minute or two. Even so, I was one girl. I couldn't barge into a nest of vampires in the middle of the day and expect to beat them.

The sisters were the ones making all the moves. They had Dylan and his pack. They could start turning cops and politicians and I wouldn't know it. All I knew was that somehow, some way, we had to stop their plan.

I'd defeated some badass vampires and some powerful gods in the past. But that was with Zoey leading the charge. Dracula was right about one thing. I needed a few more tools up my sleeve. Learning to wield a sword effectively would help, but I needed more than that.

When we left Kansas City to go after the sisters, I was headstrong and confident. The closer we got to New Orleans, the less sure I was that I could do a damn thing to stop them.

We had one address to check out. The location of Club Dracula. It had just opened in New Orleans before we left Kansas City. We didn't have any reason to believe the sisters were there, though. The place was opened and operated by humans, and Dracula had the deed to the place. He had still been his former villainous self when he started the place. There were a number of vampires who frequented the clubs.

There was a reason the sisters went to New Orleans. The club had something to do with it. Just because Dracula owned the place didn't mean much to the vampires. They knew what happened in Kansas City. The sisters came there because they knew the vampires in New Orleans had their backs. Sure, Dracula could close down the club. He could send in the authorities and have anyone he didn't want there forcibly removed. Then again, that could lead to a lot of dead cops or, worse, a few of them turned into vampires. Our best play was to let the club function. It was a place where we knew the sisters had allies. If we could catch one of them, and let Dracula go medieval interrogating them, maybe we'd learn a thing or two.

It was rather bold calling the place Club Dracula. Most people figured it was a marketing ploy. Dracula, himself, had played the role of a philanthropist back in Kansas City. He'd gained a lot of friends among politicians. That was before. That was when he was setting the stage to fulfill the plan the sisters were likely continuing now.

Dracula's club was just a couple blocks off Bourbon Street in the French Quarter. We arrived there with the sun high in the sky, just after noon.

It was a lot smaller than the club in Kansas City. It wasn't that Dracula couldn't afford a bigger place, but suitable real estate in the French Quarter is hard to come by.

"There's movement inside," Dracula reported.

I tilted my head. "How can you tell?"

Dracula chuckled. "Just listen, Sienna. You're in the sun, your senses should be acute enough to pick it up."

I huffed. "Maybe. All I can hear is my stomach growling."

"Your brooch isn't suppressing your urges?"

I shook my head. "It takes the edge off. It used to work a hundred percent. Now, if I'm in direct sunlight, the thirst really kicks in."

"Your vampirism is getting stronger. It's to be expected."

I sighed. "If I removed this brooch, I'd be insatiable. It scares me. If my vampirism keeps getting stronger, I might not be able to resist."

Dracula grinned. "Ah, to be young again."

I raised an eyebrow. "What do you mean?"

Dracula laughed. "What you're talking about isn't unusual. Every new vampire has those cravings. Most of them get it out of their system. They'll go on a binge and either get through it, with more control over their urges, or a zealous hunter will take them out first. Your brooch is only delaying the inevitable."

"Feeding helps. I don't need much. Just a few gulps and my brooch will work perfectly."

Dracula shook his head. "Again, Sienna. You're only delaying the inevitable. You have to go through it. If you're ever going to truly master your urges and have control over your vampirism, you have to let what's natural run its course."

I huffed. "Well, I can find a blood bank. Google is good for that sort of thing. I can go astral and steal as much as I want and we can have a blood bash. For now, we have to figure out what the sisters are up to."

"I'm telling you, Sienna. We have to face this thing head-on," he insisted. "How much longer do you think your vampirism might last when you step out of the sun and step into a vampire lair like my club, here, if your brooch wasn't suppressing your true nature?"

I shrugged. "I don't know if it will make any difference at all."

"You don't know it won't."

I took a deep breath. I focused as best I could through the cravings. "There are people inside. I can hear them."

"Not only people. There are vampires. I can hear them feeding."

I tilted my head. "You can hear them feeding? What, do they smack their lips, belch after a gulp?"

"I can hear the humans. Their deep breaths and moans. They aren't victims. They're volunteers."

"How many are we talking about?"

"A dozen humans, give or take. Twenty or thirty vampires, maybe more."

"Damn, that's some slick hearing you've got there, Drac."

"It comes with mastering your true nature," he explained.

I grunted. "Why would people volunteer to become meals?"

"Why do addicts return to the needle when they know it could kill them? The blood loss, the enzymes passed through the bite, it gives people quite the high. Some of them are hoping to be turned. With as many vampires, compared to how many humans there are in there, I suspect some of them will get their wish."

"And those who don't?"

"They'll likely be drained and die. Not everyone who is bitten multiple times survives the transition."

"Die? You're awfully casual about that."

Dracula looked at me with a blank stare. "Look, I might be the best version of who I used to be, but I'm still a vampire and have been for a very long time. Do the cattle who died to become hamburgers haunt humans forever?"

"You're saying humans are like cattle?"

"That's how many of our kind feel, Sienna. I may be entertaining my better demons now, but better demons are still demons. I'm still a vampire. So are you."

"We're talking about human lives, here! We have to do something."

Dracula shook his head. "We're talking about humanity itself. We can't run into a nest like this and expect to come out unscathed. Besides, the doors are probably locked. I never got keys to the facility."

"I can get in. I can go astral and walk right through the walls."

"And if they have the black lights that reveal you, what will you do?"

I pressed my lips together. "There's an emergency exit, right? I'll go through the door, if there are lights and I'm exposed, I'll run right out again. We should at least try and get a little intelligence here. We don't have any other leads."

Dracula folded his arms over his chest. "Very well. Be careful. I'll be right outside. Anything goes wrong at all, get out of there."

CHAPTER FIVE

I touched my brooch. When I went astral, I was unrestrained by the laws of physics. All that nonsense about two objects occupying one place at a time didn't apply. The only limit was my mind. That was key. My mind would react to the world around me as normal. If I thought a wall was going to stop me, it would. It also was good because if I *didn't* realize the ground was beneath my feet, I could float right through the ground or, worse, out into space. I could defy gravity if I needed to. Mindset was key. Thankfully, in my battles with Zoey, I got pretty good navigating the astral plane. So long as they didn't have black lights infused with the power of the underworld, they'd have no clue that I was there. I'd pop in, have a look around, and learn what I could. So long as I didn't do anything stupid, the sisters would never know we were there.

The emergency door to the club was around back. Fire codes required them, especially in a place like a club. Without one, they'd never be able to have the max capacity necessary to operate a place like that. There might only be one way to get into the club—for most people, that is—but there had to be multiple ways out.

The club was dark. No windows to speak of. Made sense. Most clubs didn't have a lot of windows, and if the place doubled as a vampire nest, windows could be an occupational hazard.

There were just a few cam lights overhead that gave me a general view of the place. It was like a scaled-down version of the club in Kansas City. There was a bar, a dance floor, a stage for live bands or a DJ. The floor wasn't occupied with dancers. Not in the middle of the day.

Nude bodies everywhere. Not just the humans, the vampires, too. All of them covered in blood from head to toe. It was as if all the world's most notorious serial killers got together and decided to host an orgy. I could hardly tell which ones were humans and which were vampires. Apart from the few who were feeding at the moment and those who were being fed upon, there was no way to know who was who. The victims I could identify had wounds all over their bodies. Dracula was right. They were meals, but they'd soon become colleagues. They were turning these people. Or at least, they were trying to. Not all of them would survive.

I walked around and observed. No black lights, so I was safe. It was too late to save any of the people I could identify *as* people. Even if I managed to get them out of the place, they'd turn or die. Same as if they stayed. None of the vampires were Sorina or her sisters.

Maybe it wasn't the vampires who were important. They could be run of the mill bloodsuckers. If they were sired by the sisters, and these vampires were turning others, the chain of command would play out. Who were these people? Were they really vampire groupies, looking for a fix? Or were these people targeted, important to the sisters' plan?

You can't tell a lot about someone from a naked, blood-covered body. Their clothes had to be somewhere, though. Maybe they had identification, something that would let me know who the sisters were targeting and turning.

A few jackets hung on the back of chairs. In a sitting area between the bar and the dance floor, clothes lay over the chairs and under the tables. I didn't need to examine anyone's skivvies. A wallet would be either in a coat or pants. Getting a wallet from a pair of pants while on the astral plane wasn't going to be easy. My mind was conditioned to pass through objects, not engage them.

I knelt behind one of the tables. I tried to reach into a coat pocket, but my hand passed right through it. I tried the same with a pair of slacks draped over a chair. I tried to focus my mind, to convince myself that I could do it, but every attempt failed.

I sighed. I could touch my brooch, return to form, grab someone's wallet, and go astral again. It was risky. If someone saw me, and they knew who I was, they could switch on the black lights, and I'd be exposed.

I had to balance risk and reward. What were the chances anyone would notice? It was dark, and there was a lot of blood. If I wasn't astral, I'd smell it. I'd desire it. That much blood would keep most of the vampires occupied.

I reached for my brooch. Before I touched it I felt a hand on my shoulder. I leaped to my feet and turned.

A shrouded figure in a black cloak stood there, a scythe in his hand. My heart was racing so hard I thought it might explode out of my chest.

The reaper had his hood up. If he lowered it, he'd leave the astral plane. I could see enough of his face to realize who it was.

"Morty, what are you doing here?" Mortimer Grimm was Zoey's brother, the new Grim Reaper now their father had ascended to godhood and ruled in Olympus—the realm of the gods, the "heaven" for blessed souls.

"I could ask you the same question. I'm a reaper, what do you *think* I'm doing here?"

"People are going to die."

"Several people," Morty agreed. "There's nothing you can do,

Sienna. Once someone's name is scheduled, we have to collect their souls."

I snorted. "You're the Grim Reaper. Don't you have lesser reapers, lackeys, to deal with things like this?"

Morty shook his head. "This is a special case. You know that the weird sisters are involved. You know what they did, stealing human souls before. Other reapers will be here shortly. I'm doing basic reconnaissance. I'm here to make sure we harvest the souls without a hitch. We don't want to see a repeat of the incident in Kansas City."

"What can you tell me about these people? If they were on your schedule, you know who is supposed to die. I need to find out who the sisters are targeting."

"I need you to leave," Morty insisted.

"Morty, I could really use your help here. I'm trying to do this without your sister."

"I have a job to do, Sienna. Let me do what I came here to do. I'll meet you outside when we're done."

"Don't you think about standing me up, Morty. I'll tell Zoey if you do. You don't want her giving you a piece of her mind."

Morty laughed. "You're right. I don't want that. Don't worry, Sienna. I'll be done here shortly."

I bit my lip. "Be careful. You see those fixtures on the wall? If the vampires turn those on, they'll see you. For all we know, this is an elaborate trick to capture you and a few reapers. With a few reapers, they could make more daywalkers like me. Daywalkers who could create more daywalkers."

Morty's grin was about all I could see. "This isn't my first rodeo, Sienna. This isn't the first massacre in this place. This is the third day in a row we've had to reap souls here."

I gulped. "How many people have they killed?"

Morty shook his head. "It doesn't matter. We'll talk later. I'm running out of time here. I need to bring in the other reapers.

Otherwise, these souls might get loose. No one wants to deal with wandering and vengeful spirits."

"Vengeful?" I asked.

Morty nodded. "These people might be fools, but they came here expecting to be turned, not to die. The vampires responsible aren't very up-front about the possible side effects of a few bites."

"Side effects include clammy skin, strange cravings for blood, homicidal inclinations, possibly even death. Ask your doctor if vampirism is right for you."

Morty chuckled. "Get out of here, Sienna. Give us twenty minutes to wrap this up. Give me another twenty minutes to deliver my souls to the boatman. There's a nice restaurant two blocks over. Can't miss it. Lunch is on me."

I looked back across the room at the literal bloodbath that was going on across the dance floor. "Given my cravings lately, lunch looks like it's on them."

"You can handle it. I have faith in you."

I gave Morty a thumbs-up. "Thanks for your vote of confidence, buddy!"

CHAPTER SIX

I left the club through the emergency exit door and found Dracula pacing nervously in the alley behind the club.

I snuck up behind my ancient mentor/companion. In the astral plane, I didn't have to sneak. I could have jumped up and down and waved my hands and he wouldn't know. Still, it was more fun this way.

I touched my brooch. "Boo!"

Dracula shrieked like a twelve-year-old girl who'd seen a mouse. He was clutching at his chest as he looked at me as if to say, "WTF?"

I giggled. "Gotcha!"

"That wasn't nice."

"But it was funny! The look on your face. You looked as if you'd seen a ghost."

"I always look like that. My skin lacks pigmentation."

I grinned. "You know what I mean."

"I thought I was going to have a heart attack!"

"Unless I was holding a stake, you couldn't have a heart attack. Chill out, dude."

"Dude?"

I shrugged. "Count Dude?"

Dracula chuckled and shook his head. "I'm usually the one who frightens people. You took me off guard."

"Yeah, that was the point."

"Just wait. I'll get you back. When you least expect it."

I smiled. "I'm sure you will."

"Boo!" Dracula raised his hands over his head.

I tilted my head. "That didn't work."

Dracula sniffed. "I didn't think you'd expect it right now."

I raised an eyebrow. "You can't be serious. I have to tutor Dracula on the art of scaring people?"

"I usually rely on my fangs. I spread out my cloak. I laugh maniacally. It does the trick."

"I'm sure that works for damsels in distress. I'm no damsel," I informed him. "You need to take me by surprise. That's the key."

"That didn't surprise you?"

"Not really."

Dracula sighed. "What did you see in there?"

"A lot of blood. I'll tell you what, I hope you didn't pay a lot for that dance floor. Or, I hope your janitors know how to clean up blood because there's a lot of it."

Dracula winced. "How did *you* do being around so much blood?"

"Fine. I couldn't smell it from the astral plane. I won't lie, though. It was like watching a commercial for the Golden Corral. All-you-can-eat buffet. The visual appeal was tantalizing and revolting at the same time."

"Understandable. Did you learn anything?"

I pressed my lips together. "Well, the Grim Reaper showed up."

"Zoey's brother?"

"Yep. They have some souls to collect. Nasty business. I was trying to figure out who it was that the vamps were trying to turn when he showed up. Reapers know a few things about the souls they gather. He said he'd meet us for lunch at a place a couple blocks from here. He said it would take forty minutes or so to finish his job and drop his souls off with the boatman at the River Styx."

"That knowledge could be helpful. This is a fine turn of events."

"We have a little time to burn," I suggested. "I know we're going to lunch, but gumbo isn't really what has my stomach churning right now. Think we have time for a heist?"

"A heist?"

I nodded. "There has to be a hospital or a blood bank somewhere around here. It might spoil my lunch, but if I don't get a little blood soon, I'm going to lose my freaking mind."

"Do you think you can pull that off in time to meet the Grim Reaper for lunch?"

"In the astral plane, no problem," I assured him. "Why don't you go reserve a table?"

"Mind picking me up something while you're there?"

"Sure. What's your order?"

"Type O-negative, please. I've had a steady diet of B-positive lately and I could use something different."

I smirked. "Right. Nothing hits the spot like O-negative."

"Exactly!" Dracula grinned.

In truth, I didn't know the difference. I'd had a few blood bags, stolen from blood banks, before. I knew some of them tasted different than others, but I didn't have Dracula's refined palate. I never did. Not even as a human. I wasn't of legal age, but I'd had a few glasses of wine before and I couldn't tell the difference between a Merlot and a Cabernet Sauvignon. Wine was wine. It left my mouth dry and gave me one hell of a headache. I wasn't a fan. Maybe, eventually, I'd develop more discriminating tastes. At the moment, though, I didn't care. Blood was blood.

I generally preferred to take my blood from blood banks rather than hospitals. I didn't want to be responsible for taking blood that could save someone's life. Sure, okay, eventually all donated blood could save a life, but in a hospital, the blood was inventoried and might be needed quickly. Robbing a blood bank was nothing compared to taking blood that someone might be depending on to save their life in an emergency, and wasn't comparable to grabbing a random person off the street for dinner. If I didn't steal a little blood, that's what would happen, eventually.

A quick search on my phone found a place about two miles away on Canal Street. It was called The Blood Center. It had about as much creativity as "Club Dracula," but at least if you went there you'd know exactly what it was about. Go to The Blood Center and it's all about blood. Go to Club Dracula and it's all about blood too—but they wouldn't give you a cookie afterward.

On the astral plane, I could run like Barry Allen. I was like the world's weirdest bank robber. My heists involved *blood* banks, but "bank robber" had an outlaw vibe. I knew bank robberies weren't like you saw on television. In real life, most bank robbers hand a teller a note, demand their money, and get it, no questions asked. The cameras catch them first. The cops catch them shortly thereafter. Robbing a blood bank took more finesse, especially during business hours. I wasn't sure how it would go over if I walked in and handed them a note demanding two bags of O-negative and warning them I had fangs.

Maybe it would work, but vampires hit blood banks regularly enough that most of the nurses who worked there were believers. Zoey's mom, Josephine, was a vampire hunter. She had connections at every blood bank in town. They had her business card. If the hunters in Louisiana were any good, they probably had similar arrangements. Of course, they'd never expect a vampire to show up and rob them in the middle of the day, and if a little blood turned up missing mid-day, they'd never think vampire. That meant it was less likely hunters might get a call. Then again, with vampires becoming bolder, so bold that Dracula owned a club named after himself, there were probably hunters in the area already.

Finding hunters and tipping them off was on the table as one of many strategies we might pursue if we needed a little unwitting manpower to deal with the sisters, Dracula and I had decided on the drive.

The problem was that not all hunters were as open-minded as Zoey's mother. If we contacted them, they were likely to take our information, stake us both, and go after the sisters next. They'd probably fail. There was a reason Dracula and the sisters had survived so long. Hell, Dracula even faced the original Professor Abraham Van Helsing back in the day. Many "Van Helsings," or hunters, had tried to take down Dracula and the sisters in the centuries since. For most of that time, Dracula wasn't hard to find. He lived in the same castle all that time.

None of the hunters who dared to enter that place survived to tell the tale.

Staking Dracula was the golden goose, the prize that most hunters dreamed of. If they knew he was in town, he'd be their primary target. They'd worry about the sisters after they eliminated him. Now that Dracula didn't wield the dark power of the Scholomance, the magic he'd used to defeat hunters before, he was more vulnerable than ever.

Trying to convince them that Dracula had changed, that he wasn't the villain he used to be, would be a hard sell. Even if we convinced them to listen, which was doubtful, they'd probably kill him. If a murderer gets away with his crimes for years, but reforms his life, and is later caught, he'll still be held accountable. He'll still have to pay the price the justice system demanded.

All those facts added up to one basic truth—I had to be careful how I did this. I needed the blood, that much was clear. This was the best option.

I made it to The Blood Center on Canal Street. In astral form,

I phased through the door. Donors were waiting inside for their turn. I needed to observe the operation so I could find a window of opportunity. I had to follow the blood.

I waited until one of the donors was done. The nurse took the blood bag and walked into a back room.

There were three donors in the chairs. The trick was to get my timing right. If I watched and waited, I could sneak in, grab the blood from the refrigerator they stored it in, and go astral again with the blood bags in hand before one of the nurses had reason to go back into the room. The next lady in the waiting room took the chair of the first. The other two were just finishing up. That gave me a couple of minutes. I only needed a few seconds.

I waited until the two nurses placed the bags in the fridge. The bags were all marked by blood type.

When the nurses left the room, I approached the fridge, pressed my brooch, and materialized. I reached in, grabbed two bags of O-negative, closed the refrigerator, and touched my brooch again. Since I was holding the bags of blood, they disappeared when I did.

I was about to leave when I looked up. There was a camera in the room. My heart sank. Why didn't I think of that? Of course there'd be a camera watching the supply.

"Well, shit."

No one heard me. I was astral. I could only hope that two missing bags wouldn't raise alarm, and that no one would check the cameras. Who was I kidding? These places kept a tight inventory. Maybe they wouldn't tell any hunters. If they saw a vanishing girl break in, though… I wasn't about to bank on that. No pun intended.

CHAPTER SEVEN

I hurried back to the restaurant where we were supposed to meet Morty. Dracula was there waiting with some fruity cocktail, complete with an umbrella and a pineapple-shaped plastic cup. He had another one waiting for me.

"Sienna! Check it out! It's a collector's cup."

I snorted. "Yup. Garbage collectors are a thing, too."

"It's a Long Island Iced Tea. Delicious!"

I tilted my head as I sat. "We're in New Orleans and you got a Long Island Iced Tea?"

Dracula shrugged. "So?"

"Isn't that like going to Mexico and ordering a hamburger? Like going to a bakery in Paris and ordering Italian bread?"

"It's good. You can hardly taste the alcohol."

I chuckled. "I took you for more of the Bloody Mary type."

"Ah! You have vampire jokes!"

I grinned. "Yeah. I'll be here all week. I got your O-negative."

Dracula slid his collector's cup to the side. "I was counting on that. Have any trouble?"

I bit my lip. "That depends on how you define trouble."

"Did anyone see you?"

"Not yet."

"Not yet?"

"Well, there was a camera. I didn't see it until after I took the blood."

I handed Dracula one of the bags. He hid it under the table. He gulped down the rest of his drink and took his cup under the table with the blood bag. "Great thing about these collector's cups is that they're opaque. Blood in a glass raises eyebrows. No one will be any the wiser."

I smirked. "Clever."

"Drink up. You need that cup."

I took a sip of my drink. I winced. "I thought you said you could barely taste the alcohol."

"Chase it down with a gulp of O-negative," he suggested. "You'll forget all about it."

"You seriously aren't worried at all about the camera at the blood bank?"

Dracula shrugged. "It'll take time before they notice the blood is missing. It'll take them even longer to check the camera. If they contact any hunters, well, they might not right away. Say they reach a couple hunters, and they get a look at the footage. What are they going to do with it? They'll see a girl who disappears and steals blood. They'll also know it happened in the middle of the day. The hunters will be curious, probably intrigued. They won't think vampire."

"What will they think, then?"

"Who knows? Maybe a witch looking for blood for a ritual. Most hunters won't hunt witches."

"Why not?"

"They're human, for one. They're also unpredictable. But say they start looking for witches. They'll check out local covens, they'll probably try to infiltrate a couple of them. They'll hit a dead end. They still won't know what really happened. They'll research more covens, try to infiltrate them, too. There are a lot of witches here. Mambos and houngans, mostly."

"Mambos and houngans?"

"Voodoo priestesses and priests. The hunters could spend years trying to track all of them down looking for you. Did the camera get a good shot of your face?"

I shook my head. "My back mostly."

"So that narrows it down to any redhead in New Orleans who might be involved in voodoo, witchcraft, or who knows what else. Do you see where I'm going with this?"

"You're saying we have nothing to worry about."

"I didn't say that. A mystery like that will probably bring more hunters to town. They'll want to solve the crime."

"I stole two blood bags. That's a lot of effort to go to for so little."

"They'll want to solve the crime so they can identify the culprit. In the meantime, well, hunters will do what they do. They'll start looking for vampires to kill. Might as well, you know, since they'll be in town anyway and everyone knows that New Orleans is the vampire capital of North America."

"Well, we sure can't let them find you."

"They won't be looking for me in broad daylight. Perhaps they'll find the sisters for us. We keep tabs on the hunters and let them do the leg work. In the end, Sienna, this might not be a bad thing."

I shook my head. "You said it yourself. All that is going to take time."

"It will," he agreed. "But you know, if push comes to shove, it's a card we can play."

Footsteps approached from behind and I turned my head. He wasn't in his reaper cloak this time. He was in a three-piece suit, complete with scythe cuff links and wing-tipped shoes.

"Morty? Damn, you clean up well."

Morty grinned. "I know. Think I overdressed?"

I downed my Long Island Iced Tea, hid it under the table, and filled it with the contents of my blood bag. "I don't know. This place has collector cups. It's not exactly a five-star restaurant."

Morty chuckled. "It isn't. You went to the wrong place."

"You told us where to go!"

Morty scratched the back of his head. "Yeah, there are two restaurants on this block. I didn't even know about this place. But then you weren't where I expected. I have a table waiting for us."

"Wait. We're going to a fancy place? I'm not a fancy girl, Morty. Do I look fancy to you?"

Morty laughed. "Follow me. If you must, you can take your—"

"Our drinks?" I smiled as I took my first sip. The blood hit my stomach like a piece of the best chocolate cake I'd ever had. And I'll tell you what: I love me some chocolate cake.

"Right. Your drinks."

CHAPTER EIGHT

When you're going to lunch with Dracula and the Grim Reaper, it's hard to know what to expect. For most people, a meal like that would spoil the afternoon. I couldn't think of two people that humans dreaded meeting more.

But they were my buddies!

Dracula was always dressed well. Sure, his style was dated, but no one would ever accuse him of being underdressed. Morty looked like a secret agent. Grim Reaper, 007. When I first met the guy, he had a mohawk and wore holey jeans and screen-printed t-shirts. Punk Rock Reaper. Now he was debonair, and dare I say it, attractive. He had a girlfriend, and I wasn't interested in him. Besides, he was my bestie's twin brother. It would just be weird. Still, he wore fancy well.

I was still in road-trip clothes. Yoga pants, flip-flops, and a tank top. Perfect for a place that served drinks in pineapple-shaped collector's cups.

"Why didn't you tell us you wanted to meet at a place with a dress code?"

"You look fine," Morty assured me.

"Pfffft!"

"You're about Carmilla's size."

"Isn't she your girlfriend? I'm not going to the underworld to raid her closet."

Morty smirked. "I know a few tricks. Follow me."

I expected we were going to leave the hole-in-the-wall place, but Morty led me back toward the bathrooms, where he formed a small portal with a wave of his hand. He smirked. "Perks of being the Grim Reaper. I can make portals between Earth and the underworld just about anywhere."

I tilted my head as Morty reached in and pulled a hanger and garment bag through the portal. "Carmilla won't even notice. She has too many clothes."

I rolled my eyes. "Honey, a girl always knows when something's missing from her closet."

Morty shrugged. "Not a big deal. Try it on."

I grabbed the garment bag from Morty and ducked into the restroom. I unzipped the bag. My jaw dropped when I saw it.

It was gorgeous. A black dress, befitting a vampire or, perhaps, the Grim Reaper's girlfriend. There wasn't much of a top to it. A lot of straps that I had a hard time sorting out. What exactly covered what? At least my brooch would look better with the dress than my tank top.

I untangled the straps. I was about seventy-five percent sure I figured it out. Getting into it was another matter. I was wearing yoga pants before, and I had to do a little yoga now to manipulate my body into this dress.

I was a barista who, before becoming a daywalker, saved every spare penny for community college tuition. I'd never worn *anything* like this. The mirror in the restroom was small and wasn't clean. Still, I looked damn good. Better than I thought I would. I *felt* ridiculous, mostly because my upper half was barely covered. But what the hell? This was New Orleans. It was the capital of boobs for beads. I was modest by comparison.

My flip-flops didn't go with the dress. I stepped out and saw

Morty waiting. He had a pair of knee-high boots in his hands. "Sorry, forgot to grab these before."

I tilted my head. "Carmilla is going to kill you."

Morty laughed. "I'm the Grim Reaper. She can't *kill* me."

I tilted my head. "Reapers can die, Morty. Your sister's ex died at the hand of a vampire. I was there. I saw it."

Morty smirked. "Again, perks of being the Grim Reaper. I won't say it's impossible, but if there is a way to kill me, I'm not sure what it is."

"Dude, you could totally help us kick these sisters' asses."

Morty shook his head. "I have responsibilities. I have rules to follow. I can help so far as I can help. I can give you information. The one thing I can't do is kill vampires. That's Zoey's job. She's the one who reaps supernaturals."

"Well, she's not going to help. She's got a bun in the oven."

"You've got this, Sienna. Why don't you see if these boots fit?"

You'd think wearing a dress like the one I was in would make me more refined or graceful. Nope. I hopped on one foot trying to push my other foot into one of the boots. I had to lean against the wall which, frankly, was a little gross. It felt greasy. I zipped up the boot. It fit well, so I zipped up the other one. I wrapped up my flip-flops and tank top in my spandex yoga pants. "I should drop this stuff off in the van."

Morty took my clothes and tossed them into a portal.

"Dude, what the hell?"

"I just gave you a dress that costs ten times more than your other getup. Are you really worried about it? Besides, I can get your stuff back for you later."

"Thanks, Morty." I grabbed my collector's cup off our table and chugged the rest of the blood before leaving. Dracula's cup was gone. Did he take it with him? I guess that's why they're collector's cups. You take them with you and they take up unnecessary space in your cabinets for about five years until one day you break down and wonder, *Why the hell do I have this thing?*

"Come on. They're holding a table for us."

I followed Morty out of the first restaurant. Dracula was already waiting on the sidewalk, enjoying the sun. When he saw me, his jaw dropped. He covered his mouth instinctively. Probably so no one would get a glimpse of his oversized incisors.

I had the urge to cover my upper half. This was a new look for me. I was a computer geek, with a cute face and a body I never showed off. I was a barista who wore an apron and a button-up shirt and slacks. The fanciest dress I ever wore was for high school prom—and I bought it used at Goodwill.

Now I was out in New Orleans' French Quarter, wearing a piece that was probably identifiable by a name I couldn't pronounce. If someone asked me "who" I was wearing, I wouldn't even know how to respond. I didn't like the v-word that much, but face it, "who are you wearing?" isn't something you should ask a vampire. Or Hannibal Lecter. You might not get the answer you were looking for.

Dracula and I followed Morty down the sidewalk to a single door. It was a nice door, so far as doors go. I said it before. Wine is wine. Blood is blood. Doors are doors. There's not much argument there. So long as it opens and closes, a door does what it's supposed to do. This was the kind of restaurant that people of means knew about and went to. They didn't bother with neon signs or flashy entrances. It was no wonder Dracula and I both missed it and went to the other place.

Morty opened the door to a small room with marble floors and an elevator. He pressed the call button, and when the elevator doors opened we were greeted by classical music.

"Delightful!" Dracula exclaimed. "Now that's music."

"If you're trying to fall asleep, sure," I teased.

Morty chuckled. "I'm with you, Sienna. But wait until you try their steak."

I tilted my head. "Steak?"

Dracula rubbed his hands together. "Nothing outside a jugular beats a rare steak."

"I've been to Steak n' Shake. They have good eats."

Morty tilted his head, and Dracula frowned. They hadn't heard of Steak 'n Shake. I guess I couldn't blame them. Morty lived in the underworld, and I didn't know if the chain had locations in Transylvania. Probably not. Fancy places like that are more discriminating about where they place their restaurants. It's not like they were McDonald's.

It was curious that Morty didn't know about Steak 'n Shake but did know about this place. That mystery was solved, in part, when we left the elevator and the greeter smiled at Morty.

"Mortimer Grimm! Welcome back!"

Morty smiled. "Good to be back. You never disappoint."

I tilted my head. "You've been here before?"

"I've had a lot of business in New Orleans lately."

I smirked. "I thought business was dead."

"In my line of work, that means we're busy. In Louisiana, there's an average of around a hundred and twenty deaths per day. In the last few days, we've seen that number in New Orleans alone."

"Because of the weird sisters?"

"Exsanguination accounts for the bulk of the increase," Morty acknowledged. "I don't always know who is responsible. The reaper schedule doesn't give us all those details. Sometimes things are clearer when the reapers arrive to gather the souls. Bite marks are a dead giveaway. Nearly all of the exsanguinations we've reaped in recent days can be attributed to vampires."

"The sisters aren't doing it themselves," Dracula suggested. "Older vampires rarely lose someone when turning them. They're clearly having younger vampires do the dirty work."

The host who was taking us to our table surely heard our conversation, but he didn't bat an eye.

He sat us at our table and pulled my chair out for me. I

thanked him politely, but really? Dude, I'm a chick. That doesn't mean I can't pull out a freaking chair. I'm not a weakling.

When we sat, Dracula and Morty unfolded their cloth napkins and placed them on their laps. I followed suit. Seemed like the thing to do.

"Is it okay to talk openly about this stuff?"

Morty smiled. "This is New Orleans. This particular restaurant caters to supernaturals. They're used to it."

I bit my cheek. "What a weird place."

Dracula chuckled. "You should visit Transylvania sometime. Places like this are more common than you'd think."

I grinned. "I'll add a trip to Transylvania to my bucket list."

Morty raised his hand and flicked his wrist, and a waiter approached.

"Giuseppe!" Morty exclaimed.

"Mr. Grimm. Welcome back to Laveau's."

I raised an eyebrow. "Laveau's? I didn't see a sign outside."

The waiter bowed his head. "We're named for the late Voodoo Queen of New Orleans, Madam Marie Laveau. She founded our establishment a year before she died in 1880."

"Damn," I quipped. "Talk about old school."

"Not that old," Dracula protested. "Seems just like yesterday."

I huffed. "To you, it would!"

Morty held up a menu and showed it to Giuseppe, pointing to a couple of items. "Ah, certainly," the waiter approved. "Curious to order such a drink over the lunch hour!"

Morty smiled. "It's a unique occasion. That's for my guests. I'll have the usual."

"Of course, sir."

Giuseppe left. I scanned the menu. There were some strange items there. For some reason, my eyes were drawn to the seafood. "Mermaid tail? What is that, a gimmick?"

Morty shook his head. "Not at all."

"Interesting," Dracula murmured. "The heart of a virgin. It's been years. Quite the delicacy."

My jaw dropped. "This can't be real."

Morty smiled. "I assure you they acquire their product through legitimate means."

"How do you get a virgin's heart or a mermaid's tail legitimately?"

Morty shrugged. "People and merfolk die from natural causes, Sienna. They aren't herding and slaughtering people for their menu, if that's what you're worried about."

"Are you sure about that?"

Morty stared at me blankly. "Of course I am. I'm the Grim Reaper. If they were, I'd know it."

I took a deep breath. "If you say so. I think I'll just order the steak."

"Always a fine choice," Dracula agreed. "As tempting as undefiled heart might be, I don't have the stomach for it like I used to."

"That's on the menu for werewolves, mostly, anyway."

"Seriously, Morty? I thought werewolves only ate hearts when they were shifted. I doubt many of them are refined for high society. I can't imagine them coming to a place like this."

Dracula cleared his throat. "That's true of younger werewolves. The older ones develop a palate even while still in human form that appreciates their more beastly tastes."

I shuddered. "Talk about disturbing."

The waiter, whose name I'd already forgotten, came back to the table with a bottle in his hand. He poured a red liquid until it filled my glass about a third of the way full. He did the same for Dracula.

I could smell it the moment it left the bottle. It was blood. "Only a third of a glass?"

"The bottle is yours," the waiter said.

Dracula picked up his glass and swirled it. He stuck his long nose into the glass and sniffed. "That's *nice.* What is it?"

The waiter held out the bottle and showed it to him. "A 1976 AB-negative."

Dracula took the bottle and examined it. "Grown in Bordeaux, a vegetarian. This is remarkable."

I raised an eyebrow. "You aged that shit since the seventies? Hell, I wasn't born yet. My parents were in junior high."

Dracula took a small sip and swirled it in his mouth. "Delectable!"

I shrugged and took a gulp. "Damn, that is some good shit. Thanks, Geraldo."

The waiter chuckled. "You're welcome. And it's Giuseppe."

"Right, Luigi. Well, this is weird as hell, but I have to admit, it is delicious."

"I'm pleased to hear it. Enjoy. Have you had time to peruse the menu?"

"We have," Morty replied. "I'll take a well-done steak."

"Certainly. We have the finest minotaur fillet this side of the Atlantic."

"Minotaur?"

Giuseppe looked taken aback. "What, you don't think we'd serve common bovine steak here, do you?"

I bit my lip. "I sort of assumed. I guess I'll take the same. Make mine rare."

"Make that three," Dracula chimed in. "I'll have it raw."

"Might I suggest the selkie tongue as hors d'oeuvre?"

"What's a selkie?" I asked.

Dracula smirked. "They're seals, sort of. When they're in the sea, anyway. When they come to land, they shed their skin and become human. Mostly found off the coasts of Northern Europe."

"And you cut out their tongues?" I shook my head. "When they're still seals or human?"

Dracula raised his hand. "We'll pass on the appetizer."

Morty chuckled. "Agreed."

"Hard pass for me, too." I shook my head as our waiter left us. "How many things are there that I've never heard of?"

"That depends," Dracula replied. "I don't know what things you've heard of."

Morty waved his hand through the air. "There are hundreds of species that you might classify as supernatural, or at least cryptozoological."

I raised an eyebrow. "What about the chupacabra?"

"Nasty beasts." Dracula shuddered. "Only met one, and I'm glad it was the last."

I tugged at the hem of my dress. "Bigfoot?"

Morty scoffed. "Everyone knows Bigfoot is real. That's an easy one."

"I don't think *everyone* knows that, Morty. How about Siren Head?"

Dracula frowned. "What the hell is that? I know about sirens. Never a Siren Head."

"Never heard of it, either."

"Search it on YouTube. It's a thing. Tall, murderous thing. Arms and legs as skinny as twigs. Two sirens for a head. Hangs out in the woods, looks like a telephone pole from a distance. Has a steady diet of long pig."

"Long pig?" Morty raised his eyebrows.

"Human flesh. The Dahmer special."

Morty chuckled. "I'm pretty sure someone made that shit up."

I shrugged. "You never know. To date, I've met Medusa's Gorgon sisters, gods from ancient dead religions, werewolves, vampires, banshees, ghosts, and I can't remember what else. Nothing would surprise me anymore."

Dracula took another sip of his blood wine. "Well, there's Mothman, the cyclops, brownies."

"Little girls aspiring to be Girl Scouts?"

Dracula chuckled. "Not like that. Hobgoblins, sort of like leprechauns, but not so happy-go-lucky."

"What about gnomes?"

"Wiley little boogers. Catch one in your garden, best take it out. It's rude to release it elsewhere. It'll just become someone else's problem."

I shook my head and took another gulp of the blood in my glass. I grabbed the bottle and filled it again, this time, to the brim. I was never meant to be a high-society girl. "Well, Morty, let's cut to the chase. What can you tell us about the people the vampires are trying to turn?"

"Well, the reaper schedule only tells me so much. On the surface, none of them are especially remarkable. A few of them are men or women of means. Most of them are regular folk. Respectable to the people who know them, held in high esteem."

I raised an eyebrow. "The sisters are trying to raise an army of respectable vampires?"

Morty shook his head. "Not at all. Here's the thing: every one of these souls we've reaped shared a common destination in the afterlife. All of them were condemned to Hades."

Dracula rubbed his brow. "You said they were virtuous."

"I said they were respected, held in high esteem," Morty corrected him. "It took me a while. There's only one who knows the real reason why some souls are condemned, and that's Athena, the queen of Hades, herself."

"What did she tell you?"

"They were killers, every last one of them. Murderers who got away with it. Not one of them the least bit remorseful. All of them clever and crafty enough not to get caught. Some of them killed several times."

"Serial killers?" I asked.

"Not all of them."

"Well, that's a relief. At least some of them only killed one or two people out of cold blood," I reasoned. "How many does it take before killing becomes serial, anyway?"

"They didn't all kill in cold blood. One was a drug dealer. His product killed more young people than anyone would care to count. Another was a doctor who thirty years ago had a mysteriously high number of mothers who died in childbirth. He told the families the children did, too. They didn't. He sold the babies on the black market."

I gulped. "That's horrifying."

Morty nodded. "I could keep going. Not all of them were native to Louisiana. They were brought here, lured here, with promises of immortality."

Dracula took a deep breath. "They're targeting people without a conscience. People capable of murder. People who wouldn't bat an eye about killing again once they turned."

I bit my lip. "If all they wanted was people who'd kill, the craving would do that. If all they wanted was killers, they could turn a prison guard and spread vampirism through a supermax. There must be a reason why they're going after people who not only killed but never got caught."

Dracula grabbed the bottle to pour a healthy share of blood into his glass and took a much bigger swig than he did before. "You mentioned a drug dealer and a corrupt obstetrician. Very different people, from very different lives. What they had in common was that their killings were motivated by money."

Morty considered a moment. "I hadn't thought of it like that, but it tracks. Every one of them had something to gain financially when they killed."

"Can you get us a list of names?" Dracula asked.

Morty reached into his pocket and handed Dracula a folded-up piece of paper. "Already have it. Take a look. These are only those who didn't become vampires. Those whose turnings failed. There are surely more than these who turned successfully."

"We need to do a little more digging into these people," Dracula proposed. "I know the sisters. These men must be connected to people of real means. If we follow the money, we'll find out who the sisters are after."

"Politicians?" I asked.

"It's possible. I suspect these men had something to gain, but in situations like that, there's often someone else pulling the strings. If these men were killing for profit, and someone of influence helped them cover it up, the would-be vampires also had an in."

"They'd blackmail them?" I asked.

Dracula shrugged. "Maybe. Or, they'd at least be connected enough having done the dirty work of more powerful men in the past that if they requested a meeting, they'd get an audience."

"And then they'd turn someone more powerful, who is probably connected to more powerful people, still."

"The higher up the food chain they go, pardon the expression, the more likely the sisters would be involved. I suspect that these men are more numerous than the people they worked for. If we can follow the money, and figure out who they were working for, we can identify who the sisters are targeting."

I scratched my head. "Not to overstep here, Morty, but I was roomies with your sister for a while. I know a little about how this works. You have schedules of people who will die over the next few days, right?"

Morty nodded. "In three days' time, the death rate in Louisiana will return to normal."

"So we don't have a lot of time."

Morty nodded. "There's one other thing. The exsanguinations end with last night's harvest."

"But you said the death rates don't level out for a few more days," Dracula noted.

"Mutilations come next."

Dracula and I looked at each other. We didn't have to say it. We were thinking the same thing.

I said it, anyway. "Werewolves."

Dracula nodded. "Sounds like it. It also means that the sisters have all the vampires they need to carry out their plan."

I shook my head. "We can't just ignore the werewolf killings."

"It's a distraction, Sienna. Sorina wants us to focus on the werewolves. Besides, once a name is written on the schedule, doesn't that mean that the person is going to die no matter what we do?"

Morty sighed. "Yes, and no. The people on the schedule will die. There's nothing you can do to stop it. However, names can be added to the schedule at any time. If you don't find a way to slow down the werewolves, there's a chance I'll have a sizable addendum to the schedule before the night's end."

The waiter returned to the table and set our "steaks," if you could call minotaur fillet a "steak," in front of each of us. I smiled at the waiter. "Thanks, Guinevere."

The waiter sighed. "It's Giuseppe. And you're welcome."

CHAPTER NINE

Minotaur steak isn't half bad. I can't say I would have appreciated it before becoming a daywalking bloodsucker, but it was more tender than a regular steak. A little bit gamey, I guess. At least that's what Dracula said. I didn't know what that meant. I didn't play a lot of games that had flavor. I was a city girl at heart.

Morty told us that the mutilations, which we presumed to be werewolf killings, were scheduled to occur up and down Bourbon Street. Of course the sisters would send Dylan's pack there. This wasn't my first time in New Orleans, and I'd hardly say I was an expert on the city, but everyone knew that Bourbon Street was where it was at.

Kansas City is an up-and-coming place, don't get me wrong. The downtown life is a lot more hopping than it used to be. One of America's best-kept secrets, I'd say. But it's *not* the French Quarter. It's nothing like Bourbon Street.

I'll put it this way. As revealing as my strappy dress was, I was more covered up than most of the females there. I'm not talking about prostitutes, though there were a few I suspected might be. But even the tourists—especially the tourists—let it all hang out on Bourbon Street.

Morty gave us a few names, but there wasn't any way to find them in the crowds, especially on short notice. With a little more time, maybe we could check the local hotels, make a few calls to the families of the victims and find out where they were, things like that. Hell, I was good enough with computers that I could probably even hack into their credit card records. If their hotel required a deposit, or they ordered room service, adult entertainment on their hotel televisions, or whatever, I'd be able to identify them and possibly find them.

There wasn't a point, though. Morty said you couldn't save someone if their name was already on his schedule. I didn't know how it worked. Zoey knew more than I did. It had something to do with gods and oracles. Did that mean that the future was predetermined? Did that mean we weren't masters of our own fates? Not necessarily. Morty also said that if we acted, or didn't act, in ways that the oracles predicted, more names could be added to the schedule. The names on there already were those we couldn't save. They were going to die regardless. The sisters were sending the werewolves to Bourbon Street. People were going to die. The best we could hope for was to keep the damage to a minimum.

Dracula had already given me the rundown on werewolf hierarchies. Killing the alpha would free the wolves from the sisters' control. It would also bind the wolves to an oath to avenge their alpha. They'd come after us. That's probably what the sisters wanted us to do. Of course, we didn't know how to tell for sure which wolf *was* the alpha. The best plan we had was to try to set a trap that the alpha might trigger himself. Just because it was our best plan didn't mean it was a good one. The wolves would fight it out among themselves, and some wouldn't survive. It would go on until one emerged as alpha and they'd displayed their dominance convincingly enough that the others would submit. What convinces a creature like a werewolf? Bloodshed. Dylan might not come out of it alive and if he did, several of his friends, his family, his pack, would be dead in the end.

The killings weren't supposed to begin until nightfall. There was more than one reason why that might have been the case. The werewolves didn't need the full moon to shift when they were under the sister's thrall. They were stuck as they were. The darkness of night would give the wolves a better chance of sneaking in and sneaking out when they were done with their rampage without us tracking them back to wherever they were holing up.

There was another reason. Dracula said the wolves couldn't move more than about a mile from the vampire controlling them. Presuming Sorina was the sister who had them under her control, she'd be somewhere nearby. Our chances of finding her were slim. She was smart. She'd stay well hidden. However, since she couldn't come out in the sun, neither could the wolves unless she was staying somewhere nearby during the day. While we couldn't be sure it was the case, that the wolves were going to attack at night probably meant Sorina and the sisters weren't staying in the French Quarter.

"We have some time to burn before the wolves are a problem," Dracula pointed out. "I know we just ate, but do you think there's a café somewhere nearby with Wi-Fi?"

I shrugged. "Probably. You want to try and look up some of the names of the people the vampires were trying to turn?"

"Like I said, we have to follow the money."

"It will be easier to use my laptop than my phone. Technically, though, I don't need Wi-Fi. I can connect through the mobile hotspot on my phone."

"Well, unless you want to sit in the van, a café would be nice. Besides, you like coffee. So do I."

I nodded. "I suppose we could get started. I don't know how far we'll get in a few hours. If we're dealing with politicians and people of influence, who have financial interests connected to murder, it won't be easy. Besides, I'm good with computers. I was studying computer science at a community college. I'm hardly an accomplished hacker."

"Can you do it or not?"

I shrugged. "Probably. We'll have to be careful. The last thing we want is to get caught. Hacking into a bank account, finding a credit card statement, isn't as easy as you'd think. They don't really teach you how to do that sort of thing at community college. Even then, if the money was exchanged as cash, we might not find anything even if I can get into their accounts. Not to mention, we'd have to narrow down the statements to the time around when money was moved. If we're talking about the drug dealer or the doctor, it sounds like they were tangled up in their illicit behaviors for a while."

"So that means more deposits, more frequently. Wouldn't that make it easier?"

I shook my head. "Not necessarily. Finding a needle in hay isn't hard if you only have a few pieces of hay to sort through. Bury that needle in an entire haystack and it gets a lot harder."

Dracula sighed. "They make this sort of thing look a lot easier in the movies."

I smirked. "Of course they do. They're movies."

"There's something there the sisters don't want us to find. That's why they're sending the werewolves. They need us occupied with that problem so we don't interfere with their next move."

"I have another idea. The people Morty reaped last night may not be reported missing yet. It's just a matter of time before that happens. If any of them are native to the area, we might be able to do a little digging with family or friends. These people might not have been caught, but some of them were involved in some pretty complicated crap. There have to be other people who knew what was going on."

"We're still not likely to dig much up in just a few hours, Sienna."

I nodded. "Right. But we might be able to get a lead. Time is of the essence here, right? We'd best make use of every hour we have."

Dracula handed me the list of the names Morty gave us. I pulled out my phone and started typing the names into a search engine.

"Drug dealer lives not far from here," I reported. "The doctor who stole the babies has a practice a couple hours north of here in Baton Rouge."

"We don't exactly look like the type who'd be able to get in with a drug dealer."

"What do you mean? You're emaciated and pale. You look like a druggie."

"An addict, maybe. We're looking for business connections. It would take a long time to build enough trust with any drug ring to work our way up to the top."

I pressed my lips together. "What about the doctor? Do you think we can get any further with him? I mean, we could pretend I'm pregnant and looking for a doc. You could pose as my dad. Say you're concerned, you know, because I have a rare blood disease."

"A blood disease?"

"Well, it's not far from the truth!"

Dracula shook his head. "If he has someone in his office booking appointments, they might be willing to take you as a patient. They might even know what he's doing behind the scenes. That's not going to help us sort out who, if anyone, he's connected to in politics."

I scratched my head. "Then forget the charade. We go to his office and I snoop around. Maybe I can go astral, do a little digging through some of his files, maybe break into his office computer."

"That's two hours to Baton Rouge. Another two hours back. That means you only have about that much time to find what you need."

I nodded. "Well, the death doc isn't going to be in his office today. His practice might be open, but I'd bet he no-showed and whoever runs the office had to cancel his appointments. Once I get inside, it shouldn't be hard to find what we're looking for."

"That depends on how sloppy he is."

I sighed. "He's letting mothers die and selling babies. There has to be something. Numbers of people he sold the babies to, prospective contacts on the black market. Anything we find will get us closer to knowing Sorina's plans than we are now."

Dracula nodded. "I guess we won't be going for coffee, then."

"It's a shame. After that meal, I could really use the caffeine."

CHAPTER TEN

It seemed just like yesterday when we were driving through Baton Rouge on our way to New Orleans. Oh, wait! Yesterday we hadn't even passed through Baton Rouge yet. We watched the sunrise at the Louisiana border. Sometimes, I swear, this saving the world business really gives you the runaround.

Joseph Henrickson, MD, RIP. Rest in perdition.

A quick internet search fit the profile Morty gave us. He was highly respected in the community. He was involved in countless charities. He was even an elder at his church. His clinic specialized in high-risk pregnancies. If he were a regular ob-gyn, especially in the era of modern medicine, he might go his entire career without ever losing a mother. With his specialization, it was expected that he'd lose a patient from time to time. If he had a buyer lined up, all he'd have to do is miss something, ignore a complication when it arose, or intervene only when he knew it was a little too late. He'd tell anyone who asked, family or friends, the baby didn't make it. There were probably instances when the mother legitimately died in childbirth, without his neglect or intervention. Perhaps he only killed the mothers when demand exceeded supply, when he had more buyers than his usual operation could satisfy. Since his clinic was in the state capital, it wasn't hard to imagine he might have powerful political connections.

We found the clinic two blocks from the state capitol. There was a sign on the door that indicated the doctor was on vacation.

"Makes sense," Dracula mused. "If the doctor thought he was meeting up with some vampires to become immortal, he must've figured it would take time before he'd be adjusted and ready to get back to work."

I nodded. "Even less likely that anyone will notice he's missing. From what I could find online, Henrickson was never married and lived alone."

Dracula tilted his head. "Interesting."

"I don't know. I mean, I always said if I got knocked up I'd go to a lady ob-gyn. I wouldn't want some old guy poking around in my hoo-hah. It's not so interesting as it is mildly creepy."

"It's not creepy. He is a doctor."

"Right, because doctors are immune to perversion. Think about it, if you were in medical school and you always had a hard time scoring with the chicks, when it came time to specialize, what would you pick?"

Dracula shrugged. "I don't know. I'd probably choose a specialty that was in high demand."

"Even if there was a serious shortage of proctologists or podiatrists?"

"Some people like butts and feet."

"My point exactly! How many medical students are sitting in class, studying the butt hole, and suddenly feel called to it?"

Dracula snickered. "They'd call that a booty call!"

I laughed. "Right. How do you even know what that is? Haven't you been stuck in a castle for the last few centuries?"

"I'm ancient, but I'm no barbarian," he clarified. "I had internet and the YouTube."

I snickered. "Of course you did."

"It's still a stretch to say that male obstetricians are in it for the hoo-hah, as you called it."

I pinched my chin. "Maybe, but you know, it's not about that. It's about being comfortable with your doctor. Personally, I'd just feel better if my doctor was a woman. Or maybe Channing Tatum. But I don't think Magic Mike ever got his medical license."

Dracula shook his head. "Find what you can. I'll wait in the van."

I waved at Dracula. "Tootles!"

I touched my brooch and entered the astral plane. When I got into the doctor's office I walked straight through the reception desk and into the back. The lights were off, but a little sunlight illuminated the hallway from a window at the end. I passed a few patient rooms and found Henrickson's name on a brass placard on the last door on the right.

I stepped through the door.

I checked the room for cameras. Learned that lesson. It was clear, so I touched my brooch again and resumed physical form. It was a lot easier to snoop through the doctor's shit that way.

The guy didn't even have a computer in his office. He was in his late sixties. Can't teach an old doc new tricks. He had locked file cabinets against the wall to the right of his desk and an old-school Rolodex. It was frustrating. If he had a computer, I'd probably be able to get into it. I could search all his records, contacts, anything relevant, in a matter of minutes. This guy was either stuck in his ways or he was paranoid. It's true, a lot that is deleted off a computer can be recovered. You don't have to be in the FBI to do it, either.

I didn't expect to find any names of the families who were adopting his stolen babies. It wasn't that he wouldn't have records or names and phone numbers, but I had no way to know if the names I found were connected to his operation. For all I knew, the names in his Rolodex could be family friends, other doctors and colleagues, people involved in his above-the-board business interests, or anyone. Even if there were influential people in the Rolodex, I wasn't up-to-date enough on Louisiana politics to recognize most names. Yeah, it wasn't hard to find out the major players like the governor of the state, the mayors of large cities, or the state's US senators and representatives, but even those names, especially the representatives, I'd have to look up and cross-reference. Besides, who's to say that any powerful contacts he had were listed in the Rolodex under their real names? Not to mention, having the phone number of a politician didn't mean that there was a connection to his baby-selling venture. He was a citizen of the state, like all of us, and might have other reasons to contact or support political figures and candidates.

I gave up on the Rolodex. There wasn't much point in looking further. It did occur to me, though, that since we knew the doctor was dead, I could take it with me and he wouldn't miss it.

The same went for his files. The only other items on his desk were family photos. A portrait of the doctor from several years before, standing next to a young lady. Was it a love interest, or maybe a sibling? No clue. I turned my attention back to the files. If I could bust into the cabinets. The locks on those things didn't strike me as being all that complex—if you had lock-picking skills. I didn't. On television shows, a lot of people knew how to pick locks. They made it look easy.

I had an idea. I hadn't tried it before, but I thought it might work. I rummaged around in the doctor's desk and found a letter opener. I approached the file cabinet. There was one lock at the top right corner, and I stuck the letter opener into it. With my opposite hand, I touched my brooch again.

Something snapped in the lock. I yanked the letter opener from it, pulling the mechanism with it. The file drawers opened right up.

Maybe I couldn't pick a lock, but I could destroy one. Works just as well.

"Thatta girl." Yes, I congratulated myself. When you only have a few tools in your toolbox, you have to work with what you've got.

The first several drawers contained patient files. I couldn't steal all of them. I doubted it would do any good. Most of the questionable files were doctored up—apologies for the unintended pun. The files were organized by year first and alphabetized after that. He'd been operating this clinic since the seventies. Had he been involved in selling babies all that time? It was possible.

I checked the bottom drawer. It was half full of folders, including his most recent patient files. At the very back was a single manilla envelope marked "x."

Curious, I thought. I retrieved the file and opened it on the doctor's desk.

It included a Polaroid photograph of a woman gagged and tied to a chair. I held the photo up to the framed photo on his desk. It was the *same* woman, a decade or two older. Behind the photo was a sheet of graph paper with several numbers. All the numbers were in the tens of thousands. The bottom of the sheet read, "Goal to save Violet: $5,000,000."

His numbers showed that in total he'd accumulated nearly 4.5 million. He was almost there.

I gulped, then took a deep breath. The doctor wasn't selling babies for profit. He was doing it to pay a ransom. The dates on the ledger suggested he'd been doing it for five years.

There was another small envelope in the file. It bulged in the middle. I opened it and found a single diamond ring.

Violet wasn't his sister. She was the woman he hoped to marry, even at his advanced age.

So much for thinking the doctor was working for a politician. Was Violet still alive? People had been held prisoner for ransom longer than five years. I'd seen documentaries on situations like that. It was rare, though. Someone in captivity so long would know things about her captors. More often than not, the perps would collect the ransom money and never return the victim.

I took the file along with the doctor's Rolodex and returned to the astral plane. I returned to the van, phased through the door, and stepped into the back. I touched my brooch.

"Boo!" I shouted.

Dracula almost jumped out of his skin. "Damn it, Sienna!"

I climbed over the middle console and into the driver's seat. Dracula was shaking his head. "Did you find anything?"

I showed him the file and presented my theory—he was selling babies to pay a ransom.

"I don't think there's a politician connected to this at all."

Dracula shook his head. "I wouldn't be so sure."

"What do you mean?"

"Why not turn the matter over to the police or the feds?"

I shrugged. "Maybe he was afraid the kidnappers would kill his girlfriend if he did."

Dracula pressed his lips together. "Perhaps. Or, he knew who took Violet, and the kidnappers were connected to someone of means. Someone who would know if he went to the authorities."

I scratched my head. "Five million dollars isn't that much, all things considered. Politicians raise more than that for their campaigns all the time. It's not hard to find wealthy donors looking for a tax write-off."

Dracula raised his right fist to the underside of his jaw and rested his head on it. "Sorina is working her way up the ladder. I don't think we're looking for a politician yet. Henrickson is only one person involved in illicit but profitable behaviors. We have a long list of names. We're only at the tip of the iceberg. If we keep following the money, I suspect it will all flow like several tributaries into a single river."

I raised an eyebrow. "Some kind of crime lord?"

"Maybe," Dracula mused. "Whoever it is, I imagine they have enough power and influence that they have more than one politician in their back pocket."

"The doctor was only half a million away from meeting the ransom demand," I pointed out. "Why would he be so desperate now to take the sisters up on an offer to become an immortal vampire?"

"Desperation. Perhaps the bill was coming due. He was running out of time. If he couldn't get the rest of the money together, perhaps he thought he could save Violet himself."

"If he became a vampire?"

Dracula nodded. "Think about it. If someone you loved was being held captive…"

"Not hard to imagine. I mean, I don't love Dylan. Things hadn't gone that far. But I know the feeling."

"If Henrickson was about to propose to this woman, it's safe to say that his relationship was much further along than that. What would you do to save Dylan? Would you risk your life? If someone offered you power, an ability that made you invulnerable to bullets, stronger than your adversaries, would you take it?"

I nodded. "Probably."

"This ledger only tells us a part of the story. Perhaps the doctor had the rest of the money and the kidnappers decided to change the terms. They upped the ransom at the last minute. The doctor was already working well past his prime. He could have retired years ago. What if he didn't have it in him to keep at it, if he knew what he was doing was wrong, and out of the blue comes an opportunity to save Violet without having to harm another woman or steal another baby?"

I shook my head. "This is all conjecture. We don't know that's what happened."

Dracula nodded. "All I'm saying is that it isn't hard to imagine that a desperate man might go to desperate measures at the eleventh hour if he thought it was his last chance to save the woman he loved."

I nodded. "There is also a Rolodex that I took from the doctor's desk."

"Can I take a look at it?"

I handed it to him. He flipped through a few of the cards. He stopped and pulled out a business card. "Interesting."

"What is it?"

"It's the card for an oncologist. It's stuck right where the oncologist's name should be in alphabetical order. It's not just a business card. It's an appointment card. He was supposed to come in for treatment next week."

"So it's recent. That means the doctor had cancer?"

Dracula nodded. "Looks that way. Like I said, desperate people will go to desperate lengths. Who needs chemotherapy when you could turn to vampirism and live forever?"

"Long enough to make the rest of the money he owed, *or* to rescue Violet himself."

Dracula nodded. "Precisely."

CHAPTER ELEVEN

None of what we found exonerated the doctor. It did explain his behavior. Still, nothing excuses kidnapping and selling babies. Not to mention killing their mothers or, at the very least, withholding treatment if they hemorrhaged during childbirth. It wasn't hard to imagine how someone could be pressed into doing something they knew was wrong if it meant saving someone they loved. Did he still deserve to go to Hades? Definitely. Two wrongs don't make a right. We could have pursued that rabbit hole further. Perhaps we could sneak into the oncologist's office and find Henrickson's file to confirm our suspicion. That wouldn't get us closer to finding out what the sisters were up to, though. When all this was over, perhaps we'd turn over the evidence we found to the authorities. They'd investigate and find out more about the women the doctor might have killed and the babies he sold. It needed to be done. Right now though, we had another fight on our hands and since the doctor was dead the damage was done. He wouldn't steal any more babies. I could only hope that the people he'd sold the infants to were mostly decent people who, for whatever reason, couldn't adopt a child the conventional way. They were desperate people but not innately evil. Justice would be done eventually. For now, we had to move on. We had more leads to pursue, and we had to get back to New Orleans before the werewolves started slaughtering people on Bourbon Street.

We didn't have much of a plan. Once the sun fell below the horizon and the killings began, I'd lose most of my strength.

Dracula was different. I'd made him a daywalker, but for some reason he didn't become a normal human at night. He became a regular vampire. It only takes a few hours after one is bitten for the transformation to take hold. According to Dracula, though, vampirism is a progressive condition. It takes hold over time. That's why older vampires were stronger than younger ones. If I bit a young vampire, enough of their humanity remained that they became something *close* to human at night. Dracula had been a vampire for centuries. There wasn't much humanity left in him, not even after the sisters removed the dark power from his essence.

Dracula surmised that, eventually, I might become more like a normal vampire at night. It might take years, or maybe it wouldn't. I already knew my vampirism was getting stronger. It's why my brooch wasn't as effective at preventing me from having blood cravings as it was when I was first turned. Tonight, though, when the sun went down, I'd be vulnerable. We couldn't fight the werewolves. We could try to evacuate as many people from the area as possible. We could distract the wolves. My brooch could be helpful in that regard. I'd get the werewolves' attention, lure them to chase me, then disappear. Dracula would focus on getting the people to safety. It might take all night, and the wolves might not give up even after the sun rose, but once a few rampaging beasts started terrorizing the area, people would start running for their lives. Those who couldn't get away on their own, Dracula would try to save. Eventually, with the streets clear, we hoped the sisters would call off the wolves and the damage would remain minimal.

I parked the van a few blocks away. Werewolves aren't only deadly. They can do some serious property damage. It might seem trite, but if you had a brand-new vehicle, would you leave it in the path of a pack of roving monsters?

Dracula and I retrieved our swords from the back. Killing the wolves wasn't our goal. Dracula might stand a chance with one, but probably not a pack. I could go astral and reappear with my blade in the middle of a werewolf's gut. Our primary goal was to save as many lives as possible. I still hoped to save Dylan and the pack from Sorina's thrall, but I couldn't put that ahead of protecting people. No matter how much I liked Dylan, hell, even if I *was* in love with him, which I wasn't, I couldn't let him or his friends kill innocent people. Since our blades were alloyed with silver, they'd do the trick.

As the sun dipped below the horizon, I felt my strength wane. I'd still be charged for a while, but I wasn't running on electricity anymore. I was on a battery, and I didn't know how long it would last.

We walked up and down Bourbon Street. Nothing unusual was happening yet. By Bourbon Street standards, at least. The place wasn't exactly normal. Perhaps that was the attraction. Whatever it was brought in a lot of people. A lot of people we'd have to get out of here once the—

A wolf howled in the distance, somewhere straight ahead.

Another howl echoed from somewhere behind us.

I turned but didn't see anything. It came from a distance.

"They're coming at us from both directions."

I nodded. Then a third howl came from somewhere to my right. "They're surrounding us."

"We need to get the people out of here before the wolves arrive."

"How are we going to do that? Start screaming 'werewolf'? They'll never believe it."

Dracula smirked. "If they need to see a monster to believe it,

I'll show them a monster."

Dracula turned, grabbed a woman, and bit her in the neck. He let her go. She took off screaming. "Who's next?"

He flashed his fangs, blood dripping from his mouth. Some guy thought he'd play the hero and charged after Dracula. Big mistake. Dracula backhanded the man and he went flying into the window of a nearby storefront.

No one else dared to try. They scattered.

With so many screams, I couldn't hear if the wolves were still howling. Some of the screams might have had nothing to do with Dracula. We knew some people were going to die. Morty told us as much. Hopefully, Dracula's charade, if you could call it that, would clear the streets enough that no one was added to the schedule.

These people were like sheep. Dracula was like a sheepdog, barking at them, shepherding them away from the real threat, the wolves who were encroaching on our position.

I still had enough vampirism left within me that if I removed my brooch I could have joined in and helped Dracula. Two vampires would be more terrifying than one. I considered it for about two seconds, then I saw a massive, hairy, beast run from one alley to the next.

In the astral plane, I could move faster than he could. I touched my brooch and took off after the wolf. It was after someone, probably its next meal. It was sniffing someone out. If I could get there first I might be able to get in front of the person, appear, and lure the wolf in another direction.

I ran past the wolf. All I could see as I ran up behind him was a blur and a lot of hair. The alley came to a dead end, and a young woman was huddled up and shaking next to a dumpster. I turned. The wolf was approaching. This wasn't going to be easy. If I reappeared between the werewolf and his target, all I'd do was give him a side of vampire with his human.

I ran back behind the wolf and touched my brooch, then

tugged its tail. The beast spun fast. I ran in the opposite direction. If I could just get it out of the alley, that poor girl might get a chance to escape.

The werewolf growled and took off after me. I could go astral at any second, but if I did it too soon, the thing would just turn around and go back after the girl.

I got to the end of the alley in time and turned the corner, where I ran straight into what felt like a wall of fur. It wasn't a wall.

I stumbled back and fell on my butt and looked up at the wolf I ran into. I recognized him. I'd seen him in werewolf form before. His fur was lighter than the others.

He looked at me and tilted his head.

"Dylan?"

He snarled at me and jerked his head up. I turned and saw the other wolf rear up on his hind legs. Dylan growled at him.

The way this wolf looked down at Dylan I figured he must be the alpha. He was telling Dylan something. Dylan glanced at me and shook his head.

The alpha wolf howled. Dylan fell to the ground, whimpering. He raised his front paws to his head and, with an ear-piercing screech, returned to human form.

I looked back at the alpha, who bared his teeth and lunged at me. I grabbed the hilt of my silver sword, and with just enough vampiric strength left, I thrust it into the alpha's chest.

The alpha gasped for air. His jaw fell open and he hit the ground with a thud.

I looked back at Dylan. I grabbed his hand and helped him to his feet. "What just happened?"

Dylan shook his head. He rubbed his brow with his hand. "It hurts like hell."

"What does?"

"I broke free of the pack. I disavowed my alpha. He was going to kill me."

"Good thing I got him first."

Dylan shook his head. "The rest of the pack is going to come after you now. You killed the alpha. The one who kills you takes his place."

I nodded. "I can handle myself."

"No, you can't, Sienna!"

"Excuse me?"

"I'm not saying you aren't capable. But every wolf in that pack is sworn to kill you. They won't stop until you kill every one of them or they kill you. And they're smart. They'll find a way to corner you."

"They'll have to find me first. Look, there's a girl at the end of the alley, real scared."

"Take me to her."

I looked Dylan up and down. "You're naked."

"No shit. What do you think happens when a werewolf changes back? We don't exactly come back in Gucci."

"The weird sisters were controlling your alpha."

Dylan nodded. "They were. Not anymore. Not until a new alpha emerges."

"You mean, not until one of them kills me."

"Just take me to the girl. I can get her out of here."

"It's not safe out there."

"The alpha was the only one I had to worry about. He would sooner kill a wolf than let it disavow the pack. The others won't care. Not now. They won't hurt anyone else. They only have one thing driving them now."

"If the alpha is dead, and it was the sisters' influence over them that kept them in werewolf form..."

"They'll shift back, too. That won't stop them from trying to kill you."

"Well, at least I stand a better chance if they are coming after me as a mob of naked people."

Dylan nodded. "Don't underestimate them. The drive to

avenge the alpha is primal. Even in human form, werewolves have enhanced strength. They're still dangerous."

"I'll go astral. But maybe you can help this girl first."

"All right. Let's hurry."

I brought Dylan to the girl at the end of the alley. "The wolf is gone. This is Dylan, he'll get you someplace safe."

"He's naked. I'm not going somewhere with a naked guy."

I huffed. "We're in the French Quarter, honey. A naked escort is part of the experience."

Dylan looked at me and laughed. "Meet me back at Jackson Square in the morning. I'll tell you what I know."

I nodded, touched my brooch, and disappeared to run back to my van.

Dracula was already waiting in the passenger seat for me. "I was beginning to get worried."

"Yeah, well, I found Dylan."

"You did?"

"He broke his bond with the pack. He's a lone wolf now. In human form at the moment."

"Well, that's fantastic news."

"Yeah. I also had to kill the alpha before it killed Dylan."

Dracula sighed. "They won't rest until they kill you."

I nodded. "I know. Dylan is helping someone I found in an alley. She was scared. He said he'd meet us back at Jackson Square in the morning. Let's hope the others take their hunt for me elsewhere by then."

"At least the sisters can't use the wolves now."

I shook my head. "It doesn't matter. They're going to do what the sisters want them to do anyway. What's more distracting than having a pack of wolves, in human form or not, trying to hunt you down?"

Dracula nodded. "Out of the frying pan and into the fire."

I raised an eyebrow. "Cliché much?"

"Old people speak in clichés. Get used to it."

CHAPTER TWELVE

I didn't know how many wolves were in Dylan's pack. I had visions in my mind of being hunted down by an angry naked mob, like in those old black-and-white monster movies. Only this time, it was monster-on-monster violence. Werewolves versus vampires. And I don't think anyone was naked in those movies. They'd find clothes, eventually. In the meantime, since I didn't know what any of the wolves looked like, I kept my eyes glued open as Dracula and I fled the area in my van.

Dracula sighed. "I wasn't worried about what happened at the blood bank. What I did, though, combined with the presence of werewolves in the city, is sure to attract hunters now."

I sighed. "Well, isn't that great?"

"The Van Helsings won't be looking for you so much as me. I'm pretty sure a few people got pictures of me with their phones."

"So a pack of vengeful werewolves is coming after me. Rogue hunters from who knows where are hunting you."

"Even in human form, the werewolves will track your scent. They'll get it from the body of the alpha. Van Helsings are notoriously adept at tracking vampires in most instances. So long as I don't feed, though, they'll be easier to avoid."

"They'll also be after the wolves. Even if someone got a picture of you, the bodies left behind are clearly werewolf kills. Maybe the hunters will prioritize them over you."

Dracula shook his head. "If I were any other vampire, I'd say that was the case. I'm Dracula, Sienna. They'll certainly take down any werewolves they find, but I'm the big fish."

I raised an eyebrow. "You're a fish?"

"It's a metaphor!"

I grinned. It probably wasn't the time to crack a joke, but when things got tense, I had a habit of retreating to humor. I'd faced worse than this before. Too much stress can cloud the mind. Too much anxiety can lead to desperation. So, ham it up a little, and levity can bring you clarity. "Can you make fish lips? Check this out."

I sucked in my cheeks, turned my head, and made fish lips at Dracula.

Dracula tilted his head and tried to do the same. "It's hard to do."

I giggled. "You could use that. The next time you have to feed from a real person. Rather than baring your fangs, come at them with fish lips. They'll be all like 'WTF,' and when they least expect it, you take a bite."

"That's weird, Sienna."

"Well, think about it, Drac. You flash your fangs. You hold up your cloak with both hands and loom over them. The result is inevitable. They *scream.* Not very bright, you know. Screaming gets people's attention."

Dracula shook his head. "It's my MO. My signature. That's how I approach my meals."

I raised an eyebrow. "To some, I admit, it's probably terrifying. I think it's corny."

"I'm not corny!"

"You're a little corny. You are like a walking, breathing vampire cliché."

"I'm not a cliché. I'm the vampire that inspired the cliché."

"We really need to give you a makeover. Vampires *don't* wear cloaks anymore."

"My cloak is essential. I use it to cover most of my face when I approach a meal. If they don't see my fangs straight away, it allows me to take them by surprise."

"Yes, the cloak over the face. Stalking your way toward the victim. Every movie about you ever has used that. It's not a surprise anymore because if anyone wears a cloak and pulls it over their face, the first thing *anyone* thinks is that you're doing a Dracula impression."

Dracula tilted his head. "People do impressions of me?"

"You're a character on Sesame Street. The count who teaches children numbers."

Dracula chuckled. "The count. I get it. That's clever."

"It would be nice to find a place to chill and relax. I could use a nap."

"Vampires don't have to sleep. We usually slumber during the day just to pass the time."

I huffed. "Well, I'm basically human at night. I need my rest."

"It isn't safe to stay in one place. Once the werewolves pick up your scent, they'll begin their pursuit. They probably already have."

"Look, buddy. I know it's been a couple of days since I showered, but there's no way they can smell me across the city. I don't have that much stink."

"You're right. But if you spend any amount of time in a place, they'll pick up your scent there. They'll also know that you're from out of town. Dylan was a part of the pack. They surely know more about you than you realize. The first thing they'll do is check out hotels. They'll stalk the halls. Touch a doorknob, they'll pick up your scent."

"There are a lot of hotels in the city, Drac. I think we can find something. It would take them all night to check all of them."

"They'll be working alone, individually, until the new alpha emerges. So, no naked mobs. More like several naked assassins. They won't stay naked for long, so you can't trust that. Back in human form, until we have Dylan with us, and he can identify them, they could be literally anyone."

"Like I said, it's a big city. They surely can't track me while I'm in the van. This thing is airtight."

Dracula nodded and conceded, "It will be difficult to pick up your scent so long as we stay in the van."

"We can't stay in the van forever. What do you say we do a little Hansel and Gretel in reverse? Leave them a trail of breadcrumbs, then use the van to go somewhere else."

"That would take a lot of bread."

"I don't mean literal breadcrumbs. Let me show you." I grabbed a tissue from a box on the floor between our seats. I rubbed it on my neck. I rolled down the window and tossed it out.

"They will definitely pick up your scent on that."

I smiled. "Right. So, we leave several of these leading them in one direction. Then, in the van, we go somewhere else."

CHAPTER THIRTEEN

Littering is bad. I don't endorse it, but it's hardly the crime of the century. When littering is a key to surviving a pack of werewolves that are trying to hunt you down, you do what you have to do. It would not trouble my conscience much. Besides, these were biodegradable tissues. I was environmentally conscious. What kind of monster do you think I am?

It would have been easier to do if Dracula was driving—but that would have been counterproductive to our greater goal of surviving the night. At night, you didn't have to stake my heart to kill me. At least I didn't think you did. Again, when you're the first of a subspecies you don't volunteer to become the test subject for your own limitations.

We drove all around the city dropping tissues. It was probably overkill, but this was the first time I ever had a pack hunting me down. Dracula had experience with that, and he prevailed. It was ages ago, before the advent of the automobile, and as I understood it he used his power from the Scholomance to wipe out the pack. Dracula still had power. I did, too. We'd both been through the Scholomance and passed the trials of the path of light. So far, though, I hadn't been able to do squat with that power ever since we defeated Dracula's darkness in Kansas City, and Dracula was still a bit uncertain about what he could do with that power other than dispel any dark magic cast by the sisters.

It seemed like the sisters were several steps ahead of us and taking strides to widen the gap. We came to New Orleans looking for them. Now, we were being hunted by wolves and hunters. While the sisters couldn't control the wolves, it didn't matter. They probably didn't care. So long as Dracula and I were on the run, worried about surviving more than prevailing over the sisters, they'd be able to advance their plans without much resistance.

I didn't know my way around New Orleans. I had to rely on my GPS to figure out where I was. My scent was all over the place. The plan was to lead them as far away from the French Quarter as possible. If we were going to come back to pick up Dylan in the morning, it was better if they weren't there when we returned.

Our trail of my DNA-infused tissue ended in the lower Ninth Ward. I wasn't sure of the names of the parishes or neighborhoods we led them through first. Dylan said no one else was in any danger until a new alpha emerged. Translation: until they killed me. I wasn't too worried about innocent people getting caught in the path as the wolves hunted me down. They were in human form, and the only wolfish instinct driving them was their need for vengeance, and to become the next alpha.

After that, we drove an hour or so out of the city and found a rest stop where I could get a little shuteye. Dracula kept watch.

I'd hardly closed my eyes, and the next thing I knew Dracula was shaking me and the sun was shining through the windshield.

"Damn. It's morning already?"

"Rise and shine, bloodsucker of mine."

I chuckled. "Speaking of blood, I could go for a swig."

"We could stop at Laveau's when we go pick up Dylan."

I shook my head. "Too risky. That place is swarming with

supernaturals. After what happened last night, it'll be like a magnet for hunters, too. Not to mention, if the wolves are splitting up, I'd rather not leave my scent anywhere near that place."

"I wouldn't recommend hitting any blood banks. The wolves know what you are. They'll expect you are looking for blood."

I scratched the back of my head. "All right. Well, the craving isn't overwhelming yet. Not with my brooch in place. It can wait."

"Are you sure?" Dracula asked. "It might behoove you to satisfy those cravings. The longer you go without feeding, the longer you're delaying your maturation."

"We don't even know what will happen when my vampirism gets stronger. I'm one of a kind, it's not like there are other daywalkers out there who've been through this before."

"You can feed on a live person, Sienna. One bite and a few swigs won't hurt anyone."

I winced. "It just feels wrong."

"You are what you are. Eventually, you're going to have to come to terms with it. Best feed now, while you have some control, before the cravings grow and you won't be able to stop before draining someone dry."

I checked my face in the vanity mirror. I smoothed out my eyebrows and ran my fingers through my hair, tucking a few stray strands behind my ears. "I think my eyes are getting darker."

"I've noticed. I'm telling you, Sienna. If you allow your vampirism to mature, you might not be so vulnerable at night anymore. To do that, you *need* to feed."

I smirked. "I have a need to feed. It rhymes."

Dracula shrugged. "I'm a poet and didn't know it."

I chuckled. "That's what I call a rhyme just in time."

Dracula pointed through the windshield. "There's a homeless man resting on the bench. If you feel guilty about it, hand him a twenty. He'll be grateful, even after you bite him."

I shook my head. "I don't know, Drac."

"Then give him a hundred. Money isn't a problem for me. Give him as much as you want."

"I can't buy off someone to assuage my conscience," I argued.

Dracula chuckled. "Then get his consent. A pretty girl walks up to a homeless man who probably hasn't had much action in a long time, offers to pay him a hundred bucks to bite his neck, do you think he'll refuse?"

I sighed. "I guess you have a good point."

Even if the guy consented, I still felt weird about it. The thing about remaining more-or-less human half of the time was that I retained my normal sensibilities. It wasn't just that I'd feel guilty if I bit someone. His consent would help with that. It was the whole idea of drinking blood from a person. When I had a glass at a restaurant or a blood bag from the bank, it was impersonal. No one eats a hamburger and thinks about the cow that had to die to give it to them. It's just a burger. Maybe I was afraid that if I drank straight from someone it would make me the monster I didn't want to become. I was never a religious girl, but I knew humans had souls and an afterlife. Would feeding from a person damn me to some kind of afterlife in Hades? Yeah, vampires are immortal—if someone doesn't stake them. If a wolf attacked me at night, or a hunter, I wasn't sure I could survive like other vampires might.

I held out my palm and Dracula dropped a Benjamin Franklin in my hand. "Why does this make me feel like a whore?"

"You're paying a man to bite him. He isn't paying you."

I snorted. "Right."

I was still wearing the strappy dress from the night before. I felt the homeless man's eyes on me the moment I stepped out of the van.

I approached him. He looked at me with wide eyes and his jaw agape. "Well, hello, beautiful."

"Hey there, good looking." It was a lie. The guy was repulsive. I could see the dirt seeping from his pores. His beard was caked with grease and chunks of food that he'd probably had days ago.

The man smiled, revealing a single front tooth. "Well, isn't it my lucky day?"

I held out the money. "I'm not going to hurt you."

"Please do!"

I smiled. "All right. Let me bite your neck."

"Are you serious? What kind of freak…"

"I'm the freakiest. You have no idea."

He chuckled. "Right here? Don't you want to go somewhere to play?"

I shook my head. "My momma always said I shouldn't play with my food."

The man raised an eyebrow. "Your food?"

"I told you, I won't hurt you. Not much, anyway. I just enjoy the taste of a handsome man's blood."

"And you're going to pay me for that?"

I nodded. "I'm not unreasonable."

"I've been with some weird ladies in my time, darling. None so pretty as you."

"Is that a yes?"

He shrugged. "How could I say no?"

I handed the man the hundred-dollar bill. He took it, and I grabbed the man by the back of his head and turned his neck to the side. He smelled of beer and body odor. The repulsion subsided the second my teeth pierced his neck and his blood flowed into my open mouth. I gulped it down. I sucked out more. I kept drinking. I wanted *more.*

Something grabbed me around the waist and pulled me away from the man. I turned to see Dracula looking at me. "That will be enough."

I wiped a little blood from my chin with my wrist, then licked it up.

"What the hell are you?" the homeless man asked.

I turned back to him and licked my front teeth. "Your worst nightmare or a wet dream. You decide."

Dracula grabbed my hand. "Come on. We have to get back to the French Quarter."

I winked at the man. "Don't spend all that in one place."

"Honey, you ever want another bite and have more money to give, I sleep on this bench every night."

I grinned. "Good to know."

"The name's Leeroy."

"Leeroy?" I asked.

"Leeroy Jenkins."

I laughed. "You've got to be shitting me."

Leeroy sighed. "Do I know you?"

I shook my head. "Not at all."

CHAPTER FOURTEEN

"What was that about?" Dracula asked.

I chuckled. "Ten or twelve years ago, I was really into a multi-player roleplaying game. There was a viral video of a guy whose character name was Leeroy Jenkins. They were on a raid and he charged in, shouted '*Leeeeeroy Jenkins*,' and got the entire party killed. It was hilarious."

"I don't get the joke."

I grinned. "You'd have to understand the game."

"I played Pacman once. Was it like that?"

I shook my head. "Dude, you're so old."

We got back in the van. I was energized. Maybe a little high. Fresh off a feed, straight from the source. It gave me a warm and fuzzy feeling, not at all what I expected.

I found a classic rock station. It wasn't my jam, but I figured it was a compromise. Something between top-forty music and Brahms. Dracula didn't see it that way. For him, anything produced after the turn of the twentieth century was a "racket."

We jammed down the road to the tune of *Eye of the Tiger.* Classic rock, or not, that song will juice you up for a fight. It worked for Rocky. Worked for me, too. Then again, maybe it was the fresh blood in my system that gave me a hankerin' to do a little spankerin' of the bad guys.

After *Eye of the Tiger*, Bon Jovi's *Wanted: Dead or Alive* kept me in the ass-kicking mood. It was also fitting, given our situation. Not the steel horse thing. The minivan was more like a steel hippo. But you know what? Hippos are responsible for more deaths every year than any other animal in parts of the world where they thrive. Saw that on *Animal Planet*. Horses can be domesticated. They don't kill nearly as many people. By that reasoning, my minivan was more badass than Bon Jovi's two-wheeled "steel horse."

Maybe it wasn't the best reasoning in the world, but I could roll with it. With twice the number of wheels as Bon Jovi's pansy-ass steel horse.

We made it back to the city and went to Jackson Square in the French Quarter, where the St. Louis Cathedral stood. Dracula waited in the van while I found Dylan waiting in front of a horse-back statue of Saint Louis, himself. He—Dylan, not St. Louis—was wearing spandex yoga pants and a belly shirt.

I couldn't hold back the laughter as I got out of the van.

"Yeah, keep laughing."

"You had all night, and all you could find was that getup?"

Dylan sighed. "I walked that girl home. This was all she had that I could squeeze into."

"And you didn't get something else after you left her place?"

Dylan shook his head. "All the stores were closed. Besides, my wallet was in my pants."

"Where *are* your pants?"

Dylan smirked. "Back at the home base. With those nasty vampire chicks."

"You know where the weird sisters are?"

"That's what you call them?" Dylan laughed. "'Ruthless bitches' would be more fitting."

"I agree. We still have to stop them."

"I can't say if they're still there. They've had us wolfed out for days now. Even if they are there, Sienna, they're too powerful."

"It's still worth checking out. Get in the van. I don't want one of your buddies tracking me down."

"I haven't seen any of the pack since I became a lone wolf. They took off, probably tracking you across the city."

I smiled. "Yeah, I left a trail of breadcrumbs. Technically, tissues."

"Not a bad trick."

"Dracula has evaded werewolves before. I couldn't have done it without him."

"Dracula?" Dylan raised his eyebrows.

I pointed back at the van. Dracula waved at Dylan through the window.

"What the hell, Sienna? Dracula?"

I smiled. "It's a long story. I've teamed up with the Grim Reaper, his sister, a couple gorgons, and even a god or two."

"But Dracula?"

I laughed. "I'll tell you all about it on the drive. Let's go find your clothes. If the sisters are there, maybe we aren't ready to fight them yet. But it will be good to know for sure where they're holing up."

Dylan knew the area a lot better than I did and didn't need a GPS. We followed his directions out of the city, about thirty miles to the northeast. When we arrived, Dracula and I retrieved our swords from the back of the van. You never know what you might encounter in the bayou.

"This is swampland," I observed. "The sisters are hiding in the bayou?"

Dylan winced in pain and rubbed his forehead. "They were."

"Are you okay?"

Dylan shook his head. "I disavowed my pack. That bond is forged in the mind. When I disobeyed Vance—that was the alpha you killed—it was like ripping a part of my brain right out of my head."

"It hurts."

Dylan nodded. "Like a migraine. Like five migraines, one on top of the other."

"Will it get better?"

Dylan raised both hands to his head and squinted. "I don't know. We aren't like vampires. We don't have some ancient sire who can tell us the ins and outs of our lore."

"I've never seen anything like this," Dracula put in. "Then again, werewolf lore is as much a mystery to me as it is to you. All I know is what I've seen in my encounters with werewolves in the past, and a wolf breaking from his pack isn't a part of my experience."

"How far into the swamp do we have to go?" I asked.

"It's about a mile off the road. It's going to be a trek."

I could have gone astral and skipped across the top of the water, but Dracula and Dylan didn't have much of a choice. If my friends had to march through the muck, I was going to do it with them.

We skipped across logs and the rare patch of ground where we could. We still had to wade through the water in places. The algae was thick. The water was stagnant. The mud stuck to my feet as if trying to suck me down to hell. That's what I got for trying to do the right thing and not using my special powers to avoid the nastiness.

Something brushed against my leg. I didn't know whether it was a plant of some kind or an animal. I knew there were alligators in these waters. Probably snakes. With the sun out, they couldn't hurt me. They couldn't hurt any of us. A werewolf can't be killed apart from silver, even in human form. That didn't mean any of us were eager to become better acquainted with reptiles. A bite from a snake or an alligator would still hurt like hell.

Dylan pointed ahead through a row of cypress trees. "That's it."

I narrowed my eyes. There was an old boarded-up house. It couldn't be more than a one- or two-bedroom shack. "That's where the sisters were hiding?"

"That's where they were last I saw them."

Dracula shook his head. "They won't stay there for long. I'd bet they're long gone. Those girls are as snobby as they come. They're accustomed to living in luxury."

I sighed. "Well, we didn't come all this way not to check it out."

"Not to mention, I could use a change of clothes," Dylan added.

I huffed. "At this point, all of us could."

We climbed up a ladder affixed to a small dock on the edge of the house's property. I pulled off my boots and dumped out the water.

Dylan pulled back the spandex of the waistband of his yoga pants and snapped it back. "Needed a little air."

I chuckled. "That's gross."

"Swamp foot is pretty nasty too, you know."

I grinned. "Tell me about it. Think the sisters are in there?"

"I don't think so," Dracula replied. "They're busy with their plans. When you killed the alpha and they lost control of the wolves, they knew it. I doubt they'd hang around here waiting for us to crash their party."

"Still, we should look around."

Dylan nodded. "And get my pants."

I smirked. "I don't know. Your butt looks good in yoga pants."

Dylan laughed and shook his head. "They'd look better on you."

We approached the front door of the place. It was locked. Dracula was about to kick it in when I stopped him. "I can take care of this."

I touched my brooch, phased through the door, and unlocked it from the other side for Dracula and Dylan to come in.

There wasn't anyone I could see in the small foyer or living room. There was a small hallway that led to what I assumed were bedrooms. Cobwebs covered everything. Aside from the sisters and the werewolves, it looked as if no one had been there, much less lived there, in years.

"We should search the rooms. Make sure no one is hiding here."

Dylan sniffed the air. "Usually I'd know, but I can't smell anything past your wet feet."

I rolled my eyes. "Funny. I think it's your stinky wet ass in spandex."

"My clothes are in the back room," Dylan called as he walked down the hall. "Look around. See if you can figure something out."

Dracula shook his head. "I know Sorina and her sisters. They're good. Our chances of finding any clues as to their whereabouts are slim."

Dylan opened one of the bedroom doors and stepped inside. About ten seconds later, he came walking back out with a young, dark-haired female behind him. By the look on Dylan's face, she had something sharp to his back. Probably a silver dagger.

"Let him go!" I shouted.

"Lizzie, you don't want to do this," Dylan said.

The girl shrugged. "You're right. If you were still a part of the pack, I might even feel guilty about it."

I clenched my fists. "I'm the one you want. Do you think you can take me?"

Lizzie huffed. "Sorina told us all about you, Sienna. We know what you are. Right now, fully powered by sunlight, you're right. I probably couldn't beat you. But it's you or him. Give yourself to me and I let your boyfriend here live."

I snorted. "He's not my boyfriend."

"Really?" Lizzie asked. "That's not what Dylan said."

"You told them I was your girlfriend?"

Dylan winced. "Wishful thinking?"

"I have another offer," Dracula interjected. "Take me instead. "

"No, Dracula!"

"Dracula?" Lizzie laughed. "Tempting. The sisters would love to get their hands on you."

"Where are the sisters?" I asked.

"I'm the one with the silver knife to Dylan's back here," Lizzie reminded me. "I have the leverage. I'm the one who asks questions."

"What do you want to know?"

Lizzie shook her head. "If you'll die for your boyfriend."

"That silver blade won't hurt me."

"I'm not worried about that," Lizzie said. "I have a stake in my back pocket."

"This isn't you, Lizzie," Dylan insisted. "It's instinct. The drive to claim alpha. You can resist it. I did."

"Who says I want to resist it? I could become alpha. Why would I turn that down?"

Dracula stepped up beside me. "Because if you become the alpha, the sisters will come for you. They'll use you to take control of the pack again. What kind of alpha would you be if you let vampires manipulate you and your pack?"

"They won't come after me," Lizzie claimed. "They got what they needed out of us. By the time I'm done here, they'll have no use for us. Not with the daywalker out of the way."

"I'm offering myself to you," Dracula persisted. "You don't have to take Sienna. You know what happens when you bite a vampire. It paralyzes us for a century. You can deliver me to the sisters living and breathing. Use me as a bargaining chip if you must."

I pressed my lips together. I knew what Dracula was doing. A bite from a werewolf would *usually* have that effect on a vampire.

Not one who had mastered the Scholomance. Dracula had been through the trials of the Scholomance twice. First, to master the dark path. That was the power the sisters stole from him. Zoey and I went to the Scholomance, too. We followed the path of light. It was how we were able to defeat the darkness in Kansas City. Dracula had returned to the Scholomance and went through the trials all over again—this time following the path of light. Would that power work the same way? Would it allow him to resist the paralyzing effects of a werewolf's bite? I didn't know. I didn't think he knew, either. But he was willing to make that gamble.

Lizzie snorted. "You're a fool, Dracula. I could do what you say, but I'd still be driven to do whatever it took to kill Sienna."

"You're not going to kill Dylan," I predicted. "If you did, you'd have no leverage over me. I'd destroy you before his body even hit the floor."

Lizzie tilted her head. "Perhaps. Very well, then. I'll accept your offer, Dracula."

"No!" I shouted.

"It's all right," Dracula shot back.

"The way I see it, Sienna, is that maybe you aren't Dylan's girlfriend. You must be the girl he told everyone was his girlfriend so he'd look cool to the pack. You know, like the kid in school who always said he had a girlfriend in Alaska?"

"You knew that boy, too?"

Lizzie grinned. "Boys who can't get any. Doesn't matter where you're from. There are always those who will make up fictional girlfriends to excuse their lack of a love life."

"That's not what I was doing!" Dylan protested.

I raised my hand. "It's okay. I get it."

"Seriously, Sienna. I thought, you know, the way we were talking… We just hadn't made it official, but it was basically a done deal!"

I had to play along with the act. I had to make Lizzie think I didn't care what happened to Dylan. "We had a good time in Kansas City, Dylan. That's all it was. We had fun. The fun is over."

"Take me and let the boy go," Dracula stepped past me. "I won't even resist. Bite my wrist. In wolf form or not, a werewolf's bite has the same effect. You know this, Lizzie."

Dracula extended his arm to Lizzie. She smirked, grabbed it, and released Dylan. She bit Dracula's wrist, pulled him into her, and put him into a headlock with a wooden stake to his chest.

"You didn't have a silver knife?" Dylan asked.

Lizzie grinned. "What you didn't know couldn't hurt you. But this stake will kill your precious Dracula."

"Don't do it!" I shouted.

"Do you really think I'd care to offer his breathing body up to the sisters? They're done with us."

Dracula opened his eyes. His power from the Scholomance still worked. Lizzie didn't know it.

"We're still in the same boat," I argued. "If you killed Dracula, you'd lose your leverage. I'd kill you before you could even raise your stake."

"Without your precious Dracula, do you think you stand a chance against the sisters? So what? Maybe you kill me. The sisters will kill you the moment the sun sets."

I huffed. "Well, he's already paralyzed for a century, so I'm a girl who has nothing to lose."

I pressed my brooch and disappeared. I knew it would trigger her, but she didn't know that Dracula was awake.

She tried to force the stake into Dracula's chest.

Dracula laughed. "I'm wearing chain mail, bitch."

I was about to plunge my sword into Lizzie when Dracula grabbed her and pinned her to the ground. I pushed my brooch again and reappeared standing over them. I pressed the tip of my blade to Lizzie's neck. "Now you're going to tell us how we can find the sisters."

CHAPTER FIFTEEN

"I don't understand," Lizzie gasped for air under Dracula's tight grip even as I pressed the tip of my sword to her jugular. "My bite should have paralyzed you."

"Please," Dracula said. "The sisters bit you. That should have paralyzed them for twice as long. I've been through the Scholomance. All I'd have to do is bite you and you'd be under my thrall."

"Please, don't!" Lizzie begged.

"Then tell us what we want to know. If not, it'll be your choice. Silver or slavery."

"I'm not an alpha! Even if you took control of me, the other wolves will keep hunting you."

I shrugged. "Then we'll handle them the same way we did you. It sure would be handy to have another wolf with us fighting against them though, don't you think?"

"I don't know where the sisters are! How would I know?"

"She's telling the truth," Dylan offered. "When we were together in the pack, I was with Lizzie almost the entire time. If I don't know where they are, she probably doesn't either."

"How'd you even track us here?" I asked.

"I didn't *track* you. I assumed Dylan would lead you here. I was right."

"I know you don't want to kill Sienna," Dylan tried. "It's the wolf's instinct. If you broke from the pack, like I did, you'd know as much."

"How's that going for you anyway?" Lizzie asked. "It must hurt like hell."

"It doesn't feel good," he admitted.

"Wolves are meant to roam in packs, Dylan. There's a reason lone wolves are dangerous. That pain, that's just a part of your wolf's instinct telling you that without a pack you can't live. It won't get easier. The pain will only get worse."

"You don't know that," Dylan insisted.

"Of course I do!" Lizzie retorted. "I've been a part of this pack longer than you ever were. Do you think you're the first wolf to try and leave a pack? We've taken in wolves just like you. Caleb was once a part of another pack. He disavowed his alpha. He was a real monster when Vance took him in."

Dracula tilted his head. "What do you say we kill two birds with one stone?"

I snorted. "There you go with your clichés again."

"Put your sword away, Sienna."

"Seriously?"

Dracula nodded. "Maybe the birds and the stones didn't apply. But I could save two wolves with one bite."

Before I knew it, Dracula's fangs were in Lizzie's neck. Almost immediately, he pulled away and spit her blood on the floor, gagging.

I tightened my grip on the hilt of my sword. "Why did you do that?"

"Lizzie, disavow your pack," Dracula suggested. "You have no alpha there. Submit to Dylan as your new alpha."

Lizzie's hands were shaking. She knelt before Dylan. Dylan rested his hand on her head and gasped. "The pain is gone!"

Dracula wiped the wolf's blood from his mouth with his sleeve. "Now, Lizzie, I release you from my thrall."

I grinned. "Fucking brilliant, Drac!"

Dracula chuckled. "I know, right?"

Dylan extended his hand and helped Lizzie to her feet. "I guess we're starting a new pack, then."

I smiled. "Looks that way."

Lizzie shook her head. "I'm sorry, Sienna. I had to do it."

"I know," I assured her.

Dylan looked at Lizzie. "We're going to protect Sienna with our lives. Understood?"

Lizzie nodded. "Absolutely."

"I don't suppose there's anything here I could use to rinse my mouth out is there?" Dracula asked. "Werewolf blood tastes like human excrement."

I raised an eyebrow. "How do you know what human poop tastes like?"

"It's just an expression."

"I think the sisters had some wine in the kitchen," Dylan commented.

Dracula gagged his way down the hallway. I was afraid he was going to hurl. I'd never seen a vampire puke before, but I had a feeling it was a nasty thing to witness, given our diet and all.

"Hot damn!" Dracula exclaimed from the kitchen. I walked in with Dylan and Lizzie right behind me. "It's a nineteen-twenties Polish O-positive."

"Seriously?" I asked. "They left that lying around here?"

Dracula nodded and jammed his thumbnail into the cork to pop it open. He passed the bottle under his nose. "Told you, the sisters are accustomed to the finer things."

"Did they leave any glasses behind?"

Dracula shook his head. "No, but there's a whole crate in the pantry. Take a bottle for yourself."

I tilted my head. "Why would they leave that behind?"

Lizzie cleared her throat. "I don't know how they got it here, but the sisters don't usually travel on foot. I can't imagine trying to make my way through the swamp carrying a crate like that."

Dracula nodded. "They have my power. They likely came and went in bat form. They couldn't carry much with them. Their loss is our gain. Besides, I think this is one of the crates I brought with us when we came over from Romania."

"So you're sure it's safe to drink?" I asked.

Dracula nodded, reached into the crate, and tossed me a bottle. "Drink up!"

I examined the label. "Looks like this is of similar vintage."

Dracula nodded. "Probably collected from the same source."

I shuddered. "I don't even want to imagine how this was bottled."

"I can tell you," Dracula offered. "Some vampires keep humans in their cellars for this reason. They drain them a bit, bottle the blood, and keep them well-fed. When they've recovered, they go back for more."

"That's horrifying." I shook my head.

Dracula took a swig from his bottle. "Oh, it's dreadful. Also delicious."

I fiddled around with the cork on mine. I wasn't sure how Dracula did it. I had nails. It should have been easy. Every time I tried, though, my nail pulled right out of the cork. "How did you do that?"

Dracula laughed. "Give it here. I'll open it for you. It takes practice."

Dracula popped open my bottle and handed it to me. "The trick is you have to give it a little twist as you pull it out."

"I'll try and remember that."

"Give it a taste!"

I took a sip from the bottle. "Damn. That is tasty."

"Not the same as drinking from the source, but certainly more civilized and flavorful."

Dylan grunted. "I hate to break up this tasting or whatever the hell it is you two are doing, but if Lizzie found us here, the other wolves might get the same idea. We shouldn't linger here any longer than is necessary."

I took another swig from my bottle. It really hit the spot. "I'm not all that worried about that. The wolves are mostly coming after me alone, hoping to be the first one to take me out so they can become alpha, right?"

"That's right," Lizzie agreed. "We usually operate as a unit. Until a new alpha rises, though, they'll be competing to kill you first."

I chuckled. "Delightful. I say we let them find us. We know how we can save them now. One bite from Dracula, maybe from me, and we can force them to submit to Dylan's pack."

Dylan nodded. "We stand a better chance now than before. Especially since we have the numbers advantage. Then, once we've claimed the entire pack, we can go after the sisters. We can make them pay for what they did to us to begin with."

"Careful," Dracula cautioned. "I released you. If one of the sisters bites you, it will be back to square one."

Dylan sighed. "Good point. That's why we have to work together. We have to be careful. But this is as much our fight as it is yours."

Lizzie nodded. "Agreed. I didn't like being a vampire's bitch."

Dylan chuckled. "Well, you'll always be a bitch, Lizzie."

Lizzie backhanded Dylan on the shoulder. "Watch your mouth."

"It's not an insult. It's just what you are. You're a female wolf. That makes you a bitch."

"You might be my alpha, but I'm nobody's bitch, bitch."

"Hey," Dylan protested. "I'm not a bitch in any sense of the word."

"You're wearing yoga pants and a belly shirt," Lizzie observed. "I think the word 'bitch' applies."

Dylan took a deep breath. "I see your point."

"You could make her shut up, you know," Dracula reminded him.

Dylan nodded. "That's the way Vance ran the pack. Like a dictator. That's not my style. I'm not going to deprive any wolf who is a part of my pack of a voice."

Dracula laughed. "Spoken like a genuine American werewolf."

Dylan shook his fist in the air. "Stars and stripes, motherfucker!"

CHAPTER SIXTEEN

Dylan went back to the bedroom and changed his clothes. He came out in jeans and a plain black t-shirt and had another t-shirt stuffed full of other clothes in his hand.

"Taking the other wolves' clothes?" I asked.

"I figured after another trip through the swamp we could all use a change of clothes."

"Any female clothes in there?"

"Mine," Lizzie replied. "And Dylan's yoga pants." She looked me up and down. "That's a nice dress. A bit overdressed for this sort of thing, aren't you?"

I smiled. "I have more clothes in the van. I like the dress. I wasn't thinking when I dove into the alligator lagoon wearing it."

We made our way back through the swamp. Dracula insisted on taking the case of blood wine with us and held it overhead as we waded through the water. I would have protested, but damn, that stuff was tasty. Besides, given my urges as of late, having some bottled wine that didn't require refrigeration on standby could be useful.

Dracula set the crate in the back of the van, then we tossed in our swords and covered them and took turns changing in the back of the van. We'd have to find a laundromat sooner or later. Probably a dry cleaner for my dress. For now, sweats and a tank top with a red zip-up hoodie would have to do. It was more comfortable, anyway.

We decided to make a pass through Bourbon Street. After the night's carnage, I expected the place would be a ghost town. Literally and figuratively. The place was hopping like usual. If we hadn't been there, one would think nothing had happened at all.

Dracula huffed. "The police know the truth. They're still trying to cover it up."

Dylan snorted. "How can you cover up mangled bodies in one of the most popular spots to party in the freaking country?"

"This is New Orleans," Lizzie explained. "Shit like this has happened from time to time for years."

I raised an eyebrow. "For years?"

"I'm not aware of too many werewolf rampages on nights that weren't a full moon, but vampire attacks, zombies raised by voodoo priests, ghosts, witchcraft of many varieties. It's all a part of the spice of the place."

I huffed. "And I thought they made Cajun spice from peppers, garlic, and paprika."

Lizzie giggled. "Among other things."

I scratched my head. "The sisters aren't the first vampires in New Orleans. Zoey and I fought a few others here a while back."

Dracula nodded. "Vincent and Nosferatu."

I tilted my head. "How did you know?"

Dracula laughed. "I started the club here. I knew the status of the local vampires, how they were regrouping, looking for guidance. I intended to provide that, back when I was still my old, more villainous self."

"Why did you come to Kansas City, then? This is more of a hotbed for vampires and things of that sort."

"We saw an opportunity. Ever since you and Zoey showed up and started taking out the vampires and other nasty creatures in the area, we thought it best to take you two out first, before our plan was evident."

"So you could take us by surprise? Well, it worked."

"Probably would have if the sisters didn't betray me. No matter, it was for the best. I no longer desire the things I once did."

"I know. I trust you."

"You trust Dracula?" Lizzie asked.

"You should, too. He could have killed you back there, you know. He could have left you in his thrall. He gave you your freedom."

Lizzie glanced at Dylan. "Of a sort."

"Look, I know I'm probably the least likely of our pack to ever become an alpha," Dylan admitted.

"You were the youngest of us. If it wasn't for your friends here, there's no way you would have won."

"I think he's strong. He disowned his alpha."

"Because he refused to kill you. That boy thinks he's in love with you."

I might have blushed a little. "Do you, Dylan?"

"Do I what?"

"Think you're in love with me."

Dylan sighed. "That would be silly. We haven't had time to progress that far. But our time together was pretty special, right?"

I smiled. "It was."

"Get a room, you two!" Lizzie protested. "Unless you want me to vomit all over your van."

"We'd best make the best use of the day we can," Dracula suggested. "The wolves will find us. I say we let them. In the meantime, we should do some more digging into the list Morty gave us."

"We already checked out the doctor. Things weren't as cut and dried as we hoped."

"What are you guys talking about?" Dylan asked.

"We're checking on some of the people the vampires have killed lately, the people they were trying to turn."

"Why?" Lizzie asked.

"We believe the sisters were using you and your former pack to keep us distracted. They're trying to turn powerful people, to work their way up in government in hopes of eventually claiming the presidency and, after that, the rest of the world."

"Seriously?" Lizzie raised an eyebrow. "Well, that tracks."

"What do you mean?"

"I don't think they meant for me to hear, but you know, we wolves can hear a lot better than you bloodsuckers realize. They were talking about a benefit, some charity that a guy running for Lieutenant Governor was holding. They said they already had a number of donors in their pocket and that they'd finish their plan soon."

"What benefit were they talking about?" Dracula asked. "Did you get a name of the candidate?"

Lizzie shook her head. "Well, they were talking about some guy getting elected. That means it wasn't the incumbent. Must've been the challenger."

Dracula shook his head. "I should have known. We were doing something similar in Kansas City. We were making connections through philanthropic organizations and charities."

I nodded. "So the sisters find all these people who have skeletons in their closets, things they're hiding. They use it as leverage. Their new vampires show up at the benefit with sizable donations. It gives their candidate great press. One of the vampires turns the candidate before night's end."

"Why the doctor?" Dracula asked. "It was clear he was saving up to pay a ransom."

"Money he wouldn't have to pay if he had vampire powers and could save the woman he loved himself. In exchange, he uses all the money he saved up selling babies to donate at the benefit."

"Lizzie." Dracula turned in his seat. "Did the sisters happen to mention when the benefit was supposed to be held or where?"

Lizzie shook her head. "They didn't say anything."

I pulled over and grabbed my phone. "If this was all about giving their candidate favorable press, this benefit isn't going to be a secret. Google should help us find it."

I only had to do a couple of searches. The first told me who was running for office. Some guy named Dean Carver. The second told me about a benefit he was holding the night before the election which, according to my search, was in three days.

"Monday Night. Dean Carver, candidate for Lieutenant Governor, is holding a benefit for underprivileged children. The money is supposed to pay for clothing, school supplies, all the necessities."

"That could garner him a lot of votes," Lizzie mused. "There's a huge poverty problem in the city. They're also the ones least likely to vote under normal circumstances."

I nodded. "And according to the polls, Carver only trails by one point. Something like this could give him a last-second surge and tip the vote in his favor."

Dracula grunted. "Yeah, well, by then the people will be electing a vampire to office. Since it's the night before the election, he won't have to worry about campaigning. Sunlight aversion could be a problem under most circumstances."

"And by targeting a candidate, he'll be eager to meet with said benefactors. All it would take is for one of them to ask for a private audience with the candidate in exchange for a sizable donation."

Dracula chuckled. "If only you knew someone wealthy to crash the party."

"You think you can get us in?" I asked.

"You wouldn't need me to get you in. You could walk through the walls. But money talks. I can take us in through the front door."

"The sisters will be there," I pointed out. "They'll spot you straight away."

Dracula nodded. "Counting on that. In the meantime, we could really use a few more wolves."

"How can we help?" Dylan asked.

"Protection detail. The sisters will recognize every last one of us. They won't dare do anything in public. It will be up to the wolves to make sure that none of the sisters team up with any of their newly turned benefactors to meet the candidate."

I bit my lip. "You sure the sisters are going to want to turn him themselves?"

"They'll have to be responsible for at least one bite. That will ensure that he transitions and doesn't die in the process. After that, well, someone will have to protect the candidate from hunters or us. Someone who won't freak out about what their future Lieutenant Governor is going to become. Several young vampires could come in handy in that respect."

Lizzie shook her head. "More than that. A candidate for office is going to have a lot of campaign officials. I'm guessing they'll be humans. People close enough to the candidate that they'd probably notice if he suddenly had a hankering for B-positive and stopped going outside during the day."

"That's a good point," Dracula admitted. "They aren't going to turn merely the candidate, but anyone who walks into that place and isn't already a vampire."

"That whole place could be swarming with vamps." I clenched my hands on the steering wheel. "Even with the whole pack, if we can save them, we could be walking right into a nest. If one of the sisters bites Dylan, the wolves will turn against us."

Lizzie snorted. "But if we bite the other vampires first, it's nighty night for a hundred years."

Dracula smiled. "That's the plan. Bite them before they can bite our new alpha."

"But if they do bite me, we're all screwed."

I nodded. "Pretty much. That's why I can't allow that to happen. First things first, though. We need to get the other wolves. How many are we talking about exactly?"

Lizzie sighed. "Well, we numbered twelve in total. You already killed the alpha. That's eleven. Minus Dylan and me, that means nine more wolves are out there hoping to make quick work of Little Red Riding Hood."

I huffed. "I'm not a Little Red Riding Hood."

Lizzie chuckled. "Says the girl in a red sweatshirt who has wolves trying to track her down."

I laughed. "Last night it was Hansel and Gretel leaving bread-crumbs, or tissues, all over the city. Now it's the Big Bad Wolf. What's next? Jack and the Beanstalk?"

Dracula grunted. "I hope not. If giants get involved in this affair, it might be more than we can handle."

"Seriously, Drac? Giants are real, too?"

Dracula laughed. "They were, once. Thankfully, so far as I'm aware, the last of them died even before my time."

"So far as you're aware?"

"Well, you can't ever be totally sure something is extinct. But in the case of giants, well, they liked to eat people. According to the legends I've read, anyway. I'm pretty sure if any of them still existed, someone would know about it."

I rolled my eyes. "Well, isn't that good news. No giants. That's one fairy tale we won't have to reckon with."

I saw Lizzie smiling widely when I glanced in my rearview mirror. "I say we go Three Little Pigs on these assholes. We huff and we puff and we blow their benefit to hell."

I laughed. "Amen, sister. Then we'll Robin Hood them and give the kids the money anyway."

CHAPTER SEVENTEEN

Three days to catch nine werewolves. They weren't wolfed out, so that would help. We'd still have to catch three a day, bite them all, and compel them to submit to Dylan as their new alpha. Lizzie didn't seem to think that would be a problem. They were already looking for me. All we had to do was leave a trail and hope they'd come at us one at a time.

We might be able to handle a couple at once. Possibly even three. If too many came after us and they were clever about it, they'd be hard to fend off. The problem was that they knew about my strength under daylight. They knew it would be harder to kill me this way.

Since only one of them could kill me, though, and they were all racing to do it, Lizzie didn't think they'd wait until nightfall to make a move. They'd all fear that one of the others would get lucky, stake me during the day, and they'd lose their chance. If, however, we didn't catch them before nightfall, they'd come after me with full force once I was *probably* vulnerable.

One option was to hunt the werewolves during the day and hide in the astral plane every night. The thing about going astral, though, is you can't sleep that way. Since the rules of physics don't technically apply to the astral realm, and everything depended on the power of my perception, if I fell asleep I might very well wake up just in time to suffocate in outer space, or to find myself burning up in the earth's core. I could try to stay awake, but when I was in human form at night I got tired. Three days without sleep was a bit much. Not to mention, Dracula, Dylan, and Lizzie couldn't go astral. Lizzie already tried to take Dylan, then Dracula, as hostages to convince me to give myself up to her for their sakes. The other wolves might very well do the same thing.

We drove to the lower ninth, where I had left my trail of tissues before. It had been a while, but we hoped one or two of the werewolves was still lurking around the neighborhood trying to find me.

I parked the van at a convenience store. I didn't stop for crappy taquitos or hot dogs on a roller under a heat lamp. I didn't even need any gas. This hybrid engine could go for days. It seemed like a better place to leave a new van in what was a rough part of town than on the side of a street somewhere.

Dracula and I grabbed our swords from the back. Maybe we'd need them, maybe we wouldn't. We didn't have to kill Lizzie before, but when you're dealing with werewolves who want you dead, it's best to be prepared.

Dylan stepped out of the van with Lizzie right behind him.

"Lizzie, do you smell that?"

Lizzie nodded. "It's strong."

"Smell what?" I asked.

"It's Caleb," Dylan said. "You agree?"

Lizzie tilted her head and sniffed the air again. "Yeah, definitely Caleb."

"No one else?" Dracula asked.

Dylan shook his head. "Just him. I didn't know if I'd still be able to track their scent now that we aren't of the same pack, but apparently we can."

Lizzie chuckled. "Back in the swamp, I picked up your stench from a mile away."

Dylan chuckled. "I don't have a stench. I have a fragrance."

Lizzie rolled her eyes. "Keep telling yourself that. An ass by any other name would still smell like shit."

"Harsh!" Dylan protested.

Lizzie shrugged. "Just keeping it real."

"Take us to him," I instructed. "It's pretty damn lucky that we found one wolf alone. Best add to our number before we have to deal with more."

"Follow us." Dylan sniffed at the air, and Lizzie did the same. It was a little weird. Like if someone farted, and you were trying to figure out the culprit. I didn't suspect werewolves smelled any better than that.

Dracula and I followed them into an alley. It was like the alley where I found the woman off Bourbon Street but dirtier. We passed a dumpster overflowing with trash.

Then we saw Caleb. His body. His shirt was soaked with blood.

Lizzie gasped. Dylan knelt and lifted his shirt to reveal a single two-inch gash in his abdomen.

"Who did this?" I asked. "One of the other wolves looking to thin out the competition?"

Lizzie shook her head. "We'd never do this. Not to each other. Certainly not like that."

"Sienna!" Dracula said. "People are coming."

I turned and three men approached us from the open end of the alley. They had daggers fixed to their belts and crossbows in hand. A crossbow bolt to a vampire is nothing but a projectile stake.

"Van Helsings," Dracula whispered.

One of the hunters laughed. "Looks like we hit the jackpot, boys. Two werewolves and two vampires."

"Not just any vampire," one of them noted. "That one is Dracula himself."

"Tell us," a hunter began. "How are you two out in the daylight?"

"It must be the power of the Scholomance," the hunter in the middle guessed.

"That's not it!" I shouted.

"Don't tell them anything, Sienna."

They didn't know that Dracula was wearing chain mail. I wasn't. I probably should have been. We had another set, but the stuff was heavy and uncomfortable. I didn't think we'd need it. The hunters aimed their crossbows. Before they could fire, I touched my brooch, and three bolts flew through the air.

Dracula stepped in front of Dylan and Lizzie. There was a good chance those bolts were tipped with silver.

I charged after the hunters and phased through them. I grabbed my sword by the hilt and widened my stance. I pushed my blade through the chest of one of them and touched my brooch.

The hunter gasped, spitting up blood. The other two turned to me. They weren't ready, but they reached for stakes. I yanked out my sword to swing it at one of the other two, and I caught him across his neck. His head hit the ground.

I grabbed the last one and sank my teeth into his neck. I wouldn't normally drain someone completely. I didn't want to kill, but these fuckers already killed one of the wolves and tried to kill the rest of us.

And there was something different about this guy's blood. It cleared my sinuses, as if this dude's veins were filled with Vicks VapoRub. This guy either ate a lot of eucalyptus or he wasn't entirely human.

I drank until the hunter passed out and Dracula pulled me off him. "That's enough, Sienna!"

"He deserves it!" I snarled.

"That may be," Dracula allowed. "But he might know things. These Van Helsings communicate. They work together."

"He isn't going to help us. Are you kidding? Not after I killed his friends."

Dracula shook his head. "He'll talk. I'll make him talk."

CHAPTER EIGHTEEN

My hands were trembling. I'd never killed humans—not like that. I wasn't sure what came over me. Was it rage? Was it a desire to protect my friends? Some of both. I also drank more blood in the last couple of days than I had my entire time as a daywalker before. I was so full it was like I'd just had Thanksgiving dinner.

One thing I knew for sure was that once those hunters knew about me, when they realized that Dracula and I could walk in the sun, we couldn't let them leave. They'd spread the word. They and their Van Helsing friends would come after us. We'd be at the top of the hunter's most wanted list.

It wasn't hard to imagine why they were there and why they took down Caleb. After what the werewolves did on Bourbon Street the night before, they thought they were eliminating the threat, avenging those who died. What they didn't realize was that these werewolves weren't acting of their own free will. They were under Sorina's thrall. If any of them had the slightest clue what the sisters were up to, what their plans were, they wouldn't bother with us or a pack of werewolves.

You'd think dragging an unconscious person through the streets would earn us some unwanted attention. We were traveling in a group. Dylan and Dracula carried the hunter, his arms over each of their shoulders. It looked like we were helping someone who was hurt, maybe passed out drunk. This wasn't the part of town where people called the cops. Lizzie said that half the time the cops wouldn't respond to calls in that neighborhood, and when they did, they usually showed up too late to stop whatever might have been happening. People would get arrested, usually the wrong people, and it never led to anything good. The chances that anyone would report a group of exceedingly white people carrying another passed-out white guy through the streets were slim.

We got the hunter back in the van, and Dracula bound his hands and feet with rope he had stored in the back. We tossed him in the van. Dylan and Lizzie climbed in the back with him, and we left the neighborhood.

"Where in the world are we going to go interrogate this ass hat?" I asked.

"We could take him back to our den," Lizzie proposed.

"Are you sure that's a good idea? There are still eight more unaccounted-for wolves who want Sienna dead."

"That's why I'm sure it will work. They won't go home. They won't return to the den until the deed is done. That instinct, that drive to avenge the alpha is too strong."

I sighed. "I don't know. It sounds risky."

"Do you have any better ideas?" Lizzie pressed.

"We could rent a motel room."

Lizzie huffed. "You want to take a guy and interrogate him in a motel?"

"All right, my idea sucked. I admit it."

"The den will suffice," Dracula insisted. "If any wolves come back, we'll deal with them. What are the chances they'd all come back at once, if any return to the den at all?"

"Exactly my point," Lizzie shot back. "In a roundabout way, it might be the safest place in the city. Well, near the city anyway."

She opened the hunter's wallet and her eyes went wide. "You won't believe this."

"I wouldn't count on it. I'm beyond incredulity at this point."

"Alexander Van Helsing."

Dracula's eyes widened. "Let me see that."

Lizzie handed Dracula the man's ID. "I should have seen it before. The guy is a spitting image of Abraham Van Helsing, minus the beard, and with contemporary style."

"What do you think?" I glanced at Dracula while trying to keep my eyes on the road. "How many greats are between your original nemesis and this joker?"

Dracula shook his head. "It's impossible to know. It has been a long time since I encountered someone who still bears the Van Helsing name. Still, it should not be a surprise. Abraham raised his own children as hunters. Their children did the same. Male children tended to run in the family in those days so, according to custom, the Van Helsing name was preserved."

"Well, they were never able to kill you. No reason to be afraid, right? Besides, a name is just a name."

"They came close to ending my existence more than once. Were it not for the dark power of the Scholomance, they would have succeeded on multiple occasions."

I raised an eyebrow. "On multiple occasions? Drac, if they succeeded the first time, there wouldn't have been multiple chances for them to succeed again."

"Clearly, Sienna. I only meant that there are several times I've encountered a Van Helsing when I could not have escaped without the remnant of pine stuck in my chest were it not for my dark powers."

"But you're on the light side of the force now," I quipped. "The Jedi are pretty badass in their own right."

Dylan sighed. "Even the Jedi had to train for years, for their entire lives, to master the skill."

"I'm not a science fiction character," Dracula huffed. "I'm Dracula!"

I grinned. "Horror. Science Fiction. What's the difference? I think Frankenstein is some of both. Why not Dracula?"

"Because my powers defy science!" Dracula insisted. "At least they did. And I am no fiction."

I snorted. "Just because you think vampirism is mystical doesn't mean there isn't a scientific explanation to what we are. It just means that scientists don't understand it. I imagine not many have studied it."

"Abraham Van Helsing did," Dracula stated. "He was a doctor, you know. He spent years attempting to devise a cure. When he wasn't focused on that, he studied ways to harm or kill us. His experiments produced many horrors to our kind, but none of them ever as effective as a simple wooden stake."

"What kind of horrors?" I asked.

"A synthetic version of werewolf enzyme for one. Not nearly as effective, but he managed to devise a formula that could paralyze us for an hour, maybe a little more."

"I can see how that might be helpful. Especially if you're after a vampire in chain mail or one who is elusive enough it's hard to get a straight shot. Hit him anywhere with a blade or an arrow dipped in the potion and the hunter would have an entire hour to finish him off."

Dracula nodded. "He'd only need a few seconds. Unless the hunter had *other* intentions for the vampire, hoped to interrogate him to find out the location of the vampires, or things like that."

"Ever get hit by the stuff?" I asked.

Dracula shook his head. "I wouldn't be here now if I had."

"Let's hope this isn't a mistake."

"Why would it be a mistake?" Dylan asked.

Dracula cleared his throat. "The Van Helsings are clever and unpredictable. There's no telling what methods they've devised over the years to harm either of our kind that I don't know about. We all need to be on our guard."

Lizzie gave me turn-by-turn directions while Dylan kept an eye on Alexander. He was in the back, close to our weaponry. I'd drained him well enough I didn't think he'd wake up any time soon, but Dracula said these Van Helsings were different. We couldn't be too careful.

"Turn there, the next drive on the right."

I raised my eyebrows. "That looks like an old, abandoned school."

"Great for a pack. We all have our own rooms. They were going to tear down the place if it didn't sell. We pooled our money and bought it at auction a few years back. It has everything we need. Showers in the locker rooms. A kitchen in the lunchroom. More space than we need. Plenty of room to grow if we ever expanded the pack."

"You were going to add more wolves to the pack?"

"Vance wanted to," Dylan said. "We didn't all agree, but he was the alpha. He was convinced that we were needed."

"Needed?" I asked.

"To protect the city," Lizzie explained. "We might be monsters in lore, and those without a pack, those who are young especially, can wreak a lot of havoc. But our kind has a long history of protecting villages from greater threats."

"Like vampires?" I asked.

Lizzie nodded. "Primarily vampires. We're the one thing vampires will avoid. If there's a vampire coven terrorizing a city, the wolves den up near the village, and more often than not the vampires leave before the next full moon."

"It's true," Dracula put in. "I don't know about whether the werewolves defended many villages, but I knew many vampires through the years who chose to relocate when a pack showed up in town."

"Vance thought we needed more to defend the city from the

growing threat," Lizzie continued. "We went after Sorina and the sisters the last full moon. We didn't expect they'd be immune to our bite."

I shook my head. "It's ridiculous, you know? Hunters killing werewolves. I just killed two hunters. At the end of the day, we all want the same thing."

"To be fair, all the hunters knew was that there was a werewolf attack on the city the night before," Dracula noted.

I huffed. "Yeah, but if they'd dug a little deeper, if they wondered why werewolves were attacking when it wasn't under a full moon, maybe they'd discover the wolves were forced to do that by the sisters."

Dracula nodded. "Not all vampires or werewolves are monsters. People see what they want to see. Just because I was evil and did some horrible things, and other vampires have done the same, it doesn't mean you have to become a monster, too."

"The Van Helsings won't see it that way. Not after I just killed two of his friends and almost killed him."

"In our world, the world of monsters and supernatural beings, people tend to see us for what we are rather than who we are."

"It's not just werewolves and vampires," Lizzie pointed out. "People are like that with other people, too. They like to label people. Then they look at the worst of those who fit the label and assume the worst of everyone else who shares those traits. It's a lot easier to color people with one brush than to bother to get to know people. A werewolf goes crazy and kills people. All werewolves must be dangerous monsters."

Dracula cleared his throat. "And one notorious vampire from Transylvania inspires a few horror stories and all vampires must be just like him."

"That's not you anymore, Drac."

Dracula sighed. "It is, and it isn't. Sure, I was consumed by black magic, but who do you think made the choice to follow the dark path of the Scholomance? I gave into the darkness. I allowed it to consume me. That might be in my past now, but I am still responsible."

"Well, you're making different choices now," I offered.

"That doesn't make up for what I've done. No matter how much good I do now, how many lives I save, it won't ever bring back the people whose lives I've stolen."

I took a deep breath. My eyes welled up with tears. "Now I've done the same thing."

"We'd all be dead right now if you hadn't done that," Dylan reminded me.

I shook my head. "You don't understand. I didn't just kill those men. I enjoyed it. I wanted to drain Alexander dry."

"They didn't give you much of a choice," Dylan consoled me.

"He's right," Lizzie added. "You saved all of us."

"I know. Maybe I could have just knocked them out. I *killed* those men."

"It happened fast," Dracula reasoned. "You didn't kill because you enjoyed it. You killed to protect us, to defend yourself and all of us."

"I know! But didn't you hear what I said? I liked it!"

Dracula nodded. "I can relate to that. But if you hated doing it, if it made you sick to your stomach, they'd be just as dead. Now, at least, you've learned about the darkness that's a part of you. Once you know about it, you can deal with it. You can fight it."

"It terrifies me," I admitted.

"It should," Dracula contended. "If it didn't, you'd be a monster."

"Um, guys." Dylan held out a small metal box. "Found this in Alexander's coat."

Dracula held out his hand. "Let me see it."

Dracula pulled out three syringes filled with a red liquid. Maybe it was just the sunlight passing through it, but I could swear it glowed. "What the hell?"

"You don't know what that is?" I asked. "Maybe it's the synthesized werewolf enzyme you mentioned before."

Dracula shook his head. "I've seen that stuff before. It's a clear liquid. This is different."

I pressed my lips together. "Good thing you've got medieval interrogation skills."

CHAPTER NINETEEN

We got out of the van and carried Alexander into the old school. Dracula stopped at the door and looked around.

"Something wrong?" I asked.

"It's nothing. Just a feeling."

"What kind of feeling?"

"Like someone was following us. Probably just paranoia. I'm not used to doing this sort of thing in full daylight."

We tied Alexander to an old school desk, one of those with the chair connected to it. Dracula had clearly done this before. We tied his arms to his chest and his wrists together behind his back. The legs of the desk weren't in line with his legs, so Dracula tied his ankles together.

Alexander was still out. We weren't sure how long it would take before he woke up, but his pulse had slowed to normal. It was just a matter of time.

"So, what's the plan?" I asked. "Yank out his fingernails? Poke him with your sword? Pour water down his throat? We could tickle torture him for hours."

Dracula laughed. "We tell him the truth."

"The truth? What kind of screwed-up interrogation technique is that?"

Dracula shrugged. "In my experience, the truth is more terrifying than any kind of torture."

Lizzie huffed. "He's a hunter. He'd rather commit to his biases than consider the truth."

"My point exactly," Dracula retorted. "That's because the horror of what's really going on will chill this Van Helsing to the bone. Besides, if we can put the sisters on his radar, perhaps we can use him."

"Use him?" I raised an eyebrow. "Not after I wasted his friends."

"He'll still come after us. So will whatever friends he might have in the area. A hunter, a regular hunter, might take down a doe if given a shot. Not if a buck with a nice rack passes by first."

I smiled. "The sisters do have nice racks."

"They really do," Dylan put in.

I stared daggers at him.

He chuckled. "You said it. I just agreed with you."

I smirked. "All right. Well, if this goes sour, I'm going to say I told you so."

"Oh, it will go sour," Dracula assured me. "I don't doubt that one bit. I don't know about you, though. I'd rather deal with our enemies one at a time. If we can convince the hunters to turn their attention to the sisters, we'll deal with them when this is over."

"He's right, Sienna." Dylan rested a hand on my shoulder. "The sisters pose a bigger threat. Maybe not to us, but to the rest of the world."

Alexander groaned and we turned our attention to him in unison. Dracula approached him.

"Alexander Van Helsing," Dracula began. "It's nice to be acquainted with your family again. It's been too long."

Alexander huffed. "You don't mean that."

Dracula shrugged. "Maybe I do. Maybe I don't. The truth is, your ancestor, Abraham, made me more powerful."

"What doesn't kill you makes you stronger?" Alexander smirked.

"You look awfully smug," I observed. "Considering the fact that we tied you up and your partners are dead."

A smile split the Van Helsing's face. "I have my reasons."

"We are not going to kill you," Dracula stated. "If we weren't pushed into it, we wouldn't have killed your friends, either. The truth is, we're facing a much bigger threat than you know."

"Enlighten me, then. It appears you've been enlightened, Dracula. Tell me, how did you do it? How did you manage to overcome your allergy to the sun?"

"I bit him," I explained. "I did it to him. And he's not the monster you've read about."

Alexander shook his head. "I don't believe that for a second. I've seen what you can do, young lady. He might not be the same villain of legend, but you most certainly are. To disappear like that. I'm curious. How do you do it?"

I smiled. "A girl has her secrets."

"How many of our pack have you killed?" Lizzie demanded.

Alexander tilted his head. "You don't know? I thought a pack's bond was stronger than that. I thought you'd feel it when one of your kin fell."

"We're a new pack now," Dylan informed him. "We don't know."

Alexander fixed his eyes on me. "You should thank me, you know. We know you're the one who killed the alpha. They'd still be after you if we hadn't eliminated them. All of them."

"All of them!" Lizzie screamed.

"All except for you two."

Lizzie fell to her knees. "I can't believe it. They're all dead?"

Dylan put his hand on Lizzie's shoulder.

"It was easier than you'd think," Alexander went on. "We have ways to track werewolves. Ways you wouldn't understand. I imagine more of my friends are on their way here to finish the job."

Dracula clenched his fists. "We aren't the real threat. The wolves who killed those people weren't doing it of their own accord. Didn't it occur to you to ask why they were shifted when the moon wasn't full?"

Alexander shook his head. "We're hunters, Drac. There are always mysteries begging for answers. In my experience, it's better to kill the monsters first and ask questions later."

"My pack wasn't the threat, you dick!" Lizzie jumped to her feet and charged Alexander to punch him in the face.

Alexander winced. "Damn. You really can pack a punch, young lady."

"You have no idea!" Lizzie screamed.

Dylan grabbed Lizzie's hand. "Hold it together."

Dracula cleared his throat. "The truth is, Alexander, we needed those wolves. Sorina and the sisters, you heard of them?"

Alexander rolled his eyes. "Your whores from Transylvania? Of course I know about them."

"They betrayed me. They stole my darker power. They have a plan to infect people of power, to turn them into vampires. To take over the world."

"So what if they do? Why are you telling me this?"

"Because you killed the wolves we needed to stop them. We need your help."

"A Van Helsing helping Dracula? You've got to be shitting me."

Dracula tilted his head. "I'm not shitting you. I'd have to eat you first, and I'm not going to do that. As much as I might enjoy it."

I snickered. "Don't worry. I'll be shitting you in a few hours. You were delicious, by the way."

Alexander grunted. "I'm not sure if that's a compliment or what. It's disgusting. I know that much."

"I know your kind," Dracula claimed. "Even as you think you know mine. There's nothing I can tell you to convince you to stop hunting me."

"You're right. If what you say is true, if you don't have your dark hoodoo anymore, it's just a matter of time before you're staked."

"That may be," Dracula allowed. "But we need each other right now. We can't stop the sisters without you. They have my power, the power of the Scholomance. The same magic that's thwarted your family for generations. If you want to stop them, like we do, then we'll have to work together."

"We won't work together. We might share a similar goal for a time, but make no mistake about it. We don't partner up with vampires and werewolves."

Lizzie shook her head. "And I'm not inclined to partner with reckless killers."

"Tell me, young lady," Alexander said. "How many of those bodies on Bourbon Street did you personally rip to shreds?"

"I was compelled! The sisters took control of our alpha. We had to obey."

"Not true." Alexander glanced at Dylan. "He's evidence enough that a wolf can disown his alpha and break from his control if properly motivated."

"That was different," Dylan objected. "My alpha wanted me to kill someone I care about."

"And killing innocent people doesn't motivate you enough to resist an order from your alpha?"

Lizzie shook her head. "You don't know how hard it is to do that. It's a miracle Dylan resisted at all."

"Not a miracle," Alexander argued. "Miracles don't happen. They aren't real. There's always a way where there's a will."

"What's done is done," Dracula declared. "We've both lost people. So long as we're feuding with each other, Sorina is free to carry out her plan."

"What is her plan, exactly?"

"We have reason to believe that the sisters are targeting a candidate for office. Dean Carver. He's running for Lieutenant Governor. He's holding a benefit on Monday night. They hope to turn him and use him to reach the governor himself. From there, it's not hard to imagine how the sisters might be able to reach anyone. Even the president."

"How do I know this isn't a trap? You might be able to walk in the daylight. Other vampires can't. You could be sending me and other hunters into a nest just so you can slaughter us."

"Do a little digging yourself," I recommended. "You'll find out that what Dracula told you is true. If you don't come to the same conclusion, don't come."

"We need you and your hunters to protect Carver at all costs. If you can make sure no one turns him, that the vampires don't get him alone, we will deal with the sisters."

Alexander frowned. "Say I agree to this. When this is done, when this is over, we will come after you."

"Of course you will," Dracula agreed. "Let me ask you a question."

"What's that?"

Dracula set the open metal box of syringes on the desk in front of Alexander. "What is this?"

Alexander laughed. "You'll find out soon enough."

"Is it some kind of poison?" Dracula asked.

Alexander smirked. "More like an elixir. It's incredible what's possible when you learn a little magic and combine it with genuine science."

"What are you talking about?" I snapped.

I heard a loud bang and turned in time to see two hunters run into the room, crossbows in hand. The same two hunters I thought I'd killed before. The one I beheaded had dried blood caked on his body, his shirt was still soaked. He had a scar where I'd lopped his head off before.

"An immortality elixir," Dracula whispered.

"Stand down boys," Alexander ordered. "We'll have our chance to take down these monsters later."

"How did you do it?" Dracula asked. "I'd heard of such things, but I never believed it was possible."

"I'm Alexander Van Helsing. These two are my brothers. Reginald and James. We are the sons of Abraham Van Helsing."

Dracula tilted his head. "Don't you mean *descendants* of Abraham Van Helsing?"

"I said what I said. We're a lot older than we look, thanks to our elixir. We can't be killed. As you can see, even if you chop off our heads, we can put it right back on and we're good as new."

"What the hell?" I shouted.

"Like I said, we'll get you, eventually. All of you."

Dracula took his sword out and cut through the bindings that held Alexander to the chair. "Help us eliminate the sisters and you're free to give us your best shot."

Alexander grabbed the metal box from the desk. Dracula didn't even try to stop him. He joined his brothers but stopped just before they left the room. "We'll see you soon."

CHAPTER TWENTY

"How the hell did they do that?" I demanded.

"I don't know, Sienna." Dracula paced back and forth.

"It has to be something similar to the enzyme that turns vampires, or maybe werewolves, but stripped of the monstrosity."

"I don't know. Even so, you or I couldn't lose our heads and put them right back in place. There's more to that elixir than that."

"There has to be a way to kill them," Lizzie insisted.

Dracula shrugged. "Probably. Cut off his head, put it in a box, keep it separate from the body. Burn them up. Blast them to pieces with a bomb. Mangle them so much that they can't be put back together again."

I grinned. "Like Humpty Dumpty. I think we've finally exhausted Mother Goose's repertoire."

"Not quite," Dracula said. "There are others."

"Well, we've covered all the ones I can remember. Do you think it's safe here?"

Dracula cocked his head. "Why wouldn't it be?"

I stared back at Dracula for a couple of seconds. Did he really need me to explain it? "Because the Van Helsing brothers know where we are."

"I'm not sure it matters," Lizzie said. "We could go anywhere and I have a feeling they'd find us. Hell, they ganked our entire pack, present company excluded, in a matter of hours."

Dracula chuckled. "You're looking at a vampire who has lived in the same castle for centuries. Every Van Helsing who has ever been knew exactly where I was but none of them ever got me. If these Van Helsings really are Abraham's sons, they've known where I was for years and despite their supposed invulnerability never dared enter my residence."

I snorted. "Yeah, well, you were wielding the dark power of the Scholomance."

Dracula scratched his head. "Yes, that was a part of it. I also had booby traps."

Dylan snickered. "Sounds like a really constrictive bra."

Lizzie and I stared at Dylan for a second.

"What? I mean, obviously, I wouldn't know."

I laughed. "Right. I'm pretty sure you know what booby traps are."

"I can draw up the schematics for a few," Dracula offered. "You two wolves can work on setting them up. After the benefit, we need to make sure we're ready to deal with the Van Helsings when they come after us."

"What are we going to do?" I asked.

Dracula laced his fingers together and extended his arms. His knuckles snapped and popped like a bowl of rice cereal. "Tell me, Sienna. What's stronger? Light or darkness?"

I shrugged. "I don't know. I mean, darkness is more frightening. If you're walking through a dark room you're more likely to trip over something and get hurt than in a lit room."

"In my experience, until recently, light was more terrifying," Dracula countered. "Light can burn. It consumes darkness. That's why it kills vampires. Those who aren't like us. You can't throw more darkness at a light and snuff it out. The darker a room is, the brighter even a small light shines. Light *is* more powerful than darkness. It's fear that gives darkness its power."

"And Legos," Dylan added. "You don't want to walk through a dark room if there are Legos on the floor. Trust me."

I turned to Dylan and raised an eyebrow. "Really, Dylan?"

"What? I have a younger brother who still lives at home. He's only nine. He loves Legos. I'm speaking from experience."

Dracula extended a finger. "Idea! We could put up a sign at the entrance asking visitors to remove their shoes. They'd have to walk through a dark hall. We'd cover it with Legos. Thousands of them."

I rolled my eyes. "Please tell me you're kidding."

Dracula smirked. "Of course I am. The point behind all of this is that you and I, Sienna, passed the trials on the path of light at the Scholomance. That power is within us. We just never had a master who could teach us how to use it, who could take us to the level of mastery."

"Neither you nor I have been able to do a damn thing with those powers since Kansas City. Are you sure we still have them?"

Dracula nodded. "We do. Maybe it's because we aren't confronting dark power. When I touched those syringes, I felt something."

I pressed my lips together. "I never touched them. But when I bit Alexander, there was something in his blood. Something different."

Dracula nodded. "Alexander told us the elixir was a combination of magic and science. I think we know what kind of magic the Van Helsings used."

"Are you saying a Van Helsing went to the Scholomance?"

"That's exactly what I'm saying. You felt it. I did, too. The power we have is what we need to defeat the sisters. It's also what we need to defend ourselves from the Van Helsings."

I ran my fingers through my hair. "We don't know how to access this power. We don't even know what we can do with it."

"Which is why we need to pay a visit to the one who sent us to the Scholomance and set us on the path of light. We need to return and learn whatever we can between now and the benefit."

"How are we going to do that? Athena sent us to the Scholomance. She's in Hades. We can't get there, not without Zoey and her portal."

"Morty can take us there."

"He's the Grim Reaper, Drac. It's not like I can dial him up for a chat."

"You can see reapers in the astral plane, correct?"

"Sure. If they happen to be on their way to harvest someone's soul while I'm playing the invisible woman."

"Then all we have to do is be somewhere when the reapers are likely to show up. Maybe we get Morty, maybe we don't. But any reaper who appears can get him the message."

CHAPTER TWENTY-ONE

Our best chance at finding a reaper was at either a hospice center or an ICU. From my experience working with Zoey, hospice reapings tend to be simpler. Deaths there aren't as sudden or unexpected. People in hospitals are fighting for their lives. In hospice, while the nearly departed might still be afraid of death, they know it's coming. Those spirits are less likely to resist, to flee. We stood a better chance of having a conversation with a reaper in that scenario than we would at a hospital, where his job might be more complicated.

A quick search on my phone revealed about ten hospice centers close to the French Quarter and within a few minutes of the werewolves' den. There was a string of them just south of New Orleans City Park, and Dracula and I headed there in the van. We figured if we didn't luck out at one of them, we could move to one of the others.

Dracula waited in the van. If you don't have a loved one or a friend in one of those places, it's not like you can't get in, but a creepy-looking dude like Dracula wandering around in a place like that might raise some questions. We didn't want to draw attention from hunters. Not all the hunters in the city after the slaughter the night before were associated with the Van Helsings. We also didn't know how many vampires or human agents the sisters might have out and about keeping tabs on us. It was best that Dracula keep a low profile.

I entered the astral plane before I even left the van. It was easier that way. I didn't have to make sure no one saw me when I disappeared. Reports of something like that would be problematic for many of the same reasons. Hunters were savvy. Even if none of them saw me go invisible, if someone saw me and posted on social media something about seeing a woman disappear into thin air, I didn't doubt that a hunter or two would catch wind of it. Social media didn't only help people connect. It was also a primary means hunters used to identify targets.

After I left the van, I walked right through the glass doors in the front of the first hospice center I checked.

It was a nice place. Most hospice facilities are. There were potted trees, and fresh flowers on small tables around a number of seating areas where the families of patients gathered. As I walked down the hall, I saw several gathering areas designed to give the families privacy. The patient rooms must've been farther down the hall. My eyes were peeled open looking for reapers. They wouldn't be hard to identify. The black cloaks gave them away. They rarely summoned their scythes until they were ready to reap a soul. If I saw one with a scythe ready, I knew to keep my distance. If you're asking a reaper for a favor, the last thing you want to do is interrupt him just as he's preparing to gather a soul.

I felt a hand touch my shoulder and I almost jumped out of my astral skin. The one thing you don't expect when traversing the astral plane is getting touched.

I jumped around to see a cloaked reaper looking at me. "What are you doing here, Sienna?"

I tilted my head. It wasn't a male voice. I didn't know many reapers. A lot of them knew who I was, though. The reaper lowered her hood. This was a reaper I had met before. It was Carmilla, Morty's significant other.

"Carmilla! Talk about luck."

"Morty said you were in the neighborhood. I didn't expect to see you here. We have three deaths scheduled here today, none of them caused by vampires or werewolves."

I nodded. "I needed to get a message to Morty. Dracula and I need to reach Athena."

Carmilla raised an eyebrow. "Why?"

I chuckled. "You want the short answer or the long one?"

"I have a job to do. Morty told us if any of us encountered you to do whatever we could to help. He'll still want to know the reason."

"We've encountered some Van Helsings who have somehow attained immortality. We think they've tapped into the dark power of the Scholomance. We are already facing the sisters, who wield that power in spades. We need to see Athena so she can take us back to the Scholomance so we can learn more about the path of light. We need something that will give us an edge, a chance to stop the sisters and the hunters eventually."

Carmilla nodded. "Good enough for me. I can take you back with me to the underworld when I'm done. I assume Dracula is coming with you?"

I nodded. "That's the plan."

"That will make it a bit tricker. I'll have to leave the astral plane before I form the portal. Unless he can go astral, too."

I shook my head. "He can't."

Carmilla pressed her lips together. "That's fine. We just have to find a place where we won't be seen." She glanced at a clock on the wall. "Give me ten minutes. I'll come to you. Where are you parked?"

"Just down the street. It's a silver Toyota Sienna."

Carmilla chuckled. "Of course it is."

I rolled my eyes. "Dracula thought it would be cute to get a van with my name on it."

"Dracula being cute? I'll tell you what, girl. Just when you thought you'd seen it all."

I smiled. "We can pull up in the circle drive and pick you up."

"I'm on a tight schedule with the boatman," she warned me. "We'll have to do this fast."

"We're operating out of an old, abandoned school about ten minutes from here. Will that work?"

"That's pushing it, but it should be fine. I won't have time to take the tour, but if we can duck inside and out of view, I can take you to the underworld straight away."

I smiled. "Thanks, Carmilla."

Carmilla patted me on the back and headed down the hall. She turned toward one of the rooms and summoned her scythe. It was an impressive instrument, and the crescent blade shined under the hallway lights. She walked through a closed door and out of view.

I returned to the van. Dracula had his seat reclined and his bony, pale bare feet kicked up on the dash.

I remained in the astral plane when I entered the van. I pressed my brooch.

"Boogedie, boogedie, boo!"

Dracula shrieked and accidentally kicked the windshield, stubbing his toe. "Damn it, Sienna!"

I laughed. "Sienna three, Dracula zero. You really need to work on your scare game."

Dracula huffed. "You have the advantage of that brooch. It's not fair!"

"You have the advantage of being one of the most feared monsters in history. I'd say we're on a level playing field."

Dracula shook his head. "I didn't expect you back so soon."

"I got lucky. Morty's girlfriend was there. We've met a few

times. She's going to come with us back to the school when she's done."

I watched the digital clock on my dash and timed it so that we pulled up in the circle drive in front of the hospice center's doors at exactly the ten-minute mark. Like clockwork, Carmilla appeared. She walked right through the front doors and phased through the door of the van. I tried my best not to give it away. Carmilla lowered her hood. "Hey, guys!"

Dracula jumped again.

I laughed so hard I almost snorted. "Drac is easily frightened."

Dracula shook his head. "I should have expected that."

Carmilla smiled widely. "Sorry!"

Carmilla was a pretty girl. She was a classmate of Zoey's and Morty's at the reaper academy. She had doe eyes, and her dark hair was pulled back in a bun.

I pulled away from the hospice center and headed back down the road toward the school.

"So, if you're going to Hades, you should probably be aware that Athena has made a lot of changes since she took over."

I nodded. "I've been there since. When I went to the Scholomance with Zoey the last time. We had to pass through a number of people's personal hells. We rode with the boatman through a never-ending version of *It's a Small World*. I think I still have that damn song stuck in my head."

Carmilla chuckled. "Athena has refined that idea since then. Now, as soon as you enter the borders of Hades, you'll have to pass through your own personal hell before you can see anyone else's."

"My own personal hell? I don't even know what that might be."

"You'll soon find out. Since both of you are entering Hades together, you'll have to endure both of your versions of hell before you reach Athena's castle."

I glanced at Dracula. "Any clue what your hell might be?"

Dracula sighed. "I have a few ideas."

"For condemned souls, they have to stay there a while. It won't last long for either of you, but make no mistake about it, hell will be hell."

I snorted. "Well, so long as it's temporary. Half the horror of hell is the realization that it never ends."

"It's not everlasting torment for most folks. Every soul delivered to perdition has to endure a taste of their worst nightmare, but Athena isn't as sadistic as her predecessor. Once they've endured enough, she allows damned souls to visit other people's personal hells."

Dracula grunted. "That doesn't sound like much in the way of mercy."

"You'd be surprised," Carmilla suggested. "One person's hell might be a never-ending boy band concert. Some folks might actually enjoy that."

I giggled. "That sounds like a hell populated by damned teenage girls from the early two-thousands."

"How many people merit condemnation as teenagers?" Dracula asked.

I shrugged. "I don't take it that's a demographic you're all that familiar with. Have you even seen *Mean Girls?* Girls that age can be cruel. High school was hell for me."

Dracula laughed. "Well, I guess we know one thing we might have to face when we arrive in hell."

I gulped. "Back to high school? Dear God, no!"

CHAPTER TWENTY-TWO

Dracula sketched up a plan for a booby trap before we left. When we arrived, Dylan and Lizzie were busy tearing out drywall.

"What is this going to do?" I asked.

"They're installing flame throwers in the walls," Dracula explained. "And a trip wire."

I raised an eyebrow. "Do you *want* to burn down the school?"

"Won't be an issue. The schematic includes flame retardant on the walls. Plus, if we can get the sprinkler system working, we can use that if it gets out of hand."

"All right," I agreed reluctantly. "Well, we don't have time to talk about it now."

"That's right," Carmilla said. "I'm on a tight schedule. We need to get through so I can bring this soul to the boatman and you can go to hell."

I chuckled. "I think this is the first time someone ever told me, 'go to hell,' and meant it literally."

"Are you sure this is a good idea?" Dylan asked.

"Don't worry," I assured him. "I've been to hell and back again, before. It's not pleasant, but we'll be fine. I think."

Lizzie giggled. "I was about to say, 'Godspeed,' but I'm not entirely sure that's appropriate."

I smiled. "Don't sweat it. We'll sweat enough in the hot place for all of us."

Carmilla grabbed a smoky crystal from a pocket inside her cloak. She summoned her scythe and used the golden glow from the soul she'd harvested to channel a little light through the crystal. A roughly human-sized vertical oval formed in midair, glistening with golden soul-colored energy. It was a reaper portal. "This will take us to the common gate in the underworld, so be prepared. There will be a lot of other reapers, undoubtedly curious why you're there."

"I'm no stranger to the underworld."

"True," Carmilla acknowledged. "But usually when you and Zoey showed up in the past, your presence meant something bad was about to go down."

I smiled. "I'm an omen. Cool."

Dracula grinned. "I've always been an omen."

"I imagine that's true. Most people don't see Dracula and think it's going to be a great day."

"Come on," Carmilla tapped at her wrist where her watch would be if she was wearing one. "On a schedule, remember?"

"Right." I jumped through the portal. Dracula was right behind me, and Carmilla pulled up the rear.

We landed in front of a sizable crowd of reapers, all lined up ready to use the common portal to travel to their assignments. You don't realize how many people die every day until you see how many reapers had to be dispatched all the time. The world isn't as small as the animatronic multi-ethnic bots on the Disney ride—the one I'd most recently experienced the last time I went to hell—would have you believe.

If you ever walk into a room and everyone shuts up the second you appear, it's a good sign that they recognize you and that your presence means something. When that many people are staring at you—especially when those "people" are reapers—it is chilling.

I waved at the crowd. "Hey guys, just passing through. Never mind me!"

Carmilla chuckled. "I'm sure I'll have to answer questions later. I think they're staring at you because every time you show up for the boatman, you end up cutting in line."

"Does it matter? It's not like I'm taking up any space for souls. We're just riding in the back of the boat."

Carmilla shrugged. "Not a big deal. You'll certainly churn the rumor mill. Especially now that you've showed up with me rather than Zoey. There's no telling what conspiracies folks might come up with. Especially since the infamous count is coming with us."

Dracula tilted his head. "I'm no stranger to conspiracies. I've made the front cover of Weekly World News three times now."

We made our way through the crowd, down a tunnel that looked like an entrance to the subway in New York City. No, I'd never been to New York, but I'd seen it in the movies. We weren't heading for a subway system but to the River Styx, the mystical body of water where the boatman ferried souls into the afterlife. I knew the boatman. The old boatman, Charon, had been killed in the middle of a civil war among the gods. Roy was the new boatman. Zoey and I met him the first time we went to Hades. He was a good ol' boy, a hillbilly whose only aspiration in life was to spend as much time as he could fishing. When a new boatman was needed, and the reapers made him the offer, he practically jumped at the opportunity. He had an updated boat, a fishing boat with blue sparkled paint and an outboard motor. When he wasn't working, he was fishing. The thing about being the only boatman, though, was that people don't ever take a vacation from dying. He was the Head and Shoulders of the underworld— always working. That didn't mean he didn't find time to cast a line from time to time.

Carmilla took us to the front of the line and dropped us off with the boatman, then headed back to the back of the line. She said she didn't want to give the impression she got special line-cutting privileges because she was dating *the* Grim Reaper, the lord of the underworld.

"All aboard!" Roy called as Dracula and I climbed into this boat from the dock. I had to widen my feet to steady myself. It was a fishing boat, not a pontoon boat, and it rocked when you stepped in. Dracula nearly fell on his ass.

"All aboard? Are you a conductor or something?"

Roy shrugged. "Works for boats as well as trains. Where to? Off to Olympus to hang with the gods?"

I shook my head. "Nope. We have to see Athena in Hades."

Roy tilted his head. "All right. Well, let me gather a few hell-bound souls from the reapers and we'll be on our way."

Roy had a crystal that he used to teleport souls across the River Styx. The reapers approached, touched the tip of the scythes to the crystal, and deposited their souls into it. He could take quite a few at a time. He'd have to make a trip to Hades and Olympus regardless. There was no way to know which souls were destined for which place. I wasn't sure how it worked, but the few times I'd seen it work when the boatman brought the crystal to either realm the souls were called from the crystal to their eternal resting place.

Roy fired up his engine and, with a loud "yee-haw," took us through a mist so thick that we couldn't see more than a few feet ahead of us. Roy made this trip dozens of times every day. He knew exactly where we were.

He slowed his boat and the roar of his outboard motor reduced to a purr, as he pulled up to a rickety dock on the edge of hell.

I raised an eyebrow. "You can't take us straight to Athena's castle?"

"Those tributaries are closed," Roy explained. "It's the dock for everyone, even visitors."

I snorted. "I guess Carmilla warned us we'd have to do this the hard way."

Dracula and I disembarked the boat. Climbing from a rocking fishing boat to a dock that looked like it might have been constructed of wormwood was mildly unnerving. I'd never taken a dip in the River Styx, but I knew it was infested with piranha. Roy had caught more than a few of those buggers in his day. He knew how to handle them—when they were at the end of his line. I didn't want to test my luck with the flesh-eating fish if I slipped into the river. Besides, being in the underworld without sunlight, I wasn't as resilient as I was in the light of the day.

At the end of the dock, where it met the shore, was some kind of veil. It reflected the water of a clear spring on a sunny day. The light that illuminated the water-like veil had a red hue to it.

"I guess we walk through and begin our tour of our personal hells."

Dracula nodded. "Let's get it over with."

We stepped through the portal. It took a whole two seconds to realize that we were going to go through my personal hell first.

Yes, we were back in my high school. No, we weren't in my calculus class. I thrived in math and science. We were in gym class, sophomore year.

I gulped. I knew it wasn't her. She wasn't dead. Last I heard, she was in the burger-and-fries business. Her just deserts for being a bitch and a bully in high school. She was the pretty girl who all the boys used to fawn over, who thought she was better than me, especially.

Leslie Williams. That's the form the demon, or the apparition, who'd taken the place of my torturer assumed. I touched my head. Yup, my hair was in pigtails. I was wearing the white sneakers I had when I was sixteen. I ran my tongue across my teeth. The braces were back.

I didn't take gym in my junior or senior years. I didn't have to. All those credits were satisfied. I was what you'd call a late bloomer. At sixteen, I was awkward. I'd always had a pretty face. Not a lot of boys noticed—but one did. It just so happened that the only guy who took an interest in me, a nice-looking guy named Chris, was the one guy that Leslie wanted. He wasn't shallow like a lot of guys. His dad had been a football star. Chris played on the team. But he was more interested in art and theater. We were on the debate team together. When he asked me to the sophomore year homecoming dance, Leslie decided I was public enemy number one, and for a solid year, she made my life a nightmare. Especially in gym class.

It was a basketball day, and I was assigned to Leslie's team. Lucky me. I remembered that day.

Leslie was on the girls' basketball team, and she knew how to play. She was stuck with me. Dracula was standing at the edge of the room in short shorts and form-fitting polo. A whistle hung from his neck. Of course he'd take the role of our gym teacher. From the look on his face, he was disoriented, unsure of what he was supposed to do.

I knew one thing. When I was sixteen, I was shy. I mistakenly thought that if I ignored Leslie, if I didn't respond to her torments, she'd get bored and quit. She never did.

My vampirism wasn't active in this personal hell. I didn't have that advantage. If I did, I would have drained the bitch dry. In this version of personal hell, all I had was what I had when I was sixteen—and my more recent memories.

Since high school, while Leslie had been flipping burgers, I had been kicking supernatural ass at the side of Zoey Grimm. I saved the world. Leslie delivered value meals to hungry customers. She wasn't the badass chick I used to fear. She was pretty but insecure. That's the profile of most bullies. At their core, they're scared kids who feel that the only way they can maintain their social status is by putting other people down.

Carmilla told me this was temporary. I had to get through my personal hell before I could get to Athena. That meant standing up to my former bully. She wasn't a vampire. She wasn't a threat in the least. She'd never had a hand in saving the world.

Something hit my head. The basketball bounced off my noggin and to the floor.

"Come on!" Leslie groaned. "Can't you catch?"

I turned to Leslie and narrowed my eyes. I walked right up to her. "Can't you?"

I clenched my fist and clocked her in the jaw, and she hit the ground.

"Bitch!"

I smiled. "I am. Don't fuck with me."

Leslie rubbed her chin. I extended my hand and helped her up. She turned away from me.

"Suck it up," I told her. "You want to play this game or not?"

Leslie sighed. "Whatever."

It was a two-on-two game. I didn't remember the names of the other girls. I recognized them, but they'd never been my friends and I'd attended a big school.

I didn't remember how the game turned out. I don't think we won in real life. I did recall the basketball hitting me upside the head. Several times. That wasn't going to happen now.

Leslie stood there with her arms crossed. Dracula watched from a distance. I wasn't sure why. Maybe he couldn't intervene. This hell wasn't drawn from his memory, it was from mine.

Without Leslie's help, we weren't going to win the match. I sucked at sports. Always had. Basketball was my worst.

The other two girls scored three times straight. I hit nothing but net—under the rim. It didn't count.

I glared at Leslie. "You going to play or not?"

Leslie grunted and held out her hands. I passed her the ball.

She dribbled around the other girls without a problem and laid it up for two.

I smiled. "Nice shot."

Leslie huffed. The other team took the ball, but Leslie stole it from them and hit a three-pointer. The other team got the ball again and took a shot. They missed. I took the rebound. I had to dribble to the backcourt because we were playing half-court ball. I wasn't any good, but I remembered that much.

Leslie was hardly trying. This was her thing. She didn't need to try. I passed her the ball. She barely caught it. It was my fault. My toss was off the mark. She took another shot and scored.

We eventually took the lead and won. I approached Leslie afterward. "You're pretty good. Sorry about that punch. You had it coming."

Leslie rubbed her jaw. "I guess I did."

"Truce?" I asked.

Leslie nodded. "I guess."

That was the best I was going to get. I'd take it. We returned to the locker room. Problem. I didn't remember what locker I had. That was several years ago. It didn't matter. I hoped this whole thing was over.

Leslie didn't say two words to me as she changed. We weren't going to be friends, but I'd stood up to my bully.

I left the locker room, and Dracula was waiting for me.

"Are we done here?" Dracula asked.

I shrugged. "I don't know. I hope so."

"Let's leave through the exit and find out."

Dracula and I headed to the exit and he opened the door. There was another rippling veil covering the exit. We stepped through.

We were standing in a field, surrounded by rabbits.

"What the hell?" I asked.

Dracula sighed. "This is my hell. I'm terrified of rabbits."

"Bunnies frighten you?"

"Look at them," he insisted. "Giant ears. Little gnawing teeth. Oversized feet."

"This is *your* hell, buddy. If we're going to get out of here, you have to face it."

One of the rabbits jumped out of the crowd and, flashing giant vampire-like fangs, latched itself to Dracula's arm.

He shrieked and shook his arm like a whip. The bunny went flying into the tall grass surrounding us. "I told you! These things are evil!"

"These aren't real bunnies. Rabbits don't have fangs in real life," I assured him.

"How do you know there aren't vampire bunnies?"

I raised my eyebrows. "Seriously?"

"It's possible. Most people don't think human vampires exist. Who's to say there's no such thing?"

"I can't do this for you. This is your hell. We have to get past them."

"But they're all around us! There are hundreds of those little devils."

"Either face your fear and run past them or let them close in on us. Do you want to be at the bottom of a hundred-bunny pileup?"

Dracula rubbed his arm where the rabbit had bitten him. "For the love of all things decent."

"This is hell," I reasoned. "There's nothing decent here. Not a lot of love, either."

He ran his fingers through his usually slicked-back hair, leaving it looking like he'd just had a run-in with an electrical socket. "Here goes nothing."

He took off through the crowd of rabbits, flailing his arms over his head. I don't think I could scream with such a high pitch if I tried. The rabbits dove after him as he ran. I followed behind. The rabbits didn't bother me. This wasn't my hell.

When Dracula reached the end of the field, he ran straight through another watery veil. I jumped through after him.

We appeared on a dock in front of Athena's crystal palace. I grabbed Dracula by the arm. "Watch yourself. Athena is roomies with a Gorgon. If her snake hair is loose, you'll turn to stone the second you see her."

"A Gorgon? Which one?"

"Euryale. She was one of Medusa's immortal sisters. After we tangled with your darker self and the sisters in Kansas City, she decided to stay with Athena. She liked it here."

"Makes sense," Dracula reasoned. "Didn't Athena create the gorgons?"

I nodded. "A long time ago. Even by your ancient standards."

"Well, we either go to the Scholomance by way of the Gorgon and Athena, or we go back to Romania. We'd never make it back before the benefit."

"Of course, the only way to do that is if we allow the Gorgon to petrify us. It will send our spirits to the void where Athena can manifest the Scholomance."

Dracula nodded. "All right. Let's go get stoned."

I smirked. I don't think Dracula even realized what he was saying. But when you're in hell, you take your laughs wherever you can find them.

CHAPTER TWENTY-THREE

I pressed open the two twenty-foot doors that formed the entrance to Athena's castle. The Greek goddess hadn't always been the queen of hell. She tried to usurp the throne of Olympus, and, long story short, this was her new assignment. Hell's original ruler, Hades, had aspirations of his own and was now languishing somewhere in the void, bound to a prison that suited him.

So, Athena renovated hell to something more of her liking. As horrifying as passing through our personal hells could have been, it was nothing compared to hellfire, brimstone, and demonic torture racks.

I was about eighty-five percent sure we could trust Athena. She liked her new role. She'd been a goddess of battle and strategy before, and she still had those skills. As the acting devil, she was also the mistress of the Scholomance. There wasn't a deity whose help was more befitting of the situation we were facing in New Orleans.

Classical music was echoing through the halls of the castle.

"I believe that's *A Symphony to Dante's Divine Comedy,* composed by Franz Liszt in the eighteen fifties."

I snorted. "How you know that is beyond me."

"At least Athena has a sense of humor."

"What's funny about a symphony?"

Dracula grinned. "Have you ever read Dante's *Inferno*? As the queen of hell, she chose this symphony because it was fitting."

I looked around. I didn't see the goddess or the Gorgon. "It would be funnier if she was blasting a little *Highway to Hell.*"

"I don't know that one."

"It's not a symphony. AC/DC. A classic, but not classical."

The symphony went silent. Then, *Highway to Hell* started to play.

I laughed. "Athena, you're here somewhere. You're listening to us."

The music shut off and Athena appeared in a flash of light in front of us. She was a beautiful goddess. She had fine features, was a few inches taller than me, and had an unblemished complexion. She looked like the "after" picture of a Mary Kay makeover. Too flawless to be real.

"My prized pupils of the Scholomance! Welcome back to hell. Do you like what I've done with the place?"

Dracula huffed. "Not so much."

Athena grinned. "Did little bunny foo-foo bop you on the head?"

Dracula diverted his gaze. "Shut up."

I snickered. "We need to go back to the Scholomance. Nothing we learned before seems to work. We need to learn more."

"We need to become masters of the path of light," Dracula added. "We're facing not only Sorina and her sisters, who stole my dark power, but the sons of Van Helsing."

"Ahh!" Athena smiled widely. "A Van Helsing passed through the trials ages ago."

"How do you know that?" Dracula asked. "I was a master of the Scholomance and didn't know it."

Athena shrugged. "I have the yearbooks in my library."

I snorted. "The Scholomance has a yearbook?"

"It's a school of a sort," Athena pointed out. "Of course there's a yearbook. It's more like a record than what you're thinking. After I claimed hell, the records of the Scholomance fell into my care."

"Fascinating. We still need to figure out how to use the path of light to thwart the sisters and Van Helsings. The sisters first. But after the Van Helsings help us deal with them, they'll be every bit as big a threat to us."

Athena looked at Dracula. "How much do you remember about the dark path?"

Dracula shrugged. "I remember everything. My essence was divided, but my memory remains intact."

"The dark path is to the light as an object is to its reflection. It looks very much alike but is also its opposite."

Dracula scratched the back of his head. "I'm not sure I understand. My old magic doesn't work anymore."

"You're probably trying to do everything backward."

"I don't know what that means."

"The path of darkness can allow you to turn into a creature of the night, a nocturnal bat. The path of light can turn you into a morning songbird."

"Really?" I asked. "Not nearly as intimidating as a bat, but flight could be handy."

Dracula squinted his eyes. "Doesn't work."

"That's because you're doing it wrong. It's like if you are right-handed and started writing with your left. It wouldn't be easy. You'd have to do things in a different way. Eventually, you'd pick it up, but it would take practice."

Dracula shook his head. "If I tried to write with my non-dominant hand, I could at least scribble something halfway legible. I can't use any of my old powers in the least."

"I can't tell you how to do it. Most of what I know about the

Scholomance I've observed from afar. Hades governed the Scholomance for centuries. I've been chief mistress of the devil's school for a matter of months. I've never seen someone ascend to the level of master on either the light or dark paths firsthand. In fact, I can't find anyone who's embraced the power of the path of light since the time of the biblical apostles."

I raised an eyebrow. "Those guys attended the Scholomance?"

Athena shook her head. "The Scholomance is but a school. The magic one learns there is bigger than the Scholomance itself. The power of darkness and light, of demons and angels, of death and life. These are cosmic forces that emerge in different traditions, the religions of the world, and schools of magic, in various ways."

"Why are you telling us all of this? Can't you just call up Euryale, have her petrify us, and send us to the Scholomance?"

Athena grinned. "In good time, dear girl. In good time. I have my reasons. I'll simply say this. I can send you to the Scholomance. There's much there you might learn. But never forget the power you seek is greater than the path of light that the Scholomance teaches. There are many paths. Paths of darkness find it in many and various ways. The same is true of paths of light. Any path can lead you closer to the destination, but no path is greater than that to which it leads."

I crossed my arms. "Can the Scholomance even teach us what we need?"

Athena shrugged. "Perhaps. Perhaps not. I can say with some confidence that since the vampire sisters gained their power by extracting it from Dracula, the power to defeat them can be learned in the Scholomance. I cannot say for certain that the same is true of the Van Helsings. You must consider that while it's true that a Van Helsing once studied the magic of the Scholomance, the power that they now wield was gained elsewhere."

"Are you sure about that?" I asked.

"It makes sense," Dracula reasoned. "One of the Van Helsing brothers lost his head and put it back in place. There's nothing I ever encountered in the Scholomance that could do that."

"We'll figure out how to deal with them later," I suggested. "The Van Helsings might be a threat to us. The sisters are trying to take over the world. Besides, we have a few theories about how we can deal with the Van Helsings that don't involve magic."

Dracula nodded. "Right. Blow them to pieces. Cut off their heads and separate their heads from their bodies."

"Or smash their heads like watermelons at a Gallagher show."

Dracula raised an eyebrow. "I didn't know you know about Gallagher. He was great!"

I chuckled. "My old man was a fan. I grew up watching reruns of his shows on television. Rest in peace. I'm more surprised that *you* know who he was."

"I had cable at my castle. A vampire has to do something to keep himself entertained. One can only play Candy Land so many times before it gets old."

"I never took you for the board game type."

"Chutes and Ladders, Mousetrap, Scrabble. I'm into all the classics. Nothing like a game of Monopoly to pass the time. That game takes forever to win. I used to play a lot of Hungry Hungry Hippos, too, but that was before I lost my marbles."

I shook my head. "Athena, are we going to do this or not?"

Athena snapped her fingers. "Euryale, honey! We have visitors in need of your services."

Euryale walked in from a room in the back of Athena's castle. She had a lime-green mask on her face, and her body was wrapped in a towel. She had another towel tied around her head, covering the snakes that would soon turn us to stone and send us to the Scholomance in the void.

"Sienna!" Euryale ran to me and wrapped her arms around me. "It's great to see you!"

I hugged Euryale back. She and her sister, Stheno, were roommates of mine and Zoey's for a while back in Kansas City. I'll tell you this much—rooming with gorgons presents its challenges. One thing you never want to do is accidentally walk in on them when they're in the shower and the snake hair is flowing.

"Spa day in hell?" I asked.

Euryale laughed. "You know it. The air in this place is hot and dry. Not great for my complexion."

I chuckled. "I can imagine."

Athena stepped up and put an arm around Euryale. "Our friends need a little trip to the void. They're returning to the Scholomance."

Euryale looked at me. "How much time do you need?"

"We have to be back in a couple days. How much time will that give us?"

Euryale shrugged. "Time passes differently in the void. It could give you months, maybe even years."

"The time differentiation isn't always consistent," Athena explained. "We'll bring one of you back every hour for a status report. That'll probably be a few weeks in the void."

I sighed. "I hope we won't need that much time."

"I wouldn't count on that," Dracula cautioned. "When I advanced from initiate to master on the dark path in the Scholomance, it took years of study and practice."

I took a deep breath. "Wonderful."

Euryale unwrapped the towel from around her head. "Sweet dreams."

***

"The void" was a misnomer. It was where all the gods resided. It was more like a branch of heaven, the presence into which one might enter after earning eternal bliss. Each deity who dwelled in the void had a domain that matched the kind of heaven their followers imagined. When I went to Olympus with Zoey, it was Olympus because, as a reaper, the Greeks were the pantheon that formed their worldview. I wasn't sure what I believed. The void, though, could give one access to an infinite number of heavens, visions of the afterlife, or whatever one might imagine. It was how Athena was able to create the Scholomance in the void. It was in the moment we hoped for the most. So, that's where we went.

I'm not going to pretend to understand the metaphysics of it all. All that shit was beyond my pay grade. I knew that some pantheons, and even a few remote deities from religions still practiced, were walled off in the void. No one sought them out. No souls ever entered their versions of glory. Instead, they retired to domains in the void that suited their own interests or desires.

A part of me wondered if that's what Athena meant. If there were paths of light lost to human memory, or largely forgotten, that still had a place in the void. If that was true, Drac and I wouldn't just stumble across them. We'd have to learn of them and seek them out. When we did, they'd appear. For now, the only path we knew to seek was the path of light in the Scholomance.

So, that's where we appeared. In a hallway, somewhere deep in the Scholomance we hadn't explored when we were there the first time. The air was cold and damp. The walls were made of stone. Torches illuminated by pure white flames lined the walls.

We followed the hallway down to an open room. We saw a man sitting at a desk with his back turned toward us. He was in a dusty black suit. He wore a narrow-brimmed hat with gray curls flowing out beneath it.

I cleared my throat.

The man turned. He smiled at us. "I've been waiting for this."

Dracula gasped.

"Do you two know each other?"

Dracula looked at me. "Sienna. This is Abraham Van Helsing."

Van Helsing tipped his hat. "A pleasure to make your acquaintance."

CHAPTER TWENTY-FOUR

"What are you doing here, Abraham?"

A wide grin split across Van Helsing's face and he lowered a monocle from his left eye. "You two seek to master the path of light. You require a guide, a master who has tread the path before you."

I snorted. "Of all the possibilities, we get stuck with *this* guy?"

"What other possibilities?" Van Helsing asked. "Were you expecting Saul of Tarsus? Maybe Merlin, or perhaps, the Tooth Fairy."

"The Tooth Fairy is a master of the Scholomance?"

"The transmutation of molars into money is a peculiar skill."

"You're joking, right?"

Van Helsing grinned widely. "Perhaps I am. Whatever the case, you're stuck with me."

I huffed. "Apologies if I'm not entirely hot for teacher here. Your sons want to kill us."

"We are Van Helsings. Dracula has always been our primary nemesis."

Dracula shook his head and turned. "This is pointless. He will never help us."

"Why would you say that?" Van Helsing asked.

"You said it." Dracula snapped back around. "You're Van Helsing. I'm Dracula."

I grunted. "Superman would never expect Lex Luther to help him. Batman would never beg the Joker for assistance."

Van Helsing tilted his head. "I'm the hero, not the villain, here."

I grunted. "That's a matter of perspective. Your sons just executed a pack of werewolves. Werewolves are human twenty-eight days of the month, give or take. More than that, it wasn't even a full moon. If your sons had bothered to do a little research, if they even paused a moment to ask a few questions, they might have discovered that the wolves were acting as puppets of Sorina and her vampire sisters. Instead, your boys murdered good people who'd never harmed anyone, not even under a full moon."

Van Helsing rubbed his brow. "I suppose I am not surprised. Monsters are monsters."

I raised an eyebrow. "And your sons aren't monsters? They should be long dead of old age by now. What's the difference between someone who becomes a vampire or a werewolf by a bite and someone who turns oneself into a monster by injection? At least in the case of most of us, we didn't choose to become what we are. Your sons not only *chose* to become whatever the hell they are, they researched it, they took whatever magic you must've given them and found a way to combine it with chemistry and modern medicine."

Dracula nodded. "Frankenstein, too, was made through science. No one questions if he was a monster."

I tilted my head. "Wait. Frankenstein was real?"

Dracula nodded. "The events were true. Mary Shelley changed the name of the doctor and his monster to protect the innocent."

Abraham Van Helsing crossed his legs. He rested his elbows

on his knee, pressed his forearms together, and steepled his fingers. "I suppose you two think that because you chose to pursue the path of light, and rejected the dark magic, that you aren't monsters?"

I grunted. "I know I'm a monster. But then again, isn't there a little monster in everyone? Even you, Dr. Van Helsing? Didn't you give your sons the magic they needed to become immortals? The only difference between you and Doctor Frankenstein is that you stitched together your creatures from living rather than dead bodies."

Van Helsing shook his head. "You are wrong. I did not give my sons the magic to become what they are. Nor have they passed through the Scholomance themselves. Their elixir comes from elsewhere."

Abraham Van Helsing died before Alexander and his brothers developed their elixir. They didn't get the magic they used from the Scholomance. We didn't know what power they tapped into to make it, but it was something remarkable.

Dracula crossed his arms. "Be that as it may, my interests and those of your sons currently align. The sisters have stolen my dark power. They seek to infect powerful people and rule the world through them."

Van Helsing pinched his chin. "The sisters have always wielded the power of the Scholomance."

"He makes a point," I admitted. "How do you suppose they discovered a way to overcome the sire bond?"

Dracula shook his head. "They were initiates. They never mastered the Scholomance. Their power, now, is infinitely greater than before."

Van Helsing nodded. "That may be, but the sisters have more power than that. They must. I can take you further on the path of light. I'll consider it a redemption project. You cannot remove the power they've taken entirely, but in the presence of light, the powers of darkness wane. It may give you a chance to get the upper hand."

Dracula tilted his head. "If you could do this, Abraham, why didn't you use the path of light to stop me ages ago?"

"Isn't it obvious? You came to the Scholomance by way of the void. I dreamed of the chance to learn the mysteries of light in life. This is what I was given in death."

I raised an eyebrow. "This is your personal version of heaven? You could have had a hundred virgins, or you know, since virgins can be a pain, maybe a hundred women with experience. You could have had eternal bliss, all the comforts you could imagine. Going to school for eternity was my version of hell. You're saying that's your idea of heaven?"

"Of course it is. I was a doctor, after all. I loved school. And I wished for nothing more in life than the chance to learn a power that might defeat the infamous Dracula."

"A little short-sighted, don't you think?"

Van Helsing cracked his knuckles. "I was beginning to think it was. Then you two showed up. I thought, at last, heaven has granted me the chance to finish what I never could in life."

"So you're going to kill us?" Dracula asked.

Van Helsing shook his head. "I wish I could. Trust me. When you two returned to the Scholomance, you didn't come to refine the dark powers within you. You came to reject the darkness and follow the path of light. Now, I have no choice but to help you. I'm beginning to think that this isn't my personal heaven at all. It's my personal hell."

Van Helsing led us out of his room and down a bright hallway. Chambers like these were supposed to be dark and gloomy. Not when you were on the light side of the Scholomance, apparently.

"To begin your training into the mastery of the light, you must first pass a test," Van Helsing explained.

"What kind of test?" I asked.

"To determine your suitability."

"What makes one worthy or unworthy?" Dracula pressed.

"A thousand different things could tip the scales in one direction or another. The forces of the Scholomance must examine your spirit. If you are suitable, you will be allowed to proceed. If you are not, you will remain at the level of initiate."

"What do we have to do?" I asked.

"It is not a question of what you must do," Van Helsing explained. "It's a matter of what you have done."

Dracula raised an eyebrow. "Our entire existence will be examined?"

"Not your entire existence. Only the things you've done since you passed the tests of initiation."

Dracula released a deep breath. "Good news for me."

Van Helsing huffed. "Right. You wouldn't stand a chance if your entire existence was considered. You were a real bastard before."

"I won't dispute that," Dracula grunted.

Van Helsing waved his hand through the air, and a wall of light formed at what was previously a dead end. "Pass through the light. You will be tested. If deemed worthy, you can proceed. If not, you'll return to these halls."

Dracula and I walked through the light into a white room. I wasn't sure of the source of the light until a human-shaped figure appeared. Not a shadow. Quite the opposite. He was pure energy, as if his body was powered by the force of the sun. The power within me as a daywalker welled up to the max.

"Welcome to the master's path of light," the figure said.

"Who are you?" I asked.

"I *am* the light."

This guy wasn't going to give me an answer that transcended the obvious.

Dracula tried. "What do we need to do?"

"Stand still. I will examine you both."

Dracula and I both stood still as statues. Ironic, I suppose, considering our bodies were literal statues at the moment, courtesy of the Gorgon. The figure of light placed one hand on each of our heads. A warmth passed through my body, like a cup of hot chocolate after a day out in the snow.

It was pleasant at first.

Then it burned. Hotter and hotter.

I fell to my knees, and the heat dissipated.

Dracula still stood on his feet. The light around him swelled until he looked like the mysterious light man.

"You have passed the test," the figure informed Dracula. He turned to me. "You have not."

I huffed. "Well, why not?"

"You've fed."

"He has, too!"

"But he did not feed from a living person. You have. You will remain as an initiate but cannot continue your journey on the path."

The light of both the figure and Dracula pulsed so brightly that I had to shield my eyes. Even as a daywalker, empowered by sunlight, it was too much. When I opened my eyes I was kneeling alone facing a stone wall.

"This is certainly a surprise," Van Helsing said.

I stood and turned to the famed vampire hunter. "I can't believe I didn't pass. I should have known."

"He'll be a while. It looks like we have time to burn. You up for a game of Scrabble?"

"What do you mean by a while?"

Van Helsing shrugged. "Months, probably. Maybe even years."

I sighed. "Sounds like we have time for more than Scrabble. Do you have Monopoly?"

Van Helsing smiled widely. "I call the thimble!"

CHAPTER TWENTY-FIVE

Abraham Van Helsing and I sat across each other from his desk. He retrieved his Monopoly set and opened the box. When he laid out the board it crackled as if it had hardly been used.

"Don't play much?"

Abraham shook his head. "I don't get many visitors. Those I do usually disappear into the light, and when they finish mastering the path, they come back and don't have much interest in hanging around to play games."

We played for hours. Abraham claimed Boardwalk and Park Place. He loaded them with hotels. He also got the railroads—all of them.

I had Oriental Avenue. This wasn't a politically correct version of the game, apparently. I had Baltic Avenue and most of the other avenues. I also had Marvin Gardens. I'd gone to jail more times than I could count and paid more than my fair share of income tax. I could have used a good lawyer and a savvy accountant.

Scrabble didn't go much better for me. When you're dealing with someone who lived in another era, who claimed his made-up words were "archaic" and couldn't provide a dictionary to confirm, there wasn't a good way to win. Add to that the fact that words like "internet" and "nuclear" weren't in his vocabulary, and he didn't let them count. It wasn't fair, but he insisted. His game, his rules.

He wanted to play Twister. Gee, I wonder why. Father Abraham might have had many sons, but he hadn't seen any action in a *long* time.

A girl can only lose at Chutes and Ladders so many times before she's had enough. I didn't know how Abraham got all these board games. He did know some interesting magic, but didn't show me a bit of it. I wasn't "worthy," after all.

I figured I'd best make use of the time. People love to talk about their families, especially their kids. Anything I could learn about Alexander, Reginald, and James could be useful.

A lot of what I learned wasn't relevant. None of the boys liked broccoli. Who does? Alexander was the oldest. His brothers followed him around like two annoying yippie puppies when they were kids. Again, that the two younger brothers idolized their older brother wasn't exactly a revelation. That sort of thing is common. It's natural to look up to your older siblings. Especially since Alexander took up the role of father-figure when they were teenagers and Abraham died. He carried his father's flag in more ways than one. He was the one who kept the anti-vampire sentiment alive. At least, that was what Abraham believed.

Being dead and all, he hadn't seen his sons since they were young. He'd trained Alexander from a young age in the art of vampire slaying. Reginald inherited his father's love for science. Abraham didn't know if he ever became a doctor, but if one of the boys devised a chemical compound that could carry mystical energies, it was Reginald. James was who Abraham believed was most likely to be the one who dove into the world of magic. The boy had always taken a keen interest in spellcraft of many sorts. Even as Abraham sought the power of light in the Scholomance, James was right there, digging into dusty old books and grimoires, looking for alternative ways that his father might be able to gain an upper hand against Dracula's power.

In short, if Abraham Van Helsing was a jack-of-all-trades and that made him a formidable threat to Dracula, his sons were focused on individual interests each inherited from their father. Alexander had all his father's passion and dedication to the elimination of vampires. Reginald inherited his father's intellect and exceeded him in academic rigor. James inherited Abraham's fascination with mystical arts and knew more about various paths and crafts even as a teenager than his father ever did in life.

All that added up to a deadly combination. The apple hadn't fallen far from the tree for any of Abraham's sons. Where Abraham had a variety of interests and combined them in his repeated but failed efforts to defeat Dracula, his sons had a laser-like focus on their particular gifts. They were experts in their chosen disciplines. That alone made them deadly, especially together. Add to that their immortality elixir, and I wasn't sure we stood much of a chance. Depending, of course, on how juiced up Dracula was once he emerged from the Scholomance.

Of course, Abraham wouldn't tell us how to fight them. I don't think he even knew the best way to stand against them. He didn't want us to win, strictly speaking. We were vampires, after all. Even if we were different, daywalkers on the path of light.

All that said, I think he came to like me. He even told me about a fourth son, his youngest, Samuel, who had been abducted by a coven of vampires. Abraham never saw him again. He believed the vampires drained and killed him. He'd tracked down the coven some time later and his son wasn't among them.

Tears fell from Abraham's eyes when he spoke of the incident. Samuel was a promising young man. A jack-of-all-trades, more like his father, but with a presence that tended to illuminate a room. He was the sort of man everyone loved, even if no one could tell you exactly *why.* He hadn't spoken of Samuel in centuries. Even in Abraham's earthly life, he couldn't bring himself to talk about his long-lost youngest.

I ached for him. I also was honored that he opened up to me like that. I suppose even in death, love endures, the pangs of loss linger, and the connections we forge in life remain.

After Abraham got past the fact that Twister wasn't going to happen, he started to see me as a young lady, more like a daughter than a bloodsucker who needed to be slain. He didn't want us to kill his sons, even if they had outlived their human lifespans several times over. He also wished me the best, taking a keen interest in my brooch, how it silenced my urges and the like. I didn't have it in the void. I looked like I did, just as I appeared in all the clothes I was wearing when the Gorgon turned us to stone. It didn't have power there, though. There was nothing he could study or examine. If he could, he thought it might be possible to develop a cure, something that made vampirism dormant with repeated dosage. I didn't think it was likely, but he *was* a master of the Scholomance. If anyone could figure it out, it was him. Or, his sons. Fat chance they'd give me enough time to explain their father's interest in something like that before thrusting a stake in my chest.

I didn't know how much time passed. They didn't have clocks in the Scholomance. There weren't windows or even a sun in the void that I could use to count the days. I did count the stones that formed the walls in the hallway. Eighty-three thousand, four hundred and fifty-two. It was a long hallway, and I had time to burn. I counted them twice just to make sure. The second time, I was three bricks short of my first total. I was going to do it a third time to determine the final answer when I realized it was pointless.

Still, I was impressed. I once counted the ceiling tiles in the dentist's office. That wasn't so hard. I multiplied length times width. It wouldn't work with the stones since they weren't all the same size or shape. I'd achieved quite a feat, which came with absolutely no reward other than the satisfaction that I burned time doing it.

I also didn't have any hunger or urge to feed while in the Scholomance. I'm not sure if that was better news for me or Van Helsing. I didn't know if I'd even have a chance to get a bite out of him if I tried. He was Van-freaking-Helsing, after all. I assumed my lack of blood craving was because I wasn't in my body.

It wasn't just my cravings. My fingernails weren't growing. Neither was my hair. My body wasn't a body. It was a manifestation of my spirit. I didn't know how it worked. Weird shit governed the spiritual realms.

It could have been a few weeks, maybe months, possibly a year when the light at the end of the hall illuminated again. I didn't dare walk into it. Not again after Captain Glowstick rejected me the last time. I watched it intently.

A light flashed behind me. I only knew because it was so bright it radiated on the walls around me.

I turned to see Dracula standing there. He wasn't dressed in black. He now had a white cloak. His eyes glowed like the sun. All his skin radiated light. For the first time in the devil knows how long, I felt the vigor that the sunlight gave me. Funny, you know, since nothing else about my vampirism functioned there. Light still affected me, though. Perhaps it was because what made me a daywalker wasn't a property of my body, it was something fused to my spirit.

The light faded and Dracula returned to normal, except for the fact that he was dressed in white. The dude looked like a beardless Colonel Sanders with fangs. The way he was glowing, I'd say he was extra crispy. Definitely not original recipe.

I stood in the hallway, looking at Dracula with my jaw halfway between my head and my chest. He opened his arms and I ran up to him to give him a hug.

"You're warm. I'm glad you're back."

"How long has it been?"

I shrugged. "Feels like an eternity."

"Given your age, not long, then."

I smiled. "Long enough. What happened?"

Dracula grinned. "I'm not even sure I could explain it with words. I can do a few interesting things that I couldn't before."

"Like what? Anything that will help us with the sisters?"

"Well, darkness can't thrive in the presence of light. Their power should be useless on me. I can radiate sunlight now, which, for most people, isn't good for much more than a cheap tan. For you, though…"

"That could be enormously helpful. Anything else?"

"There's the songbird form. I got that down, too. And I can teleport, as you just saw. However, I can't do it much. I can jump once a day, maybe twice if my jumps are more like little hops. And I can only move somewhere in plain view of where I'm standing so, no, I can't beam myself between New Orleans and the Bahamas. Sure would love to go there, though, now that the sun agrees with me."

"Well, welcome to the party. This Van Helsing guy isn't as bad as I thought he'd be."

Dracula pressed his lips together. "We won't be staying long."

"Are you sure? That old fart has beaten me six times straight at Monopoly. Maybe you could best him."

Dracula grinned. "We don't have time for that."

I raised an eyebrow. "Until Euryale brings us back, *all* we have is time."

"That brings me to the last thing I learned. Disembodied souls, like us, aren't complete. We were born human. We were meant to be embodied. That's why we manifest like this, as if we had bodies here. We don't need the Gorgon to bring us back, Sienna. All she does is call our souls back to where our souls want to go. All we have to do is make the call."

I raised an eyebrow. "A call? Like 1-800-THAT'S MY BODY?"

Dracula chuckled. "That's too many numbers. And there aren't any telephones here."

"Then what does the trick? A little pixie dust and happy thoughts?"

"Not that far off, actually. You spent a lot of time with a reaper. You're the Grim Reaper's sister's best friend, for Pete's sake. You've met a few ghosts. You even rescued one from hell and made him the new boatman at the River Styx."

I nodded. "That's Roy. Loves to fish."

"Exactly. Spirits look for something in the physical world that connects them to their earthly life. Some obsess over their corpses. Kind of pointless. Others bind themselves to things that make them feel alive. Places that have intense memory, activities that brought them pleasure. For Roy, that's fishing. Happy thoughts."

"So all I have to do is think about something that makes me happy, makes me feel alive?"

"Yes, and no. As a disembodied spirit, think too much about your childhood home and that's where you'll go. You'll have to ghost your way back to hell, somehow, to find your body. I don't recommend going into hell without a body. You might get lost in the shuffle."

"You're saying that spirits here, in the void, those who think they've reached their own heaven, can visit Earth again?"

Dracula nodded. "That whole thing about our loved ones looking after us isn't too far from the truth. They can do that, you know."

"Fascinating. What do we do to get back into our petrified bodies in hell?"

"Think of something visceral. The most pleasurable experience you can recall in the body. Maybe that's a sexual experience. For me, it's that day at the Louisiana visitor's center when the sun hit my face. I can't think about it too hard or I'll zap right back into my body. Though, now that I think about it, that could work. I could just wake up and have Euryale bring you back the old-fashioned way."

I shook my head. "No, don't do that. I want to try it. If it doesn't work for me, then we can go with that plan."

Dracula nodded. "All right. What is the thought? What is your pleasure?"

I winced. "It's personal, Drac."

Dracula chuckled. "Sexual experience. Right."

I sighed. It wasn't that. I was ashamed to admit it. It was a tie. It was when I drank from Leeroy, the homeless man, or when I bit Alexander. The feeling, the surge of energy, when I tasted blood from the source. There was nothing like it.

The memory came to mind, the sensation of all that energy coursing through my body, and the next thing I knew I was stiff. I stretched out my arms and pieces of granite fell from my limbs.

Athena and Euryale stood there staring at me with furrowed brows.

"Looks like someone learned a few tricks," Athena greeted me.

"I didn't know that was possible! In all these years, no one I've petrified has come back on their own," Euryale added.

I heard another hunk of stone hit the ground. I turned and Dracula was standing there, shaking the dust from his cloak, which somehow had turned white, matching the one he had in the Scholomance.

I raised an eyebrow. "A few tricks is right."

CHAPTER TWENTY-SIX

The trip out of Hades was easier than our arrival. It helped that Athena escorted us to the dock herself. It wasn't long before Roy showed up with a few damned souls to deposit. Drac and I hopped aboard, and he took us back to the underworld.

Dracula struck out like a sore thumb. His black cape and getup blended in with the reapers before. Now he marched through the underworld looking more like the Easter bunny—his own worst nightmare—than a reaper.

There was only one way to go back home. We couldn't use the common reaper portal. We didn't have assignments to harvest souls and we weren't reapers. We had to find Morty. He, alone, could form portals anywhere in the world on a whim. Thankfully, this wasn't my first trip to Reaperville. I knew where to go.

My phone didn't have service, but it kept time. We'd lost two days in the Scholomance. It was like an eternity in board game hell for me, but we got back in time.

The Grim Reaper had a castle of his own. Any time I'd been there before was with Zoey, so I didn't know what kind of security measures they had. I was a little surprised to find the doors to the castle unlocked. Dracula and I made our way up what felt like a thousand stairs spiraling their way up a narrow tower with Morty's office at the top.

Again, his door was unlocked. We found him at his desk with his feet kicked up.

"I was wondering when you were going to show up. Cutting it a little close, don't you think?"

I sighed. "You have no idea what we've been through."

"I probably don't want to know. Did you find what you were looking for?"

Dracula nodded. "I did."

"I didn't get the mojo," I reported. "I wasn't worthy."

Morty tilted his head. "Well, that's bullshit. If I were to pick between the two of you, I'd figure you were the one who had all the virtuous credentials."

"It's complicated," I offered.

Morty pressed his lips together. "It always is."

"Any insights into what we might be facing?" Dracula asked.

Morty unrolled a scroll on his desk. "I've examined my list and checked it twice. A tip I picked up from Santa Claus."

"Santa is real?" I frowned.

Morty laughed. "Ask your parents. I wouldn't want to spoil it for you."

I smirked. "It was a joke."

Morty nodded. "Bottom line is I don't see anyone dying in the entire state of Louisiana over the next couple days who appear to have been murdered by vampires or werewolves. Nothing here is at all extraordinary. Just the usual collection of heart disease, cancer, and automobile accidents."

I sighed. "I'd say that's good news, but your schedule doesn't include vampire deaths."

Morty shook his head. "It doesn't include the passing of any immortal, any being whose soul has what you'd call supernatural qualities."

"Can you send us back to the school?" I chuckled. "Not a question I thought I'd ever ask anybody."

Morty nodded. "I know the one. Where Carmilla formed the portal that sent you here before."

Dracula nodded. "Make it quick. We're running short on time."

Morty stood from his desk. He formed a golden portal in the middle of his office. "Be careful, Sienna."

I nodded. Dracula went through the portal first. Before I stepped through, I looked back at Morty. "I'll try. Thanks, again."

My feet landed back at the entrance to the school. Dracula immediately pressed his hand to my chest. "Don't take another step. Tripwire."

"Right." I stepped over the wire and avoided becoming barbecue.

Dracula grabbed me by the arm. "Wait. That tile in front of you is a pressure plate."

I raised an eyebrow. "What the hell is a pressure plate? Sounds like something I had to deal with growing up at dinnertime. Eat all your green beans or you get no dessert. Talk about pressure."

Dracula pointed at the ground. "I gave the wolves a schematic for this. Step on that and you'll get a dart shower. All the darts infused with different kinds of poison. Holy water, colloidal silver, tranquilizers. If the wolves were able to track all that stuff down. I'm impressed they did all this in just a couple days."

"So, holy water works against us?"

Dracula laughed. "Not us. It's more effective against demons. Fire can deal with vampires, of course. That's the first trap. It won't impact demons at all. Colloidal silver is for werewolves, and I'm hoping that a tranquilizer will work to slow down the Van Helsings or anything else that they might send after us."

"What about salt? Won't salt keep demons and ghosts away?"

Dracula nodded. "They have an aversion to it, especially ghosts who used to have high blood pressure. The best way to set that up is to mix salt with paint or varnish. It will create a more permanent barrier. Otherwise, a salt line is too easy to break. A good breeze, a blast of water, or just a broom can be used to create an opening. We aren't dealing with ghosts or demons right now, so far as we know, but we have to try it all. At least until we know what kind of magic the Van Helsings used. It wasn't from the Scholomance, we know that now. It was something dark. If it is demonic in origin, salt should dampen the effects of their elixir. If it isn't, well, at least we'll be able to say we tried."

I nodded. "And we'd be able to check demonic power off the list. I really hope that's not it. I've encountered a demon or two. Back in Hades, before. We met Sloth."

"Ah, yes. There is a demon for each of the deadly sins. What does Sloth do?"

"Absolutely nothing. He's Sloth."

Dracula chuckled. "Well, that's not too scary."

"Except for the fact that he infects everyone he encounters with the urge to do nothing at all. At least that's what I understand. I only encountered him *in* Hades, but it's said that he can be a real problem on Earth. He makes people so lazy they won't even get up to go to the bathroom or to eat or drink. Eventually, Sloth kills."

"Sounds like a powerful ally. Imagine if we could just send Sloth to deal with the sisters and Van Helsings. If they do nothing at all, we'd have nothing to worry about."

I chuckled. "Yeah, well, I don't know that Athena is interested in loaning out dangerous demons."

"Probably for the best," Dracula admitted. "If a demon ever helps you out, you'd better know that they will expect something in return."

"Like your soul?" I asked.

"Sometimes. They also require vessels on Earth. So, they might demand someone's first-born son. They usually pick a vessel close to the person who requests their aid."

"Why someone close?"

"Because demons are dicks. And because parents can consent on the behalf of minors. Until puberty begins, a parent has responsibility for a child's soul."

"Damn, Drac. You sure know a lot about this stuff for a guy who never got out much."

Dracula nodded. "Why do you think I don't go out much? The sun is only a part of it. Demons and bunny rabbits are also high up the list, though not necessarily in that order."

I nodded. "Well, it's a good thing we didn't meet any in Hades."

"Are you sure about that?"

I shrugged. "I don't remember seeing one."

"The people in your personal hell meant to torment you had to be played by someone."

I gulped. "That's terrifying. I'm just glad we're back in the land of the living."

We continued down the hall. It was a school building, so it took a while to find Dylan and Lizzie, but finally I found them working together to assemble what looked like a bed in one of the classrooms.

"Hey, guys."

"Sienna!" Dylan jumped to his feet. "You guys are back."

Lizzie looked Dracula up and down. "What's up with the whole Gandalf the White look?"

"He mastered the path of light. They wouldn't take me. He's the virtuous one."

Dylan cocked his head. "Really?"

I sighed. "Long story. Apparently, my feeding habits since the first time we went to the Scholomance were more reckless and vile than his. Crap, if you ask me. I fed from one guy who agreed to it. I even paid him. The other guy I bit was trying to kill me. I think I was justified."

"That's not it," Dracula said. "The fact is that no matter the reason, feeding directly from a human awakens a darkness within our kind. It's not that they didn't accept you, Sienna, so much as it was that they couldn't."

"Well, whatever. While Dracula was off at Hogwarts, I was stuck playing board games with Abraham Van Helsing."

"The Van Helsing brothers' father?" Lizzie asked.

I nodded. "Dracula's old nemesis. Nice enough guy, but he confirmed that his sons didn't develop their elixir from magic there. Dracula and I fear it might be some kind of demonic power."

"Good thing we set up those traps," Dylan said.

I nodded. "Even so, that might not be enough. And we can't say for sure if that's really the magic that empowers their immortality elixir."

Dylan changed the subject. "Do you like your new bed?"

"This is mine?"

"Got it from Ikea. Really splurged. This is the Haugsvär mattress, the Idanäs frame, and I even got you the Kärnmott comforter."

"I'm impressed you can pronounce those words at all. Now do it three times fast," I teased him.

Dylan shook his head. "I don't think I said any of those words correctly."

"Well, that was thoughtful of you. Thanks for that. I see you got the queen size."

Dylan smirked. "Just in case you ever want to share your bed with someone."

I chuckled. "You dog, you!"

"Down boy," Lizzie ordered. "Watch out for this one. He'll hump your leg if you aren't careful."

"A leg man, eh?" I winked at Dylan.

"Don't you know it!"

Lizzie cleared her throat. "We should probably get ready for the benefit. I took the liberty of getting your dress dry-cleaned for you. Any chance you can reimburse us for all this crap?"

"Did you save your receipts?" Dracula asked.

Lizzie nodded. "Every one of them."

"It won't be a problem."

"Every penny counts!" Lizzie offered.

Dracula raised an eyebrow. "Was that a count joke? You should know, I've heard one, two, or three in my day."

I snorted. "I see what you did there."

"Come, Sienna. We still have the bottles of blood from before. We should make sure you are well-fed before we arrive. The benefit starts shortly after sundown. The longer you can retain your strength, the better."

I nodded. "I agree. After that, we'll get dressed and hit the road. Let's hope the Van Helsing brothers will stick to their end of the deal. If they don't, this could get nasty."

"On the bright side, the Grim Reaper didn't know of any deaths to occur tonight," Dracula reminded me.

I nodded. "That's not necessarily a good thing, Drac. It could just mean that every human in that place becomes a vampire before night's end."

"Or it means we are bound to prevail."

"You're one of those always-half-full kinds of vampires, aren't you."

"It's certainly better than leaving a person half-empty when you feed."

CHAPTER TWENTY-SEVEN

Dracula and I shared a 1963 Southern Californian B-positive. Since he was intent on being the half-full optimist, it was fitting that we chose to *be positive*.

The key to getting into the benefit was to present ourselves as wealthy donors. That meant we all had to look presentable, and Dracula had to show up with the big bucks. Not a problem for him. A seven-figure cashier's check would get us in. For Drac, that was a drop in the bucket. When you live as long as he has, and invest wisely, it's incredible how much you can make. I didn't ask him much about *how* he invested or accumulated his riches. Asking people—or vampires—about their money seemed tacky. A bit invasive. All I knew was that as an old-timey count, he was at the upper echelon of Romanian society back in the day and he'd maintained that status through the industrial and technological revolutions. Probably through timely investments. Back when Dracula had dark magic, he had hypnotic abilities.

It didn't go so far as mind control, but he could convince people to tell him the truth and give them powerful, nearly irresistible suggestions. It wasn't absolute, but I imagined those abilities could be handy when it came to savvy investing. Whatever the case, he had boatloads of money and didn't think twice about a million-dollar check to charity. Most people didn't make as much money their entire lives as he was willing to give away. Besides, while the benefit was compromised, the charity was real. The money was going to a good cause.

I'm not the sort of girl who is usually all that focused on her appearance, but in the dress Morty had given me, I looked hot. With as much as I'd fed recently, I had more color in my cheeks than before. My hair was fuller and its red hue was deeper and darker. Lizzie helped me with my makeup. As a bookish girl by reputation, the art of "putting on my face" wasn't one I'd mastered, but Lizzie was damn good at it.

Dylan was in a black tuxedo, complete with a vest and bowtie. He thought he looked like a penguin. I've never been attracted to penguins. That's just weird. But when I saw him step out of the dressing room at the tuxedo rental place, for a moment I thought the demon Lust might have possessed me. Dylan was steamy, and I was already looking forward to breaking in my new Haugsvär.

We pulled up to the community center where Dean Carver's benefit was supposed to take place. The parking lot was already filling up, and we had to park in the back of the lot. I didn't know if the Van Helsings had arrived yet, or what their plan was to get in. Dracula wasn't worried about it. The only thing I was worried about was whether they'd stick to the plan. This was an "enemy of my enemy" situation. Our alliance with the Van Helsing brothers was temporary. If they had a chance to defeat the sisters and take us out, they'd take it. We had to be ready for anything.

The other thing we didn't account for was the number of police officers serving as security for the event. We were so focused on the sisters and the Van Helsing brothers that we hadn't considered it. We had to leave our weapons in the car, because they had metal detectors at the entrance. We couldn't even sneak a dagger in. Carrying a wooden stake might also raise red flags. If we had a shot at the sisters, we'd have to find something we could use in the building. Anything wooden that could be broken to a point would do the trick. A chair leg. Even the handle of a toilet bowl plunger could work if push came to shove. There was always my fist, too. I could go astral, reach into a vampire's chest, and touch my brooch again. I'd ripped out a vampire heart once or twice before. It's messy but effective.

The sun was setting as we passed through the security checkpoint, and I hoped the blood I'd consumed would sustain me long enough that I'd have the advantage of my daywalker strength to face the sisters when the time came. If not, going astral was my only option. Either way, I was confident I could make it work. There was a good chance I'd use the astral plane regardless. Still, we had to take down *three* powerful vampire sisters. I might get lucky and eliminate one of them that way, but I'd still have to deal with the other two. The sisters already knew what I could do. They surely had a plan to stop me if it came to that.

After we got through security, Dracula approached a man at a table who represented the charity. He gave the man his cashier's check. The man's eyes widened. He stood and shook Dracula's hand before he welcomed our group to the party.

I surveyed the room. I didn't see the Van Helsings, the weird sisters, or candidate Carver. It was a matter of time before each made their appearance. If the Van Helsings were sticking to their plan, they were focused on protecting Carver from the sisters.

There were a lot of people in the place, and as best I could tell, they were human. I wasn't sure if that was good or bad news. Morty said he didn't expect any deaths—but couldn't guarantee there wouldn't be a few turnings. If the sisters were involved, and the turnings didn't depend on youngling vamps doing the deed, anyone they took would turn. If that happened, no matter what powers Dracula gained, we'd find ourselves outnumbered in short order.

Dracula didn't think the sisters would be so bold as to turn folks in plain view. They'd find ways to lure donors elsewhere, presumably under a promise to meet the candidate, and turn them behind closed doors.

Several servers wandered the room with platters full of appetizers and drinks. I grabbed a martini from one of the servers as he passed. Dracula had a glass of red wine and Dylan passed on the drinks, but Lizzie hit up the same waiter I did and grabbed a martini like mine.

I'd never had a martini. I only knew what it was because of the shape of the glass. I took a sip and winced.

"Good Lord. That shit is strong."

Dracula laughed. "What did you think a martini was?"

"I don't know. I hoped it was similar to a daiquiri."

Dylan chuckled and shook his head. "There's a reason I passed on that."

"I like it," Lizzie remarked. "A lot of people do."

Dylan rolled his eyes. "That's because you're a lush."

"Am not!" Lizzie protested. "I just appreciate the finer things. In abundance."

Dracula made his way through the crowd, shaking as many hands as he could. He insisted he'd know upon touch if anyone was a vampire or wielded any dark magic. So far, though, everyone was clean and nothing out of the ordinary had occurred. I was beginning to think it was a bust. There was always a chance that the sisters knew that the wolves might spoil their plan and had changed their strategy. Worst-case scenario, Dracula was out a million dollars that went to a good cause, and we'd be back at square one trying to sort out the sisters' new plan.

Several Louisiana state flags, alternated with American flags, formed the backdrop on a small stage at the front of the room. A podium on the stage featured a whole bouquet of microphones, some of them sporting the logos of various local news stations, and a couple of television cameras stood at the opposite side of the room. This was a benefit, sure, but it was also a campaign event. We should have assumed that television reporters would be there. That added a layer of complexity to the issue. Anything that went down might be caught on camera. That was probably part of the plan. The sisters knew we wouldn't expose ourselves or make a move on them in full view of cameras. Some people believed in vampires—the authorities certainly did—but we weren't in any rush to provide the public with a spectacle to confirm our existence. Not to mention, every hunter out there, not just the Van Helsings, would recognize Dracula if he was caught on camera. Very few of them would be able to identify the sisters. Though they were famous, their likeness wasn't as well circulated among hunters.

More than a few creepy rich dudes undressed me with their eyes as I wandered the room, looking for something, anything, that might indicate what the sisters were up to or their where-abouts. Dylan picked up on it, too, and extended his arm as if to play the role of my escort.

Lizzie took Dylan's opposite arm, and I huffed a little. Look who came out looking like the womanizer in all this. I didn't have time for pettiness, though. We had more important things to focus on.

Dylan stopped in his tracks. "Do you smell that?"

Lizzie sniffed the air. "You've got to be kidding."

"What are you two talking about?"

No sooner did I ask the question than the door behind the stage opened and Dean Carver stepped out. He was flanked on one side by Caleb, the werewolf whose body we'd seen mangled and dead in the alley. On his other side stood Alexander, Regi-nald, and James Van Helsing.

"Holy shit," I whispered.

"He's not the only one," Lizzie replied. "They're all here. The whole pack. They didn't kill them."

Dylan grunted. "That damn elixir. They used it on Caleb then killed him to make it look like the pack was gone."

"Does that mean they're still going to try and kill me?" I asked.

Dylan shook his head. "I don't know. There's no telling what that elixir could do to the werewolf's instincts."

"If they killed and revived the entire pack, I'm guessing the pack itself dissolved," Lizzie ventured. "They're a new pack now. Just like us, but larger."

"Are the wolves still in the back?"

Dylan shook his head. "I can't tell. The smells in this place are swirling. All the hors d'oeuvres, the drinks, the bodies, and the natural odors that accompany large crowds. It's all one big whirlwind of fragrances."

I felt a cold hand on my shoulder. I didn't have to turn to recognize the touch.

"We have to get out of here," Dracula urged. "It's a trap."

"Are you sure?" I asked. "Just because the Van Helsings didn't really kill the wolves doesn't mean that they still don't want to stop the sisters."

Dracula shook his head. "The Van Helsings and werewolves are protecting Carver like they promised. But we're too late. Carver is already turned."

"He's a vampire?"

Dracula nodded.

I clenched my fists. "Well, shit. Why would the Van Helsings help the sisters?"

Dracula sighed. "Probably for the same reason we thought they'd help us. The enemy of my enemy. I should have known better. To the Van Helsings, I'll always be the bigger threat, at the top of their list."

"But they're protecting the candidate? He's a vampire. Why not stake him and be done with it?"

Dracula pressed his lips together. "These Van Helsing brothers are more like vampires than even they'd care to admit. Like vampires, they've seen the atrocities of the twentieth century. They've seen the worst of humanity and the worst of vampires. So far as body counts go, humans have us beat by the millions."

"Then why go after you?"

"Other than the fact that I'm Dracula and they've sworn to kill me?"

"Right. Other than that."

"The same reason they are coming after you. We are the biggest threat to the sisters. To their new world order. To everything that they want to accomplish."

I huffed. "You're right. We have to get the hell out of here and regroup."

Dean Carver was already speaking. Our conversation garnered a few annoyed stares. I don't know what people really cared to hear. Campaign speeches were predictable. A mixture of pipedreams that the candidate would never have the power to fulfill, half-truths, and platitudes. It was the platitudes, the hollow references to American values, patriotism, and the like, that earned the lion's share of applause.

Dracula, Dylan, Lizzie, and I pressed our way through the crowd, now gathering around us closer to the stage. It took a while to get to the back of the room, especially with more and more people crowding into the space going in the opposite direction.

Dean Carver was wrapping up his speech. I wasn't paying much attention, but his tone of voice changed for a moment.

"Now, friends and supporters, I have exciting news. It's not common for someone of such stature to endorse a candidate for Lieutenant Governor, but his support testifies to what's at stake for the future of our state and how pivotal the success of Louisiana is for the state of our nation. Ladies and Gentlemen, it is my privilege to introduce to you Robert Brandon, the president of the United States."

We stopped in our tracks as cheers erupted all around us. We turned to see the president, along with a cadre of secret service agents, approach the stage.

Dylan sighed. "I guess that explains the enhanced security."

Dracula shook his head. "And it speaks to the ambition of the sisters. This isn't a start-small-and-work-their-way-up plan to take over the world. They're taking the fast track."

I shook my head. "They plan to turn President Brandon into a vampire?"

Lizzie chuckled. "He doesn't get out much as it is. Who would really notice?"

I glared at Lizzie. "Show some respect. That's the president you're talking about."

Lizzie shrugged. "I didn't vote for him."

"You voted for the *other* guy?"

"Nope. I voted for the Libertarian."

"It doesn't matter," Dylan pointed out. "Politics aside, we can't allow the sisters to turn the freaking president."

"I agree," Dracula said. "We can't trust the Van Helsings to protect him. The sisters already turned Carver. That means, he'll have arrangements for them to meet the president before he leaves the building."

CHAPTER TWENTY-EIGHT

The sisters had a clear plan. Turn the president, do it behind closed doors, and deliver us to the Van Helsings in the process. I shouldn't have been surprised when a group of eight people blocked the exit. I didn't recognize them, but Dylan and Lizzie did. I could see it in their faces. It was the rest of their former pack.

"Dylan! Lizzie!" one of the wolves in human clothing stepped out from the others. "I'm so glad you could make it."

"What are you doing, Charlie?"

"The rules still apply, Lizzie. You two might have disavowed the pack, but we're still on a mission."

"To kill me," I sighed.

Charlie waved his hand in the air. "Don't be such an eager beaver. We'll get around to that. It's already agreed who will do the deed."

"Tell us," Lizzie said. "We saw Caleb die. Was it the Van Helsings that revived him?"

"They injected all of us. Funny thing, you know, when you inject a werewolf. Even death by silver is temporary."

"You won't hurt anyone here," Dylan predicted. "Not in public. Not like this."

Charlie grinned. "You're right. Sorina would never allow it. That whole dying and rising thing took the edge off. We aren't compelled to avenge our alpha like before. But the rules still apply. Thanks to the Van Helsings, and our vampire mistresses, we're working together now. We're free to take our time, to strategize. It seems that you four fell right into our trap, just like Sorina said you would."

Dracula grunted. "I knew we shouldn't have trusted the Van Helsings to keep up their end of the deal."

"They knew their chances to defeat you before were uncertain. With you here, Dracula, Sienna, all of you, we'll all get our vengeance. You four won't stand a chance against the sisters, the Van Helsings, and our pack all standing together."

I looked past the wolves through the glass doors to the parking lot. I nudged Dracula. "You just need a line of sight, right?"

Dracula nodded. "But Dylan and Lizzie."

"What are you two talking about?" Charlie asked.

"We'll come back for them."

Dracula nodded. I touched my brooch. He disappeared in a flash of light. We met back out in the parking lot by the van.

"I can't do that again," Dracula said. "Not until tomorrow."

I unlocked the van and retrieved my sword from the back. "It's okay. The sisters want you. The wolves want me. The Van Helsings want us both, but mostly you."

"Are you sure they won't kill Dylan and Lizzie?"

I scratched my head. "If I were in their shoes, I wouldn't. They've used Dylan to bait me before. They know I'll come after him."

"And Lizzie?"

I shook my head. "I don't know. She was a part of the pack."

"Right, and one who disowns the pack is usually hunted down

and killed."

"They're strategizing. That Charlie guy said as much. Two hostages are better than one."

"So, what's your plan? Walk through the walls and gank them all? That won't work."

"You're right. I can't do it alone. I'm going to get the pack back on our side."

"How are you going to do that? You don't seriously think you can convince them to disavow the pack and follow Dylan, do you?"

I rubbed my brow. "All you need to know is I had a lot of time to think while you were in the Scholomance. Abraham and I talked, and I learned a lot. More than I can explain now. I have an idea and if it works, the first thing we'll do is try to give you an opening. You can neutralize the sisters' power, right?"

Dracula nodded. "I can, Sienna. But going in there alone, astral or not, without sunlight no less, it's suicide."

I patted Dracula on his shoulder. "You're only half right. See you soon."

Before Dracula could protest, I touched my brooch. I grabbed another dagger from the back of the van. I didn't want Dracula to know I was taking it. If he knew what I was about to do, if he had any inkling of it, he'd try to stop me. But he didn't know what I felt or what I was learning about my nature. The Scholomance was right. I wasn't pure. I wasn't all light. Van Helsing sensed it in me, too. The truth is, none of us are pure light or dark, good or evil. There's a little good in the worst of us and a little bad in the best of us. The only real evil emerges when we try to realize pure goodness, perfect virtue, and find ourselves blind to the darkness within. I saw it now. There was no sense denying it. That's how I knew this was going to work.

If I was patient, if I had the opportunity. If I could convince him to do it. That was the only flaw in my plan. *He* had to do it.

I passed through the walls of the community center. The

president was still talking. He wasn't making a ton of sense, but bless him, he meant well.

Walking through people in the astral plane is always a little awkward and dangerous. Even with my mind right, there was a chance I'd lose focus. I wouldn't rematerialize if I didn't touch my brooch, but I could interact with the physical world. Sort of. Lose focus while passing through someone and I could do some serious damage.

The power of sunlight wasn't invigorating me anymore. It faded at some point after I took the sip of that martini and before the president took the stage. I still had strength. More than I had any time before at night. The vampire within me was there, lurking beneath the surface, waiting to burst through whatever humanity remained and take over when I walked through the night.

I tried to move between people as much as possible. I still had to pass through some arms and shoulders. So long as I didn't walk straight through someone's torso, if I lost my focus, the worst I'd do was injure someone's rotator cuff or trigger someone's funny bone.

I walked right up on stage. No one could see me, of course, but I couldn't resist holding up two fingers to give the president bunny years. No one else saw it, but I got a kick out of it.

No more time to waste, I turned and walked into the room behind the stage. Two secret service agents stood guard and there wasn't anyone in the room. There was a door off the room. I was pretty sure it wasn't a closet.

Since Charlie and his Oompa Loompas weren't watching the entrance anymore and I knew they went back inside the building, they had to have Dylan and Lizzie somewhere. Unless they paraded two hostages on stage behind the president they weren't there. Still, reconnaissance was necessary before initiating any plan. Learned that bit from Zoey. It was standard operating procedure for reapers, and we co-opted it in our fights in the past. When you're dealing with enemies like vampires or even gods, it's important to know where all the players are before you launch your opening salvo.

I pressed my hand through the door. It met resistance. I couldn't get through. That could only mean one thing. My hand was trying to materialize the second it reached the other side of the door. The sisters had black lights, technically powered by something harvested from the underworld, that made it impossible to go astral. If the lights were on back there, and they were expecting me to show, that was where the sisters were hiding.

It was also where they'd turn the president after he finished his speech. I didn't know how long the president planned to talk, but he wasn't as long-winded as some of his predecessors.

There weren't any other doors in the back. No other way to get through. Not unless there was an exit somewhere in the mystery room. I could have gone outside to check, but it wasn't worth the fifteen or twenty seconds it would take. I might not have even have that long before the speech was over and the president returned to begin his new existence as the sisters' progeny and puppet. I knew enough as it was. If this worked, it wouldn't matter if there was an outdoor entrance to that room. We'd make one if we had to.

I skipped back across the stage. The president was talking about his forthcoming budget proposal. Thrilling stuff.

There was another door close to the entrance. Just before the security checkpoint. I wasn't sure where it led, but it was the only place I could imagine Charlie and his pack could have taken Dylan and Lizzie without drawing too much attention. Everyone else in the place was focused straight ahead, surprised and enthused to see the president take the stage. They could have snuck my friends through that door without anyone noticing a thing.

I made my way back through the crowd. I was a little less careful this time, but I maintained focus.

Charlie and the wolves were back in the entryway. They had their backs turned to the door in question. Whatever they did to Dylan and Lizzie in there they were done—for the time being. They were guarding the door.

No problem for me. I slipped right past them and walked through the door.

It was a medium-sized room. It was filled with mops, cleaning supplies, and fold-up tables and chairs. Behind all the mess, I heard a few grunts. I moved through the stack of tables and saw Dylan and Lizzie each tied to chairs.

I touched my brooch and reappeared. I cut Dylan's bindings loose first. I removed the gag from his mouth.

"Thanks, Sienna. But how are we going to get out? There are too many of them."

"I don't have time to explain. Can you recommit yourself to your old pack?"

"I don't know."

Lizzie grunted. I turned and removed her gag.

"You going to cut me loose?"

I nodded and cut her bindings.

"Why do you want him to do that? We're making a new pack."

"Because I want Dylan to become the new alpha."

Lizzie shook her head. "That won't work. The only way he could do that is—"

"If he killed me."

"Sienna! I can't do that!"

"Be quiet," I snapped. "They'll hear you. I need you to trust me. This is going to work. I killed your alpha at night, I was in human form. My vampirism is growing in strength. All I need you to do is kill my humanity."

Dylan looked at me with wide eyes. "Sienna, you don't want me to do that."

"It's the only way. Besides, it doesn't matter. We aren't good or evil because of what we are, it's because of who we choose to be.

My humanity is failing anyway. The vampirism will take over even under the cover of night. I'm ready. I've fed enough that this should work."

"It *should* work?"

I nodded. "If I don't come back, meet Dracula out back. Use the force of the pack under your control to go after the sisters. The Van Helsings are on stage guarding the president. Once he stops talking, this is going to get a lot harder to pull off."

"How are we going to get to the sisters?" Lizzie asked.

"There might be a door on the south side of the building. The sisters are in a room on the southwest corner. If you can't get through a door, you wolves are strong. Do whatever you can to break through."

"I don't know if we can."

"Look, it's the only plan we have. And if we don't do this now, we won't stand a chance even with the pack if the Van Helsings are back there. Not to mention if they turn the president, the entire world is screwed."

Dylan grunted. "I don't like this. You're asking me to kill you. How confident are you that you'll make it?"

I shrugged. "It's a sixty-forty situation."

In truth, I had the odds reversed. I was only about forty percent sure I'd survive. It didn't matter. If we didn't do that, and quick, it was a hundred percent that they'd turn the president and the sisters, and the Van Helsings would kill all of us. Dracula and me for sure.

"You don't have to disavow the new pack," Lizzie said. "Any wolf who avenges the alpha whether he was a part of the pack to begin with or not will be the new alpha."

I smiled. "That makes this even easier."

"There's no other way?" Dylan asked.

I shook my head. I placed the knife in Dylan's hand. "Do it."

I kissed Dylan on the lips. He kissed me back even as tears fell from his eyes. Then, he jammed the knife into my heart.

CHAPTER TWENTY-NINE

I gasped for air. I was alive. The two chairs where Dylan and Lizzie sat before were empty. They left. They were proceeding with the plan. I touched my stomach. My dress was wet with blood, but my wound was healed.

I was strong. The power I felt wasn't nearly what I experienced under the light of the sun, but it was a lot more than I usually knew at night. My humanity was gone. I was a vampire—a real vampire, now.

I grabbed a mop and snapped it in two. I had stakes in the van, but you can't ever have too many. There was a chance, depending on how long I was out, that I might not even make it back to the van.

I pressed my brooch for safe measure. It wouldn't work once we got inside the sisters' room, but it could ensure that the Van Helsings didn't catch me before I got there.

The wolves weren't guarding the door anymore. The only explanation was that Lizzie was right. Dylan took control of the pack.

I ran around to the south side of the building. Dracula was there, standing with Dylan and the pack.

I looked around to make sure no one was spying on us from afar. So far so good. I touched my brooch and appeared in the middle of them.

"Sienna!" Dylan wrapped his arms around me.

I smirked. "Told you it would work."

Dracula looked at me. He met my eyes with his and tilted his head. "You turned."

I cracked my knuckles. "Sure did. Now, how about we bust in there and take care of those bitches?"

Dracula pointed straight ahead. "Small problem. We've got a wall. No door. The only other way in is if we fight through the crowd, the secret service, and the Van Helsings."

I shrugged. "Not necessarily. I can bust the wall open."

Dracula shook his head. "A vampire doesn't have that kind of strength."

"No. But a daywalker does."

Dracula grinned, flashing his fangs. Then he extended his hand. A ball of sunlight formed in his palm. The power rushed over me.

I ran headlong toward the wall and with all my strength thrust my shoulder against it. The wall crumbled around me.

I saw the three sisters, their eyes wide and jaws agape. Sorina, Ana, and Elena.

Blood was dripping from Sorina's mouth. The president was in her arms. Three secret service agents lay dead on the ground.

"We're too late," Dylan said.

"Not too late. That's just one bite. He won't turn from that."

I charged after the sisters. Sorina stood and backhanded me. I touched my cheek. "That hurt."

Sorina snapped her fingers. I don't know what magic she was trying to do but nothing happened.

I smirked. "Sorry. Your powers won't work around Dracula. Not anymore."

I grabbed Sorina by the shoulders and threw her out through the hole in the wall. The other two sisters chased after her. I picked up the president in my arms.

Dracula had a stake in his hand. A blast of sunlight would hurt them, most likely, but they could fight through it. Even a full-on blast might not waste them immediately. They could do a lot of damage before they burned up. Dracula was going through the kill. He went for Sorina, but she dodged him. Lizzie grabbed her and threw her to the ground. Ana dove at Dylan and sank her teeth into his neck.

"No!" I screamed. I almost dropped the president on the ground. If she bit Dylan, the new alpha, she'd take control of the pack again.

Ana fell to the ground, paralyzed.

Sorina and Elena clenched their fists.

Dracula smirked. "Your dark magic won't work around me. That means you can't bite a wolf without going nighty-night."

Sorina laughed. "We have a few more tricks up our sleeves. How do you think we ever broke the sire bond?"

"Another kind of magic," Dracula said.

"Yes, I suppose you could call it that. A little bit of science, too. Death breaks the sire bond. The Van Helsings have a clever way to defeat death."

"They injected you?" Dracula asked.

"Then they killed us. Staked us each in the heart. Thing is, in a few hours we were back up good as new. By the way, we have that juice running through us now. I'm not sure it's enough to wake up Ana here, but you can't kill us."

"You can't take the president!" I screamed.

Sorina laughed. "How are you going to stop me?"

"We will!" Dylan screamed.

The wolves gathered around Sorina and Elena.

"Have at them, boys!" Dylan commanded.

Then several gunshots sounded in the distance. Lizzie fell to the ground. Charlie did next. I dropped the president as gently as I could and dove after Dylan and tackled him to the ground. A bullet hit me in the back. It hurt, but silver bullets wouldn't do me in. I was a vampire, not a werewolf.

Bang!

Caleb took a bullet to the back and fell to his knees, coughing up blood.

"Stay down," I whispered in Dylan's ear. I took off after the Van Helsings. I touched my brooch just in time for a crossbow bolt to fly through my astral chest.

I moved fast. A lot faster than the Van Helsings could. They wouldn't even know what hit them. I reappeared just in time to take my blade across James's neck. Still invigorated by Dracula's light I stomped his severed head.

"RIP Gallagher," I smirked.

I touched my brooch again. Alexander and Reginald took off running. I was about to chase them when I heard Dracula scream. I turned to see Sorina with a stake in her hand, the sharp end in Dracula's chest.

I took off back toward them. I threw my fist through Sorina's chest and touched my brooch. I ripped her heart right out and threw it to the ground.

She was dead.

Someone screamed behind me. It was Elena. She had a stake in her hand. I couldn't move fast enough. Then she stopped and gasped. Dylan had his teeth in her neck. She fell to the ground, paralyzed like her other dark-haired sister. Dylan pounced on Sorina's body after that and gave her a bite for good measure. I yanked out Elena's heart. The power of the Scholomance could thwart the effects of the werewolf bite, the elixir could revive them. We wanted to make sure we have our bases covered. The only way to keep them dead was to keep their hearts separate from their bodies. If the hearts got close, hopefully the werewolf bite would keep them paralyzed and they wouldn't recover. The way I understood it, the power of the Scholomance necessary to overcome a werewolf's bite required a conscious effort. It wasn't a latent effect of being a master of the Scholomance.

I yanked the stake from Dracula's chest. He was breathing but just barely. Usually, a stake will take down a vampire straight away. Dracula wasn't like other vampires. Then it dawned on me —if that Van Helsing juice was coursing through the sisters' veins it was worth a shot. I dragged Sorina's body to Dracula. I forced her wrist to his mouth.

"Drink!"

Dracula bit her. He swallowed her blood. One gulp, then his eyes plastered open wide.

"Damn it! Come on, Drac!"

I shook his body. I pounded on his chest. "Wake up, damn it!"

Dylan put his hand on my shoulder. "He's gone. I'm sorry, Sienna."

"No! Get your pale ass up, you stubborn son of a bitch!"

I sat there shaking his body, slapping him in the face, just looking at his face, waiting for it to move. It felt like an eternity had passed. I was about to stand up. There was too much at stake to take the time to mourn. Then Dracula gasped. He looked at me, confused.

"Sorina's blood! Oh my God, Dracula! It was one hell of a long shot. I can't believe it worked!"

Dracula cocked his head as he sat up. "Did you just call me a son of a bitch?"

I laughed and wrapped my arms around him. "I sure did."

"And my ass is not that pale."

I let Dracula go. "Please."

Dracula laughed. "All right. It is pretty damn white, but you wouldn't know!"

"I couldn't let you die."

"And *I'm* the stubborn son of a bitch?"

I laughed. "Well, daughter of a bitch doesn't have the same ring to it."

Dylan cleared his throat. "Um, Sienna?"

I turned to him. "Yeah?"

"Where did the president go?"

CHAPTER THIRTY

We lost Lizzie. My heart was still racing from the fight. At least we put down the sisters. Dracula stayed with their paralyzed bodies. He didn't have the heart to smash Sorina's heart *or* head. She didn't have a heart at all. I suppose smashing it would do the same thing. He asked one of the wolves to bite her body. I don't know what he was planning to do with them. Even with the Van Helsing elixir in their bodies, we could kill them. Especially now that they were comatose and couldn't resist our efforts to chop them into bits. Instead, we'd lock them up for a hundred years and see what makes them tick. Just like Sandy Claws.

That was Dracula's business. I had to find President Brandon. Had someone taken him while we were occupied fighting for our lives? We only saw one bite on his body. That didn't mean there weren't more. There was a chance he was up and about with a serious craving for long pig.

Dylan came with me. We climbed back through the wall. I sighed.

The president was feeding from the corpse of one of his secret service agents. Dean Carver, the candidate for Lieutenant Governor, was standing beside him, nodding with approval.

There were more bites on the president's body than before. The sisters might have started it. Carver finished the job.

I clenched my fist. "What did you do?"

Carver turned and looked at me. He laughed with a fang-exposing, open-mouthed smile. "What does it look like?"

"You're a youngling. You can't control yourself. Both of you are. We can help you."

Carver pinched his chin. "A youngling? You *think* I'm a youngling? Sweet girl, I know who you are. I've been watching you for some time."

I raised an eyebrow. "You have?"

"I'm like you. I've been like you for centuries."

"You're a daywalker?"

Carver nodded. "Like you, I was abducted and bitten by vampires. While I didn't have a reaper friend to harness my soul while my body tried to recover, I had three brothers who used magic and science and tried their best to save me. Their efforts were only partially successful."

I gulped. "You're Samuel Van Helsing?"

Carver laughed. "Carver was a nickname I earned in the nineteenth century. You've heard of the ripper. I was the carver. I was more artistic than Jack when it came to my mutilations.

"My brothers and I reunited ten years ago. Their immortality had altered their perspective. They'd already developed a plan with Sorina and the sisters, and I was to play a role when the time was right. I got involved in politics. I waited to announce my candidacy for Lieutenant Governor until the time was right, until I became something of an up-and-coming celebrity in my party. I was immensely popular among politicians and talking heads all around the country, but I was running for office in a state where my party rarely wins. An endorsement from the president could tip the polls in my favor. I imagine it will. It also brought the president to me."

I narrowed my eyes. "The sisters are gone. We took them out. You won't get away with this, Samuel."

"Carver. I'm still the carver. And I will get away with it. I already have. The sisters provided a bite. Their track record of ensuring a successful transition is better than mine. I provided the subsequent bites necessary to complete the transition. Thanks to you, I won't have to share control over the president with those vile sisters."

I touched my brooch. Nothing happened. I was going to rip Carver's heart out of his chest. It wouldn't work. Those damned black lights.

I charged Carver. I didn't have a stake on me, but I had Dylan. If I could restrain him and Dylan could bite him we could deal with him later. My body ran right into a wall. I flashed with red magic when I collided with it.

Carver laughed. "Do you really think I'd make it that easy? I'm standing here gloating like every idiot villain in every movie you've ever seen. I wouldn't bait you like that if I wasn't prepared."

"You'll never get away with this. The president was attacked. Secret service agents are dead."

"You don't think I'll get away with it? I'm the candidate who *saved* the president. Oh, and since I bit him, he'll be able to walk in the daylight just like us. I'll be a hero. I'll win my election in a landslide. Everyone loves a hero. Meanwhile, the president will do *my* bidding. We're taking over the world, and there's not a thing you can do to stop us. Especially when the full force of the government will be looking for you and Dracula, the two vampires who tried to assassinate President Brandon."

I narrowed my eyes. "Your father would be ashamed of you."

Carver laughed. "The weird sisters are handled. They played their role perfectly. You could revive them, I suppose, but if you do, it's your funeral. Now it's just a matter of time with the full force of the government before Dracula is killed. I will have finished what my father never could. He wouldn't be ashamed of me. He'd be proud."

I shook my head. "You're wrong. I met your father at the Scholomance. He'd never endorse turning the world's leaders into vampires."

"Do you really think I care about my father's approval? My father is dead. This isn't the world that my father used to know. He didn't see the evils of the twentieth century. He died before the World Wars, before the nuclear age. You should embrace my efforts. You should be my most vocal supporter. I'm going to make a better world for our kind. The age of the vampire has begun. Don't forget what you are. It's your choice. Give me Dracula. He has to die. He's been a thorn in our side for too long. Join me at my side. You could be my intern. You could help me secure a better world for all vampires."

I huffed. "I know what happens to politicians' interns. No thanks."

Carver laughed. "I'm a gentleman, Sienna. You can't get to me. You can't kill me. You can either join the winning side or become the hunted. Public enemy number one."

I clenched my fists. A tsunami of rage washed over me.

"I'll tell you what, Sienna. I'm a generous man. I've lived a long time and I've learned to be patient. There will be an investigation. It will take some time before the suspect responsible for the attempt on the president's life is identified. I can tell you right now, Dracula will be a suspect. You have thirty days to decide. Go down for the Count or join the revolution."

Carver helped the president to his feet. He grabbed a handkerchief from his pocket and wiped the blood from the president's mouth.

They left the room together.

I stood there speechless for a good fifteen seconds.

"You aren't seriously considering this, are you?" Dylan asked.

I huffed. "Please. I'm already dead. Besides, he gave us thirty days."

"If Carver controls the president, he can do a lot of damage in a month."

I nodded. "Then we'd better get to work."

CHAPTER THIRTY-ONE

We drove slowly back to the school. The bodies were stacked in the back. The sisters were on the bottom. We brought the fallen wolves with us, too. I didn't know Charlie or Caleb well, but Lizzie was a part of the team. The girl gave her life helping us stop the sisters. She deserved a proper burial. Even if it was six feet under what used to be a school playground.

Dylan sat in the back with the bodies. With the seats down to accommodate our "cargo," it was the only option.

I said we were driving slowly. The one thing you can't afford when you have a van full of bodies is a speeding ticket.

Dylan was quiet. The loss of Lizzie and the other wolves was sinking in now that the adrenaline of the battle was waning. Shock would turn to denial, and denial would turn to anger. The wolves—Dylan included—would want revenge before they got to acceptance. I was more than eager to help them get it. But we couldn't start talking revenge yet. Not now. Not until it sunk in a little and we had time to come up with a plan.

I filled Dracula in on the details—everything we'd learned from Carver.

Dracula didn't hesitate.

"We have to wake up Sorina."

I grunted. "Are you serious? She was working with those Van Helsing assholes."

Dracula shook his head. "She is a vampire. She's already broken the sire bond. If we can find a way to cure her of the werewolf paralysis, and there's enough of that elixir in her system to get her heart back in her chest cavity and pumping again, you can bite her. You can turn her into a daywalker. She is one of the president's sires. With two different sires competing to influence him, we might not be able to completely stop Carver, but we can certainly complicate his efforts."

I shook my head. "We don't even know if it's possible to wake her. Not for a hundred years. I hate to break it to you, but in a century it will be too late for the world."

"If there's a way, we'll find it."

I raised one eyebrow. "In one month?"

"More than enough time in the void."

I raised an eyebrow. "Seriously? We have to go to hell again?"

Dracula laughed. He reached into his white cloak and pulled out a crystal. "Perks of being a master of the path of light. I can take us straight to the Scholomance. Let's hope your buddy Abraham isn't keen on a vampire apocalypse."

"Even if he wants to help, he died before his sons devised their elixir. He's never had reason to cure a vampire of werewolf paralysis. What are the chances he'll know how to do it?"

"He doesn't need to know. He just has to be willing to babysit a corpse for a hundred years."

I bit my lip. "How does that translate to earth days?"

Dracula shrugged. "It's hard to know. Let's hope a month will do the trick."

I scratched the back of my head. "Say it works. What if the elixir expires over a century? We don't know if she'll even rise again once the paralysis wears off."

Dracula shook his head. "Do you have any other ideas?"

"Sure. We find Carver and kick his ass."

"We don't know what magic he's wielding. That barrier you described, it's nothing like any magic I've ever encountered. Even if we could get to him, it would be suicide."

I swallowed hard. "You're right. I don't like it. It means trusting Abraham with Sorina. It also means I'll have to turn her. I'm not all that inclined for a hundred years losing Monopoly games with Abe."

Dracula laughed. "You won't have to stay there."

"Dracula, Sorina is a master of the Scholomance. She has your power. If she wakes and I'm not there to turn her, do you really think she's going to play nice with old man Van Helsing?"

Dracula grinned. "Abraham is a master of the path of light. Her power will be dormant in his presence as much as it is in mine."

"So what do we do? Drop off Sorina's mangled corpse and check in every couple days to find out how much time has passed?"

Dracula nodded. "Pretty much. In the meantime, we fortify the hell out of that school and prepare for war with the Van Helsing brothers."

I raised an eyebrow. "And the US Government."

"If all goes according to plan, it won't come to that."

***

We arrived back at the school. It was best to bury all the bodies before sunrise. Dracula gave me a little sunlight to give me the strength to do it.

I don't care how strong you are, or what kind of supernatural abilities you might have. Digging graves is nobody's idea of a good time.

It also makes you hungry.

I sipped on a bottle of blood between shovelings. More Southern Californian B-positive. Refreshing.

Dylan and the other wolves worked together to dig a grave for Lizzie, Charlie, and Caleb. I handled the grave for the two dark-haired sisters. They wouldn't stay down forever, but hopefully, by the time they rose, we'd have a better solution. It would have been easier if we'd burned them, smashed their heads, or thrown them into a woodchipper. Dracula wasn't on board with that. Despite their treacheries, the count was sentimental. He wanted to try to save them. The way I saw it, if a century passed and we didn't have a solution, we'd dig them up and burn their bodies then. I was more worried about surviving the next month. We'd tackle the next century when the time came.

There was also a chance, if things got rough, that we could use the sisters. We could do the same for them that we planned to do for Sorina. They could serve their sentence in the void and I'd bite them when they rose again. Two sisters with dark power, subject to my will, could be helpful.

Sorina and the sisters knew how to break a sire bond. They'd do it again. Dracula told me that I could command them not to. I still wasn't entirely comfortable with the plan. Sire bonds aren't absolute. Chaining up Sorina with a sire bond was sort of like putting a lion on a leash. I could pull her chain, tell her to sit, and she'd sit. If I wasn't careful, though, and she figured out a way to turn on me or compromise our plans that didn't directly defy one of my orders, she'd turn on me.

It was a risk we had to take. There was too much at stake. We could only hope we got what we needed out of her, that we stopped the president from spreading the vampire apocalypse to the rest of the world before she got a chance.

We also couldn't control what Carver and the president might do in the coming month. Without the sisters, Carver said many of the people he tried to turn died. It wasn't a foolproof plan, but if we kept tabs on the news, even checked in with Morty regarding any world leaders whose souls were coming due, we might at least know what we were facing and how far around the globe the new world vampire order had spread.

After the bodies were buried I went inside to shower. The gym showers at an old school brought back some awful memories, but I made do. It's funny how you can face evil vampires and hunters without flinching but still find yourself haunted by the metaphorical ghosts of high school bullies.

We wrapped up Sorina's body in a blanket and put her heart in a paper grocery bag.

Dracula pulled out his crystal. He held it with one hand and formed a ball of sunlight in his other hand. An oval portal of white light formed in front of us. I threw Sorina's body over my shoulder. Dracula grabbed the grocery bag. Then, we stepped through the gateway to the Scholomance.

We appeared in front of Abraham Van Helsing's desk. He was playing solitaire. His countenance brightened as soon as he saw us. I wasn't sure if it was purely on account of the fact that he was happy to see us or if it was the light still radiating from Dracula's portal.

"Sienna! You came back to see me!"

"What?" Dracula asked. "No greetings for your old rival?"

Abraham nodded. "Hello, Dracula. What's in the bag? Did you bring takeout?"

Dracula chuckled. "Something like that."

CHAPTER THIRTY-TWO

"Samuel is alive?" Abraham shook his head in disbelief.

I nodded. "If you think that being a vampire counts as being alive. He's like me. He's a daywalker."

"Then he can be saved."

I sighed. "I don't think so. He's trying to take over the world, Abe. He already has the president of the United States in his thrall."

Abraham shook his head. "I can't believe it. I mourned his death. A father should never have to go through something like that, but I did. Now you're telling me he's alive and he has to be stopped?"

Dracula nodded. "I'm sorry, Abraham. I can't imagine how hard this must be for you."

Abraham grunted. "You turned from the darkness, Dracula. No one has ever fallen so far, embraced the dark power so deeply, as you. If you can be saved, so can he."

"That's different," Dracula said. "The sisters took my power."

"Then someone can take his. He can return here. I can guide him on the path of light."

Dracula shook his head. "I don't know, Abraham. Stopping Samuel will be hard enough."

"He prefers to go by Carver, now," I added.

"Exactly my point," Dracula said. "He's let go of his old life. He's become a monster."

"As did you, Dracula," Abraham said.

Dracula grunted. "I see your point."

Abraham rested his elbows on his desk and pressed his hands together. "I'll watch Sorina. I'll babysit her paralyzed corpse for a hundred years if that's what it takes. But you have to promise me that you'll bring Samuel to me. You will do what you can to save my baby boy."

I nodded. "We'll do it."

"Sienna," Dracula said. "We can't promise that."

"I promised we'd do what we could. We'd try to save him. If there's a way, we'll find it."

Dracula and I returned through the portal. We landed back in the school.

"I know why you promised that Sienna, but you shouldn't make promises you can't keep."

"I didn't!" I insisted. "All I promised was that we'd try."

"And while we're trying to save Carver, how many people will die? How far will he spread his influence around the globe?"

"Look, Dracula. If I didn't agree to try, Abraham wouldn't have agreed to help. This was your plan."

Dracula sighed. "I know. I'm sorry. It's just breaking a promise with Abraham Van Helsing isn't wise."

"He's dead, Drac. He's a master of the Scholomance, sure, but only in the void. He's a ghost."

Dracula shook his head. "I'm not sure that would stop him if we killed his sons."

"We only made the deal for Samuel. We already killed one of his boys."

"And it was a good thing we didn't tell him that. Trust me,

Sienna. He might be a ghost, but he's a powerful ghost. Do you think he's *stuck* there at the Scholomance?"

I shrugged. "I sort of figured he was. He is dead, after all."

"The same rule applies to how you and I returned to our bodies, how we broke free from the Gorgon's spell. Abraham Van Helsing is in the Scholomance because that was his idea of heaven. There was nothing so far as he knew that tied him to Earth. Now he knows his children are still alive. If he wants to, if he has the right motivation, he can leave. Ghosts aren't as power-less, especially those who can wield power like Abraham, as you might think."

I nodded. "Then we'd best uphold our end of the bargain."

"And when we do, when Samuel goes to the Scholomance and tells Abraham that you killed James, what do you think he will do?"

I sighed. "I hope he'll understand. We didn't have a choice."

"I wouldn't count on that."

I snickered. "It's always funny when you talk about counting, Count Dracula."

"I'm not joking around here. But you're right. That's a battle to fight another day. And stop with the counting jokes. I've heard them all. My whole life."

With Dracula footing the bill, we turned that school into a fortress. Every kind of trap you could imagine that might ruin a vampire's day if one ever tried to come in after us covered every entrance to the place. Carver knew where we were. He must have since his brothers had been there. Besides, as the new Lieutenant Governor, he had ways of finding out even if his brothers didn't tell him. Technically, the werewolves owned the place. The deed was in the name of their former alpha and the property was willed to the rest of the pack in the event of his death. I suppose there was no way to know in advance who the new alpha would be, so he bequeathed the property to all of them.

I traveled back to the Scholomance with Dracula every week at first. As the month drew closer to an end we popped in more regularly.

I polished off the bottled blood within a week. Dracula helped, but I fed more often. I was younger, I required more frequent feedings. After that, our friend Leeroy was happy to provide all the blood I required in exchange for adequate compensation.

We had to deal with a full moon situation during that month. The wolves went out to the swamps, the same one where we found Lizzie before. They came back smelling like wet dogs. I could tell, though, that Dylan was reinvigorated by the experience. It was good to get out, run through the breeze, and howl at the moon.

Everything depended on Sorina waking up in time. If she didn't, well, I'd have to fight. That, or agree to work with Carver. That wasn't an option, but Dracula thought I could agree to it and try to go undercover, do what I could to stall his progress. I hoped it wouldn't come to that. Carver was too smart to be fooled by something like that. If I joined him, it would be a matter of time before he'd find out. He'd probably suspect I was a mole from the start. It still gave us a better chance than trying to take him down head-on. If I got on the inside, I could try to find a vulnerability and give Dracula and the wolves an opportunity to go after him.

I was glad it didn't come to that. Three days before the month was up, Dracula and I returned to the Scholomance. We found Sorina awake and chained to a wall.

"Look what the cat dragged in," Sorina muttered when she saw us. "Isn't this how you like it, Drac? I'm all tied up. Now you can have your way with me. I'll even let you call me Mina."

Abraham looked at Dracula with wide, horrified eyes.

"That's not me anymore, Sorina. I'm not the one who has come here to play."

I smirked. "Don't you look delicious."

Sorina raised an eyebrow. "That's your plan? You're going to bite me and turn me into a daywalker?"

Dracula shrugged. "What? Carver wouldn't do it for you?"

"He can't turn vampires into daywalkers. Not permanently."

I scrunched my brow. "Carver said that being a daywalker meant that the president would be able to go out during the day. How does that make sense if he can't make daywalkers?"

Sorina sighed. "I suppose you'll *compel* me to tell you the truth so there's no use fighting it. It's true. When he turns someone, the daywalker condition lasts for a short time. Eventually, it fades away. Whatever it is he passes along through his bite has an expiration date. When it passes, they become regular vampires."

"By a short time, let me guess, that's roughly a month?"

Sorina nodded. "About that long. Maybe a little longer, but not much."

I sighed. "This is starting to make sense."

"It's why he's so eager to recruit you to his cause."

"We'll need your help, Sorina. You're going to be a good little girl, won't you?"

Sorina lowered her head and laughed. "I won't have much choice in the matter, will I?"

I smiled widely, exposing my fangs. "Nope."

Dracula formed a ball of light in his hands. To turn a vampire, I had to be in my daywalker form. I moved to one side of the room so Dracula could blast me without hitting Sorina. The last thing we needed was to complicate her change. When I felt the power wash over me, I sank my teeth into Sorina's neck. Her blood flooded my eager mouth. I gulped it down. Vampire blood wasn't my meal of choice, most of the time, but as a daywalker, I had a taste for it.

Sorina gasped for air. "My God, I can feel it! It's glorious!"

"First things first," I said. "You will do nothing to harm Dracula, me, the werewolves, or anyone else without my expressed permission."

Sorina nodded. "Of course I won't."

"Can you reach the president?" Dracula asked.

Sorina smiled. "You have my body. Tell me you still have my phone."

I nodded. "It needs a charge, but we have it."

Sorina nodded. "I can get ahold of him. Our plan was to give the president a phone. We had it all set up and I have the number."

"You realize, Carver set you up. He wanted you out of the way so he could be the only one to manipulate the president. Who's to say he hasn't changed the president's number?"

Sorina shrugged. "Well, if he has, getting ahold of the vampire in chief is going to be a lot more difficult."

"It's worth a try," Dracula said. "It's the best option we have. Besides, Carver thinks Sorina is dead."

I shook my head. "He also knows we have her phone."

"I don't think he'd worry about that much," Dracula said. "After all, he's still hoping you'll defect to his side. What's the worst you could do, anyway? You don't have any influence over President Brandon. He's in Carver's thrall."

"Remember your promise," Abraham said. "You will not harm Samuel. You will bring him to me."

I nodded. "That's right. I promised we'd try. First, we have to save the president."

"You might be too late," Abraham said. "A lot of damage can be done in a month if a vampire is manipulating a powerful man."

I nodded. "We've been keeping tabs on the situation. I know the Grim Reaper. He's been checking the schedules. There's a meeting scheduled with the United Nations next week. So far as we can tell, the vampirism hasn't gone beyond the United States. If we don't succeed soon, though, this could spread very quickly."

"Don't you see what he's doing?" Van Helsing asked. "That's why Samuel gave you one month. He needs you. If you could turn the world's leaders, including the president, into daywalkers, it would make it a lot easier to spread vampirism around the globe."

I nodded. "I thought of that. That's a risky proposition, though, from Samuel's perspective. I'd be able to control the new vampires during the day. He'd maintain control at night. Even so, all I'd have to do is command them to stake themselves and I could end this nightmare before it spread further."

"That's right!" Sorina laughed. "Come nightfall, I'll be a free agent!"

Dracula grinned. "So long as I'm around, I'll make sure you stay bathed in sunlight. Don't think we hadn't thought of that."

Sorina raised an eyebrow. "You're going to babysit me with your ball of light forever?"

Dracula nodded. "If that's what it takes. Or, you know, we could chain you up at night. All Sienna has to do is command you to do it."

I nodded. "That's right. Every day you are to bind yourself in shackles. We have it all set up in the girls' locker room. Don't think about pocketing the key, either. I have the key and you are never to try and take it from me. I'll unlock you every day when the sun comes out. At least until we know we can trust you."

Sorina smiled. "Look at you. Impressive for such a youngling."

I glanced at Dracula and smirked. "I have a pretty impressive mentor."

"You'd better stay vigilant," Sorina said. "Once you're staked, you know, I'll be free forever. No one will be able to stop me."

I nodded. "Good thing I don't plan on getting staked anytime soon."

"No vampire ever plans to meet the true death, love. Most do, eventually."

Dracula narrowed his eyes. "And if it comes down to that, I'll end you myself."

Sorina smirked. "I love it when you talk dirty to me. Besides, Dracula, my *love,* you and I know that you don't have the heart to do it. If you did, you would have killed me a long time ago."

CHAPTER THIRTY-THREE

We brought Sorina back to the schoolhouse. We were met with stares when we showed up in the old gymnasium. The wolves weren't thrilled to see her. I understood that. She wasn't the one who pulled the trigger, but she was a part of the picture. All her plans, her alliance with the Van Helsings, including Carver, led to that moment—when the other wolves lost their lives.

If Dylan wasn't their new alpha, I suspected they'd feel the same way about me. I killed James Van Helsing, after all. Smashed his skull under my heel.

Our little alliance depended more than I'd like on sire bonds, alpha bonds, and the compulsions that accompanied such things than I'd like.

Dylan fought beside me because he wanted to. Lizzie did eventually, too, even though it wasn't initially by choice. Now that Dracula had died, it didn't matter that I'd made him a daywalker. I wasn't his sire in any sense anymore. We fought side-by-side because we shared a common goal. Not to mention, old Pale Face was growing on me. He was the closest thing to a vampire father— more like a grandfather—that I had. I'd learned more about my true nature, how to feed, and to do so without becoming a bloodsucking monster in the short time we'd been together than I had in all the months before when I fought alongside Zoey in Kansas City.

Josephine, Zoey's mother, taught me a few things. Still, Josephine was a hunter. Learning how to be a vampire from a hunter is like asking a Republican to teach you how to be a good Democrat. They might know the general ideas and philosophies, but they didn't embrace them, and their views of the "other" were always skewed toward the negative. With Dracula, it was different. He didn't see my vampirism as something to fear so much as to understand.

When all this started, I got the brooch hoping I could have a normal human life. It worked for a while. It suppressed my urges, even in direct sunlight. As my nature evolved and grew, the brooch still took an edge off and allowed me to go astral, but it couldn't mask what I was. Not anymore.

I was afraid of what I was. Head shrink that shit. It's one thing to be afraid of monsters, it's another thing when you are terrified of the monster that you're becoming. I came to realize that my nature wasn't something to fear anymore. I embraced it. I couldn't control my urges. I could control how I satisfied them, and what I chose to do with them. When you think about it, being a vampire isn't that different than being human. I mean, sure, we can't swear off blood indefinitely. It's not like a human who can live just fine without alcohol, drugs, or porn. If we don't feed, and control our feed, our nature will take over and bite the first blood bag with legs we can get. That's how most people who are killed by vampires die. It's usually by young vampires who try to suppress what their human nature tells them is repulsive. Until they can't. Most vampires, especially the older ones, catch and release. Sure, for some it's out of self-preservation more than due to conscience. A body count tends to attract hunters. Still, whatever the reason, most vampires aren't all that interested in killing people. Even fewer have world-dominating aspirations.

Even the sisters thought they were doing what they did out of survival. They feared that as humanity learned about us, eventually they'd slaughter us. I had more faith in people. Maybe I was naive. Still, I had to believe that coexistence was possible with humans without ruling them.

"This place smells like dog," Sorina huffed.

I narrowed my eyes. "Watch your mouth. Don't think for a second these 'dogs' wouldn't like to get their revenge. Especially after you manipulated them and got half the pack killed."

"I'll stop by Laveau's and see if I can get a couple bottles of your favorite O-negative," Dracula said. "Just mind your manners."

Sorina narrowed her eyes. "I don't have to listen to you."

I smiled. "Mind your manners, Sorina."

Sorina huffed. "Humiliating. I've gone longer between bowel movements than you've been a vampire."

I raised an eyebrow. "That's concerning. You really should lay off the cheese."

Sorina laughed. Then she stopped herself and coughed to interrupt her chortles.

I smiled. "You like me. Admit it."

Sorina smirked. "I find you amusing. There's a difference."

I nodded. "You like me. Might as well give in to it. This whole thing will be a lot easier if you're let loose. Also, couldn't hurt if you dealt with that constipation problem."

"I'm not constipated. I just don't eat solid foods! I haven't had anything aside from blood in a decade."

I tilted my head. "Really? We can eat, you know. Doesn't provide much nutritional value, but what the hell. We don't gain weight either. All the ice cream you could eat, and you won't even end up with dimples in your thighs."

Sorina laughed. "Yeah, but you'll have gas for days."

I winced. "Yeah, there's that."

"I'm going to tell you something. Not because you're making me. Because I think you should know."

"What's that?"

"Be careful with Dracula. I took his dark power, it's true. But he was a brute long before he mastered the Scholomance. Have you even asked him about his human life? All the things he did, the unspeakable violence he committed *before* he was a vampire?"

I shook my head. "It never occurred to me to ask him about his life before. Kind of crazy, all that time in the car it never came up. He's been a vampire so long sometimes it's hard to imagine a time when he was a regular man."

Sorina shook her head. "Trust me, there was nothing regular about the man he once was."

I sighed. "The key phrase is *once was.* I don't know the things he did before. What I do know is that he's been nothing but a gentleman, noble and virtuous, ever since we left Kansas City."

"A tiger can't change its stripes. I'm not saying he isn't trying. I'm not even saying he's not a better vampire now than he was before. Perhaps he's even nobler than he was as a human. Speaking of tigers, Siegfried and Roy had a tiger they thought they'd tamed. They performed with him for years. Then one day, out of the blue, the tiger attacked Roy. It took four men and a fire extinguisher to get the beast off of him. It left him partially paralyzed on one side of his body."

I grunted. "I could say the same thing about you, you know."

Sorina nodded. "You're right. Somehow, I think you're far less likely to let your guard down around me."

Dracula returned sooner than I expected with a whole crate of blood wine. I don't know how much it cost, but apparently it was from the Rhine, circa 1945. A combination blend, each bottle containing every blood type. I didn't know how they collected the blood, or if the donors gave it willingly. Whatever the case, it was bottled a long ass time ago. It was scrumptious. Sorina finished an entire bottle alone. I suppose after a century, from her perspective, paralyzed by werewolf enzymes, she was more than a little hungry. Dracula and I split a bottle.

"Your phone should be charged by now," I said. "Ready to make the call?"

Sorina nodded. "What should I tell him?"

"Tell him not to do anything Carver says."

Sorina laughed. "I can't do that. I shouldn't. Not unless you want to drive the old man insane."

"She's right," Dracula said. "Conflicting commands between sires will drive a man right out of his mind. It will force his consciousness to split into multiple personalities."

Sorina cleared her throat. "And we'd never know for sure which personality was listening. We couldn't trust that he'd fulfill my demands."

I bit my thumb. "All right. Well, we don't know what Carver has told him to do. Say you tell him to come here but Carver told him not to leave Washington."

"The same problem would occur," Dracula said. "Besides, if we told the president to come here, he'd come with an entourage."

Sorina nodded. "The first step in the plan, as Carver and I discussed it before all this went down, was to turn the president's cabinet. They're all loyal to Carver. If the president comes here, they'll know it. That means Carver will also know."

I shook my head. "Carver gave me a month. I suspect he'll be showing up here soon, one way or another. He didn't give me a way to contact him."

Sorina shrugged. "He's the Lieutenant Governor. At least he's the Lieutenant Governor-Elect. He's in Baton Rouge. Perhaps he expects you to do your invisible girl routine and tell him your answer."

I chuckled. "If he's not a dimwit, and I hardly think he is, he wouldn't let me go astral anywhere near him. I could rip his heart out before he realized it."

Sorina winced. "I know. It doesn't feel good."

I bit my lip. "Sorry, not sorry."

Sorina laughed. "I'm not looking for an apology. You couldn't have taken me without the use of mystical devices. Woman to woman, I'd take you every time. But anything goes in love and war."

I chuckled. "Love had nothing to do with it."

"I wouldn't be so sure about that. Your feelings for that wolf and his feelings for you were all a part of the plan. My plan, before, I mean."

"A plan that ended with me ganking your heart and you taking a very long nap."

"It doesn't matter," Dracula said. "We need a plan to reach the president without alerting Carver."

Sorina shook her head. "It doesn't matter. Say we reach President Brandon. By now, I imagine the vice president is also in Carver's thrall. I hate to tell you this, but even if we feed the president some of my blood, and supposing there's some of that elixir pumping through my veins, and we kill him and he revives, Carver will have the president assassinated, Probably by one of the vampires in his cabinet. The vice president will take over and we'll be back at square one."

I folded my arms in front of my chest. "Then we need to lure Carver here."

"You promised Van Helsing we wouldn't kill him."

I nodded. "You're right. And we won't. One of the wolves has to bite him. He won't be able to control any of the vampires in the president's cabinet, but we'll still be able to keep tabs on the president through Sorina."

Dracula nodded. "That might just work. Then, we deliver Carver to his father in the Scholomance. We let Abraham worry about rehabilitating his boy."

Sorina reached into the crate and pulled out another bottle of blood. She shoved her thumbnail into the cork, twisted her hand, and popped it open. "I have an idea. It may or may not work. It all depends on what Carver has told the president. If you really want to lure Carver here, then fine. We can ask the president to arrange a visit. Maybe he shows, maybe he doesn't. But if Carver knows I'm here, that I *tried* to reach the president, you'd better believe he'll come after me."

"Are you sure about that?" I asked. "He double-crossed you once before. He let you fight us, knowing there was a chance we'd kill you."

Sorina nodded. "We weren't supposed to bite the president. Carver was supposed to become the next president, the candidate in waiting once the current president's term was up. Then Carver's brothers showed up. You and Dracula pushed the issue. We had to push our agenda forward. It also made both Carver and I dual sires for the president. An arrangement I was willing to live with. I'm betting he wasn't willing to allow me to. He has to realize if I'm back that I'm a threat. He'll come. Partially, I'm sure, to see if you'll join him. He still needs you, Sienna. But he doesn't need to come here to get your answer. He'll come after me."

"You're suggesting we use you as bait?" I asked.

Sorina nodded. "That's precisely what I'm suggesting."

I raised an eyebrow. "Why would you suggest that? I didn't compel you to get creative."

A half-grin formed at the corner of Sorina's mouth. "This wasn't Carver's plan. It was mine. I'll be damned if I allow Samuel Van Helsing to become the emperor of the world. He might be a vampire now. But he was a Van Helsing first."

I furrowed my brow. "I thought the plan was to make him the next president. The original plan. After this president's term was up, Carver would be the candidate in waiting."

Sorina nodded. "I cannot be president. Carver has established his citizenry already. I had plans of my own to take a place of influence representing Romania in the United Nations. We were supposed to keep one another in check."

I shook my head. "You were working *with* the Van Helsing

brothers. You have been for centuries. You said they were the ones who helped you break the sire bond with Dracula."

Sorina took a deep breath. She let her lips flap when she exhaled. "That was a long time ago. The Van Helsings were a means to an end then even as they were supposed to be now. I never intended for them to take the reins. Not the way he now intends. Not unchecked by me."

I watched as Sorina put the bottle of blood to her lips and gulped down half of it. She placed her hand to her chest and belched.

"Excuse you."

Sorina giggled a little. "Sorry. I'm still so thirsty."

Dracula grunted. "How about you make that call?"

"On speaker," I added.

CHAPTER THIRTY-FOUR

We arranged a bunch of old school desks together so that they formed a table. They weren't the desks with chairs attached. These were the kind that were open in the middle, where young children could cram all their assignments and then go digging for them later when they came due. More bad school memories.

I arranged several chairs around the desks. They were too small for us. We couldn't get our legs under the desks, so we all sat sideways around the makeshift table. I placed Sorina's phone in the middle.

Sorina dialed the president, put it on speakerphone, and set the phone back on the table. The phone rang a few times. That was a good sign. If Carver changed the number, we wouldn't have gotten that far. We would have been greeted by one of those "the number you have dialed is out of service" messages.

"What do you want, Carver," the familiar deep but gravelly voice said on the other end.

"It's not Carver," Sorina said. "It's your mommy!"

"Excuse me?"

"You're going to listen to me," Sorina said. "I made you. I bit you first."

"Of course."

"Tell me the truth. Did Carver forbid you from coming back to Louisiana? Did he give you any commands at all that would restrict your travel?"

"He did not."

Sorina smiled widely and rubbed her hands together. "In that case, you're going to plan a trip. I'll text you the address when we get off the phone. I want you to come by tomorrow."

"Of course, but it's quite the ordeal when I travel. A lot of arrangements have to be made."

"That's fine," Sorina said. "Arrange what you must, but you will come to the address I'm sending you. You'll arrive just after sunset."

"I will be there."

"Good boy. Now, one more thing. Make sure Carver knows you're coming. Don't speak to him yourself. Have one of your aides send him a message."

"I understand."

"Did Carver order you to pick up the phone when he calls?"

"He did."

"Did he forbid you from breaking the phone?"

"He did not. He only told me not to lose it."

Sorina winked at me. She was showing off her compulsion skills. "Good. When we get off the phone, you will wait for my text message. You will write it down so you don't lose it. Then you'll smash the phone you're talking on to pieces."

"Absolutely. Consider it done."

Sorina hung up the phone. "That was easier than I expected."

"Clever," I smirked. "Now we have to get ready for Carver."

Dracula nodded. "We should disarm all the traps. We don't want him dead. We want him paralyzed."

"Do that," I said. "I'll brief the wolves on the plan. We'll lure Carver into the gymnasium. The wolves will be waiting just outside the door. The first wolf to bite him wins."

"What about me?" Sorina asked.

"Wait here. Drink as much blood as you'd like. If you need more, find Dracula and let him know. Don't hurt anyone. Don't set up any traps. Don't scheme in any way to undermine our plan."

Sorina rolled her eyes. "I think you covered it. It's unnecessary, you know. I want to remove Carver from the equation as much as you do."

I nodded. "I know. But someone told me recently that a tiger can't change its stripes."

Sorina chuckled. "Clever girl. We're more alike than you know."

I gathered the wolves in the gymnasium. I gave them the rundown of the plan. The plan that everyone *else* thought we were enacting, anyway. I saw Carver's power. I didn't know how it worked or what the source of his magic was, but I knew it was something beyond what we could handle if he unleashed it on us.

A young child could kill even the greatest of the world's warriors if the child catches him in his sleep. With the right weapon, catch a mighty wizard doing his business on the john and any regular Joe can take him out. The element of surprise is the great equalizer.

I pulled Dylan aside.

"Excuse us. We could use a moment alone."

The wolves hooted and hollered. They thought Dylan was about to get some. Maybe he would, after this was over. They could think whatever they wanted. So long as they didn't know the real plan.

I took Dylan's hand and led him into the girls' locker room.

Dylan chuckled. "I always wondered what it looked like in

here. It's disappointing. Just like the boys' room, without the urinals."

I laughed. "What were you expecting? Floral arrangements and potpourri?"

Dylan smirked. "Hello Kitty posters and statues of unicorns."

"You forgot the seashells on the back of the toilet."

Dylan scratched the back of his head. "What's the deal with that anyway? What about taking a dump makes someone think, *gee, I wish I was doing this on the beach?*"

I removed my brooch. I reached into one of the lockers. I'd planned this in advance. I pinned the brooch to Dylan's shirt and tossed him a jacket.

"What is this about?"

I slipped a jacket on myself. "I can't handle Carver myself. I need you to bite him. He can't see you coming."

"In the gymnasium?"

I shook my head. "He can't get that far. He'll be waiting for a trap. Do it in the hallway before he even walks in. You have to catch him when he least expects it."

"How do I work this thing?"

"You touch it. You disappear. You'll want to practice. I can give you a quick tutorial. You can't give Carver an inch. You will have to rematerialize with your teeth already sunk into his skin. You'll get a mouthful, but he'll drop."

"What are you going to do?"

"I'll talk to him. We'll negotiate a partnership. I know what he wants. I'll tell him that I'll agree to join him if he agrees to a few terms. He'll ask me what those terms are. Before he gets his question out, you bite. The second I tell him I have terms."

Dylan nodded. "How much time do I need to practice?"

"You won't have to walk through walls or anything crazy. All we really have to do is make sure you don't have any crazy thoughts. We have to keep your feet on the ground. I'd say a few minutes on the astral plane, just to get your bearings, will be sufficient."

Dylan grinned. "Everyone thinks we're doing it, anyway. What do you say we make the most of our time?"

I grabbed Dylan by the waist of his pants and pulled him into a kiss.

Talk about a great way to redeem one's memories of school locker rooms.

CHAPTER THIRTY-FIVE

Dylan picked up astral walking like a natural. He got it almost as quickly as I did. Sure, he accidentally got his rear end stuck in a chair when he tried to rematerialize while sitting in one. He just didn't quite have his focus right. A quick touch of my brooch and he shook it off his ass in a hot second. I don't imagine it felt good. Getting things stuck in your butt usually doesn't. Not that I'd know anything about that.

I had my jacket zipped up tight. So did Dylan. We didn't want anyone to know that he was wearing my brooch. The zipper still gave him quick access. Any tip of the hat, any odd glances from one of the wolves, Dracula, or Sorina could raise suspicions.

Carver pulled up to the school well before the president was due to arrive. I expected that. It was a much shorter trip for him. I was watching and waiting.

Dracula disarmed the booby traps. I expected Carver to walk through the front doors. Instead, he wandered the perimeter. I had to run from classroom to classroom to catch a glimpse of him out the windows. He stopped right over where we'd buried Sarina's sisters. He chuckled and shook his head. Could he sense them down there? There wasn't any other explanation. What was he looking for? He was probably expecting a trap. If I was in his situation I'd want to do a little recon on the property before I walked through the front doors.

I grabbed Dylan in the hallway. "It's time. I don't know if we'll be able to get him inside. We might have to do this out in the playground. Same rule applies. When I mention my terms, you bite."

Dylan kissed me on the cheek. "Got it."

Dylan reached inside his coat and touched my brooch. He disappeared. I didn't realize how creepy it was to other people when I did my disappearing act. To know that Dylan was right there, beside me, but I couldn't see him was strange. Not freaky, really. If it was anyone else, maybe it would be.

Carver stood in the middle of the playground and looked up at the sun. I forced one of the windows open. The thing was so stiff it caused enough of a racket that Carver heard it and turned to me.

"You coming in or not?"

Carver laughed. "Why would I do that? You didn't invite me."

I smiled. "I don't have to invite you in, you know. This isn't a home."

"It sort of is. But you're right. That lore is crap. I could come in. I'm really just here to see Sorina, to talk."

"We can talk. Just come on in."

"Don't get me wrong, Sienna. We're overdue for a conversation. But you know as well as I do that Sorina is in there. I need to talk to her."

"Well, she isn't going to come out in the sun, Carver." Technically, Carver didn't know she could. As far as he knew, she was still a regular nights-only bloodsucker.

Carver shrugged. "I could wait."

"Do you want to talk to her before or after the president gets here? Seems to me things will be a lot messier if you two don't sort out your issues first."

Carver chuckled. "I suppose that's a fair point."

"Besides, I'd like to talk to you about your proposal first. I know why you need me."

"Do you?"

I nodded. "Your daywalker juice doesn't last as long as mine."

"No tricks, Sienna. Anything is off, be warned, I don't play nice when I'm deceived."

"No tricks."

"Then why'd you call the president here?"

I shook my head. "Sorina wanted to talk to him. She said she has a stake in all of this."

"A stake?"

I winced. "Bad pun. Didn't mean anything by it. She's not planning to stake the president if that's what you meant."

"Wouldn't do any good and she knows it. I'm more worried about her trying to stake me."

"She's barely come out of werewolf paralysis. Trust me, Carver. She's not herself. I don't think she could stake you if she wanted to."

"That's the thing, Sienna. She should be sleeping for a century. How is she awake?"

I smiled. "You have your magic, Dracula has his. You'd be surprised what's possible for a master of the path of light."

"All right, Sienna. I'll come in. But I'm staying at the door."

"Good enough for me."

Carver walked around to the front of the building. I opened the front doors.

"I need to talk to Sorina. But first, what do you want to know about my plans?"

"That's just it, Carver. If you're doing this to keep vampires safe, to ensure that the world doesn't start wiping us out, I get it. But you're also a Van Helsing."

Carver chuckled. "I was once, a long time ago. That was another life."

"You can't blame me for asking."

"Look, Sienna. You're right. There is a little Van Helsing in me. But we Van Helsings weren't all about killing vampires for the sheer thrill of it. It was about protecting humanity. That's still my agenda. But I'm also a vampire, just like you."

"Not *just* like me. Your mojo is different."

"Be that as it may, I might be the closest thing to you on the third rock from the sun. My dream is peace. If I could control how the world treated everyone without turning everyone into vampires, I would. But this is the only way. The sire bond is key."

"You're still turning people against their will."

"A necessary evil to ensure a better world."

I huffed. "Yeah, there was a German asshole with a funny mustache who made the same argument. Remember him? You lived through it."

"Don't compare me to Hitler, Sienna. That's the cheapest trick in politics. Trust me, I'd know. Whenever one party wants to smear the other, they always make Hitler comparisons. It's cheap, and it's inaccurate."

"You can't do this without me."

"You're wrong. I can. It won't be as convenient once all the world's leaders become reclusive during the day, but I can still do it. I'd like to have you on board because it would make things a lot easier. It would help prevent a panic. Think about it, Sienna. Once people learn that vampires rule the world, there will be riots in the streets. Anarchy across the globe. Millions of people will die. I'd like to avoid that. You can save lives if you join me, Sienna."

I narrowed my eyes. Then I took a deep breath. I hoped Dylan was ready.

Someone stepped up behind Carver. It was Sorina. Before I could open my mouth, she slammed a stake through his back and into his heart.

"Sorina! What the hell! I told you not to hurt him! I commanded you not to hurt anyone!"

I caught Carver as he hit the ground.

"Sienna, I meant what I said. I like you. But you can't control me."

"I bit you! I turned you into a daywalker!"

Sorina laughed. "I should win an award. I played along. I did what you said. You were never my sire. You can't turn someone who is already turned."

"You were already a daywalker?"

"I have been for some time. I stayed out of the light. I had to keep up my ruse. How do you think the Van Helsings learned their magic? They didn't teach me. They didn't help me break the sire bond. I made them a deal. When the sisters and I left Dracula all those years ago, we pursued sorcery of many kinds. Nothing quite so useful as the dark path of the Scholomance, but we learned enough. I gave the Van Helsings the knowledge they needed to create their elixir. You see, the magic I learned, the kind that Samuel used to become a daywalker himself, the same kind of magic that the Van Helsings used to create their elixir wasn't something I could control with the wave of a wand."

"So you made a deal with them. You provided the mystical source they needed, and they harnessed it through science."

"It was a bit more complicated than that, but that's the short version."

"So what's the plan? You complete the plan that Carver set in motion?"

"More or less. The thing is, Sienna. I don't need you. I know the science that the Van Helsings used. I didn't give them all the magic I learned. I gave Samuel a weaker version of the same daywalker spell that I used on myself. He can't turn daywalkers for much more than a month. I can do it permanently."

"How do you know Carver won't come back?"

Sorina shrugged. "He probably will. It doesn't matter. Even if he does, you'd be wise to deliver him to Abraham. You don't want that ghost on your tail, trust me."

"So you're going to leave us here? You're not going to attack us?"

"You're lucky. I need you to deal with Samuel. I can't have him coming back and screwing with my puppet president. The way I see it, Sienna, I've got you by the balls. I might be a nightmare, dear girl. The ghost of Abraham Van Helsing would be a night terror."

Several red and blue flashing lights appeared around a corner. A police escort with an armored limousine not far behind.

"I've got work to do. You'd best deal with Samuel here before he wakes up. He'll be a lot harder to handle, then."

"I should kill you right now!"

Sorina laughed. "I'd like to see you try. You'd lose. Even with Dracula coming up behind you to help."

I turned and saw Dracula standing about fifteen feet behind me. I was glad he was there. His power, his presence, was our only chance to stop Sorina.

"Don't think about sending those wolves after me, either. I'm faster than they are, I'm full of blood, and the sun still hasn't set completely. I have more than enough silver on me to do them all in. Do you want any more wolves dying on your watch?"

I sighed. "All right, Sorina. You win. I won't come after you. I won't even move from where I'm standing. But I have one request."

"Are you really in any place to make a bargain?"

"If you don't want all those police and secret service agents out there seeing a bloody fight and getting involved, you'll hear what I have to say."

"What is it, girl? The president is arriving, and I'll be leaving with him."

"I just have a few terms."

The second I said "terms" Dylan appeared with his teeth

already in Sorina's neck. She gasped and looked at me as if to say "you bitch" but the words didn't come out.

She fell to the ground, paralyzed.

I nodded at Dylan and took a deep breath. "Nice one!"

Dylan spit Sorina's blood from his mouth. "Disgusting."

I laughed. "You might need Listerine. Before that, Carver might wake up any minute. I need you to take him to Dracula. He can bring him to his father in the Scholomance."

Dylan was still gagging, but he knelt and picked up Carver. He threw the man over his shoulder. Werewolves are stronger than the average person—even in human form. I grabbed Sorina's slipping body and pulled her inside. The president was free. He was a vampire, sure. But he didn't have a sire. The last thing I needed was for anyone in his motorcade to see a body lying at the door.

CHAPTER THIRTY-SIX

The motorcade stopped in front of the school. A few secret service agents stepped out first and surrounded the president's door. He stepped out next. I approached him.

"Where is Sorina?" the president asked.

"She can't control you anymore, sir. Neither can Carver. You're free, but I know what you're going through. You and your entire cabinet. I want to help."

The president looked at me for a second. "What's your name, young lady?"

"I'm Sienna. And I might be the only person on earth who can help you right now."

President Brandon and I had a nice conversation. I had butterflies in my stomach the whole time. Meeting a president is surreal. I'd met gods before, but this was different. I explained what happened to him. He knew he'd become a vampire. He knew that his whole cabinet and the vice president were turned. I also told him how he'd soon be unable to go out in the sun. He dismissed the secret service agents and while I still had enough sunlight coursing through my body I bit him. I also promised never to use my bond to control him in any way. To make sure of it, I commanded him never to listen to any command I make. I didn't want to rule the world. Sure, politics suck. I didn't agree with half of the president's platform. But who was I to impose my will on a man who was elected by the people? I had to believe that since he was a vampire, perhaps he'd take a sympathetic stance to the rest of our kind. He'd find out that we aren't all monsters and that he didn't have to become one either.

I offered to travel to Washington with him to bite everyone else who was infected. I'd free them from my bond the same way I did him. He said he'd make arrangements in the coming days. I'd never been to Washington, DC, and I was looking forward to it.

I gave the president my phone number. He said he'd be in touch. I also sent him with a bottle of the blood wine Dracula brought back for Sorina. Something to take the edge off for the trip home.

I closed and locked the doors and headed back down the hall just in time to see a bright white light. Dracula reappeared in the room.

"Did you take Samuel to his father?" I asked.

Dracula nodded. "Abraham was grateful. Samuel woke up moments after we arrived. He's not exactly thrilled about being holed up with his dead dad in the Scholomance, but Abraham is confident he'll come around. I suppose they have all the time in the world to sort it out."

I nodded. "That's good to hear."

"There's one thing that you might not have thought about."

"What's that?"

"Samuel knows you killed James. If he tells Abraham, I don't know how he'll react. He could come back himself or, just as bad, send Samuel back to avenge his brother on his behalf."

I gulped. "Surely Abraham will be grateful that we gave him his youngest son back."

Dracula nodded. "He is. But remember, Sienna. Time passes a

lot faster there. I can't say if his gratitude will eclipse his anger forever. Even worse, if he does come after us, if he comes after you specifically, he'll have a lot more time to come up with a plan than we have to prepare for it."

I pressed my lips together. "I spent a lot of time with him in the Scholomance. Hopefully, he understands. Hopefully, he knows that I only did it trying to protect my friends."

Dracula nodded. "I hope you're right. If I know Abraham Van Helsing as well as I think I do, I wouldn't count on it."

AUTHOR NOTES - THEOPHILUS MONROE

MARCH 1, 2023

Something very *strange* happened while I was writing this book. It had to do when I described how one might go about killing a Van Helsing whose immortality elixir renders him nearly invulnerable: "…smash their heads like watermelons at a Gallagher show."

I grew up watching Gallagher specials on television. My father always put them on. He was a fan. Sadly, I never went to one of his shows. When I wrote that line, though, I wanted to double-check to make sure I was spelling the comedian's name correctly. When I googled it, the first thing that came up was an article indicating that Gallagher died earlier *the very same day* I wrote the line.

I almost removed the line, but then I figured why not give the comedian whose antics kept my father laughing, and my younger self entertained, an homage. So, R.I.P. Gallagher.

As I reflected on that I had to wonder—what were the chances? I hadn't thought about the comedian in years. The one time I do, and include a reference in one of my books, happens to be the same day he passed away? Was it merely a coincidence? Probably. Still, there's a small part of me that can't help but wonder if there's more to it than that. Especially since that isn't the first time something like this has happened.

Back to this book...

I hadn't planned on this story until I wrote *The Chronicles of Zoey Grimm* and so many readers expressed their affection for the quirky, but resilient, daywalking vampire, Sienna. When Dracula made an appearance in *Soul Harvest (Zoey Grimm #7)*, and his character took on an equally quirky flare, I figured, why not tell more of their stories?

There was something fun about the interplay between a young woman who doesn't know much about her vampirism, and has spent the last couple years of her life fighting vampires, gods, and devils of various kinds, teaming up with the most notorious vampire in history... who has had something of a change of heart.

While Sienna is struggling to embrace her vampirism, Dracula is wrestling with that last spark of humanity that the Scholomance revived within him. He's also old, sheltered from a lot of the modern world, and couldn't be any more different from our spunky young heroine. The dynamic between those characters was a lot of fun to write and I hope you found it entertaining.

Thank you to Michael and everyone else at LMBPN who got behind this project. Thank you to everyone who read and enjoyed *The Chronicles of Zoey Grimm* and demanded more from that world. Will Zoey return to this series at some point? You'll have to keep reading to find out. She just might. But this is Sienna's story.

Thank you, also, to my wife who never reads my author notes. She usually waits for my books to come out on audio (the audio for this series is coming, by the way) so she can listen while she's out and about in the car. She's put up with many nights alone in the house while I went out to my studio to write, pressing deadlines, so I could get these books into your hands.

I hope you enjoyed this book! Sienna's adventure isn't over yet. As always, I'm grateful to you, my readers. Without you, I'd be stuck doing a regular job. I'm not built for that. Mostly because I have authority issues and don't deal well with bosses. Spending my days crafting stories for all of you is a dream come true.

-THEO

AUTHOR NOTES - MICHAEL ANDERLE

MARCH 20, 2023

Thank you for not only reading this book but these author notes as well.

Today, I want to take a moment to appreciate and acknowledge the unsung heroes behind every author.

Author spouses (or Significant Others)

Living with a writer can be a unique and, at times, bewildering experience. Here are a few challenges author spouses often face and a word of warning for those considering a relationship with (almost all) creatives.

Sharing Time with the Muse

When an author is in the throes of creativity, it can feel like we're having an affair with our muses. Our passion for writing can consume damn near everyone, leaving our spouse to wonder if they've been replaced by the characters and storylines living in our heads.

It takes a patient and understanding spouse to accept that sometimes, we need to get lost in our fictional world to bring our stories to life.

(Editor's Note, written as an author's wife: And a very patient one not to snap the fifth time in an hour that the author insists on reading

some choice snippet from the new creation to you. It generally isn't half as interesting to the wife/SO as to the author.)

In short, we *are* in the middle of an affair, but I promise, it's consensual and benign.

Deciphering the Half-Formed Conversations

Trying to have a conversation with an author can feel like participating in a game show where you're only given half the information.

We authors often lose ourselves in thought and forget that we haven't verbalized key parts of the conversation. It takes a special kind of spouse or significant other to learn the art of mind-reading and fill in the blanks of these half-formed discussions.

Hell, sometimes we are having multiple conversations with our multiple muses, and if *we* are confused, I can just imagine what Judith (my spouse) is dealing with. I happen to know she doesn't enjoy the conversation whatsoever.

Social Events and the Reluctant Author

For many authors, social events can be daunting since we would much rather be at home, exploring our fictional worlds, than out in public.

At least, that's true for many of us. Some of us would like to be out talking about…ourselves.

Author spouses know that bringing their partner to events can be a challenge since authors tend to delve into their stories and characters, leaving "normal" humans bewildered and questioning said author's sanity.

In these cases, author spouses are often the ones who bridge the gap between the author's world and reality, translating their partner's enthusiasm for their work into relatable conversation topics to the best of their abilities.

And shutting us down when we don't get the hint.

So, author's spouses are the unsung heroes who support, love, and tolerate the quirks of living with a creative partner.

They navigate the delicate balance between encouraging our passions and ensuring we stay connected to the real world.

(*Editor's note, again written as an author's wife: That's is the gods' honest truth!!!*)

So, let's raise a glass to the spouses and significant others of authors everywhere, for without their support and understanding, our stories might never make it to the page.

Oh, and thanks for not murdering us in our sleep. That's a solid you do us every night.

Ad Aeternitatem,

Michael Anderle

MORE STORIES with Michael newsletter HERE: https://michael.beehiiv.com/

ALSO BY THEOPHILUS MONROE

Scared Shiftless

Bat Shift Crazy

No Shift, Sherlock

Shift for Brains

Shift Happens

Shift on a Shingle

The Vilokan Asylum of the Magically and Mentally Deranged

The Curse of Cain

The Mark of Cain

Cain and the Cauldron

Cain's Cobras

Crazy Cain

The Wrath of Cain

The Blood Witch Saga

Voodoo and Vampires

Witches and Wolves

Devils and Dragons

Ghouls and Grimoires

More to come!

FREE URBAN FANTASY ADVENTURE: DRUIDESS (GET IT HERE!)

GoE OMNIBUS COLLECTIONS [in Chronological Order]:

The Druid Legacy

Wyrmrider (Books 1-4)

The Voodoo Legacy

The Legacy of a Vampire Witch

The Legend of Nyx

The Vilokan Asylum of the Magically and Mentally Deranged

Other Theophilus Monroe Series

<u>**Nanoverse**</u>

[Also Available in an Omnibus Edition]

<u>**The Elven Prophecy**</u>

[Also Available in an Omnibus Edition]

<u>**Chronicles of Zoey Grimm**</u>

[Also Available in an Omnibus Edition]

<u>**The Daywalker Chronicles**</u>

<u>**Go Ask Your Mother**</u>

AS T.R. MAGNUS

<u>**Kataklysm**</u>

Blightmage

Ember

Radiant

<u>**FREE EPIC: DARKWORLD (GET IT HERE!)**</u>

CONNECT WITH THE AUTHORS

Connect with Theophilus Monroe

Website: www.theophilusmonroe.com

Social Media
https://www.facebook.com/pages/category/Author/
Theophilus-Monroe-Urban-Fantasy-Author-101469961530864/

Connect with Michael Anderle

Website: http://lmbpn.com

Email List: https://michael.beehiiv.com/

https://www.facebook.com/LMBPNPublishing

https://twitter.com/MichaelAnderle

https://www.instagram.com/lmbpn_publishing/

https://www.bookbub.com/authors/michael-anderle

www.ingramcontent.com/pod-product-compliance
Lightning Source LLC
Chambersburg PA
CBHW020135310726
48970CB00006B/1888